BAD LAW, A Novel

By WILL NATHAN

Ferry Press, LLC
San Francisco

Publisher's Note

Bad Law, a Novel, is a work of fiction. And all fiction, by definition, is a lie.

Consistent with the above, person(s) and/or events portrayed in *Bad Law, a Novel*, are either entirely a product of the author's imagination or are utilized fictitiously and/or hyperbolically.

Put another way, *Bad Law, a Novel*, does not purport to portray any real person(s) and/or event(s) in any factual manner and it lays no claim that it would have any basis in fact for so doing.

Rather, and put yet a third way, *Bad Law, a Novel,* tells tall tales in the hope of achieving a philosophic insight into the high priests of the state religion and the justice system where they worship.

Synopsis

Boomers. From a bad war. To bad acid. And, finally, to *Bad Law*. A novel of the *not* greatest generation and the law.

Advance Praise for Bad Law

"Wonderful book. I tried to persuade my wife, Kim, that some of the *Bad Law* stories were fictional, but she didn't believe me," says attorney Richard Plumridge, Esq., former senior partner at Brobeck, Phleger & Harrison, LLP.

"Hard cases, it is said, make bad law. But they can also make good novels, and Will Nathan has done so with a gripping tale of the seamy side of law practice; replete with ethical crises and missteps; heartless firm politics; and the brutal, fragile road to success. The story may make you uncomfortable because the fiction is only a disguise for reality, a reality many of us have faced. But, fiction or fact, Mr. Nathan's crisply written, insightful and unyielding novel holds you until its conclusion—and even then it stays with you," says attorney Jerome Shestack, Esq., former United States Ambassador to the United Nations Commission on Human Rights, Past President of the American Bar Association, and 2006 winner of the American Bar Association Medal.

"*Bad Law* invites speculation about whose lives and careers the novel's outrageous characters are based on. But real insight, rather than real characters, is the real point of *Bad Law*," says attorney Ephraim Margolin, Esq., Past President of the California

Academy of Appellate Lawyers, as well as 2004 winner of the State Bar of California Trial Lawyer Hall of Fame Award.

"Will Nathan takes us on a disturbing ride through the underbelly of big-city law practice, along with a cast of characters much too close for comfort to the real thing" says attorney Robin Meadow, Esq., Past President of the Los Angeles County Bar Association, as well as Past President of the California Academy of Appellate Lawyers.

Historical Note Regarding Title of Bad Law, a Novel

"Hard cases, it is said, make bad law." General Sir John Campbell, 4th Duke of Argyll (c. 1693-1770).

Dedication

Bad Law, a Novel, is dedicated to my lawyer-grandfather, VJM; and to his youngest son, my uncle JAM—a member of the greatest generation and a brave soldier—who was killed in action in Northern Italy in 1945 while serving with the 10th Mountain Division.

Hard Cases

Bad Law

Hard Cases

Chapter One
McLean Hospital
Belmont, MA
{Dawn, Friday, February 3, 1969}

Shane Sullivan howled. Malcolm, a black guy who worked night security on Shane's psych ward, wasn't in the mood for these all-too-familiar noises. He slipped into Shane's locked room, which smelled like a zoo. Inside, he punched Shane in the gut.

"Fucking shut up, college boy; fucking shut up or I'll come back and kill your white ass."

Then, to make sure his threat had sunk in, he kicked Shane—who was already down and somewhat dazed, lying in his own shit—squarely in the kidney. After that Malcolm left, figuring the violence would maybe buy him twenty or thirty minutes peace, enough time to get to sleep and hopefully stay that way through the rest of his shift. It was time to find another job, he knew, when you start beating on the crazies, but what job could an old man like him find anyway.

Things were not going so well for Shane in early 1969. Not only was he locked away, naked and screaming at the moon, with Malcolm making increasingly frequent visits to administer corporal punishment; he was also having an increasingly difficult time remembering who he was. Sometimes he was Christ; sometimes he was Winston Churchill. Then he would be George

Patton or Julius Caesar. The only common denominator was that it was always some powerful male figure. Certainly nobody who'd ever been involuntarily committed to a psych ward by an assistant dean of Harvard College.

As his delusions grew more acute, Shane had begun living full-time in that medieval secret of psychiatric hospitals everywhere: the seclusion room. The place where all the various abstract theories of psychotherapy were thrown out wholesale. Where otherwise unmanageable patients were simply cast naked into bare cells and then left there indefinitely to smear feces and otherwise work out their problems for themselves. Pathetic, raving souls abandoned to the tender mercies of the Malcolms of this world, who had their own old-fashioned ways of dealing with problems like bad smells and too much screaming in the night.

The events that led up to Shane's forced psychiatric hospitalization had begun two years earlier. In the spring of 1967, with the Vietnam war in full swing, Shane decided to stay out of the draft by obtaining a graduate school deferment available to students who volunteered for a two-year accelerated Army Reserve Officer Training Corps program.

It was his experience in the Army since then that had started him on the road to his breakdown. That and falling in love with a military brat whose brother was at West Point and whose Dad was an infantry general.

Shane had been a ridiculous soldier. At Georgia's famed Fort Benning, his initial summer posting in 1967, he was generally thought of as mildly retarded. Certainly no one believed he was attending Harvard. Even the Sergeant Major, who had access to an official list of the various cadets' colleges, had his doubts. He'd decided Shane must be a commie, playing some commie trick by enlisting and then fucking everything up so thoroughly all the time. This was why he finished Shane and another obvious commie, a Jewish guy from the University of Chicago, last in their platoon at the end of that summer.

Shane's junior year was spent in love with Catherine Herman, a Wellesley girl whose family was then living at Fort Bragg, North Carolina. All he'd admitted to Cathy when they'd first started dating was that he'd had a few bad moments while at Fort Benning that previous summer. Something she'd casually told him to take in stride, just the way her twin brother John was then handling Beast Barracks. So, Shane had gone along, pretending that he was just as tough as John, a guy who'd gotten his own set of paratroop wings at West Point Prep before being appointed to the Point itself.

Inevitably, however, Cathy had figured out that Shane wasn't any soldier. And since Cathy wanted to stay in the Army life she'd grown up with, she needed to marry one of the string of admirers she'd picked up among her brother's classmates, whatever good points she saw in Shane. This she told Shane, more or less honestly, at the end of the spring semester of 1968. When Shane left for his second camp that summer, this time in Pennsylvania at

3

the Indiantown Gap Military Reserve, Cathy's rejection had made him an emotional wreck.

And then The Gap, as it was called, had turned out to be a much bigger nightmare than Fort Benning. At least Benning, for all of its frightening reality as the living, breathing heart of the Army during the Vietnam conflict, had the virtue of being a well-organized regular post, not some harem-scarum ROTC camp like The Gap. At Fort Benning, too, the training cadres were good people, not ideologues. They cared about keeping their people alive in combat, nothing more and nothing less. They didn't care how you got there, didn't care where you went from there. Just "we eat this shit up"—WETSU, from dawn to dusk. Good for you, good for them.

At The Gap, it was mainly ROTC officers from one Eastern college or another, guys who had been shat upon all day on the campuses, losers hiding out from the war themselves. And Shane, he got Major Proviso, an ex-bank clerk then teaching ROTC classes at Norwich University in Vermont, a school so obscure that at first Shane didn't believe it really existed.

But two guys in his platoon actually went to Norwich, and they confirmed that, like the better-known Virginia Military Institute and its South Carolina cousin, The Citadel, Norwich was an actual four-year private college, one where everybody was forced to wear an Army uniform all day, every day.

4

After observing how Major Proviso changed into freshly starched fatigues and newly spit-shined combat boots at least twice each day, Shane realized his lack of passable military bearing would inevitably doom him in the Major's eyes. So, Shane decided to use the tools he did have at his command to avoid being washed out.

In the event, he'd pretended to be the most gung-ho advocate of killing the Viet Cong imaginable. He was still a fuck-up, of course. Couldn't bring his boots to a spit shine; couldn't get his brass to gleam; couldn't march in step; couldn't do any normal Army shit. No telling exactly why. Probably an utter lack of any patience with such tasks. But he loudly proclaimed all the politically correct answers about the war. And Major Proviso was dumb enough to buy it and cut him some slack.

His fellow cadets despised him, of course, both because of the pro-war heresy he was spouting and mainly because he was so screwed up on every practical level. And it was during that summer—feeling totally isolated by the end of his relationship with Cathy, his soldierly ineptitude, and his crazed baby-killer charade—when Shane really began to come apart.

At the end of the camp—after he'd been rated 10 up from the bottom, and had thus succeeded in not being washed out of the program for finishing in the bottom five, two camps in a row—he first cracked. He and a group of cadets were gathered for departure, standing around their bags in mufti. Their bags as well as the bags of the many guys who hadn't arrived at the sign-out area yet. The mass of luggage was blocking a line of march for a company still in the training cycle, and an unknown officer had approached Shane and the others and told them to move everything out of the way. Now.

His fellows went right to work, but Shane pretended not to have heard the order. The officer, who had already started walking away, looked back and saw something odd in Shane's insouciant attitude.

"Didn't you hear me, mister?" he demanded, striding rapidly back, getting up in Shane's face in an all-too-familiar way. Shane looked the man up and down. The officer, a first lieutenant, was about twenty-five, trim, well-turned out. Probably Regular Army, not just another sad sack Reservist. But you never knew since, at The Gap, as opposed to Fort Benning, Regulars were so few and far between.

What was clear was the guy had no idea who Shane was, as Shane had no identifying badges on. And Shane's car was parked only about ten feet down the street, not blocked by any traffic. His 1965 Mustang, a ticket home.

So, Shane said nothing. He picked up his own bag, sidestepped the furious first looey, and jumped into his waiting car. He started the engine, lowered the driver's window, and then, as he pulled out, gave the sputtering officer—still standing dumbfounded in the same spot where he had first confronted Shane—the finger.

He'd just stopped caring what happened to him, if only for the moment, and as things turned out, the offended officer, who had a full company of men standing there, impatient for direction, never got around to pursuing the matter. But it had been attempted suicide, no doubt about it. And when Shane was a half-hour from the post, he stopped and threw up, thinking of the two summers' worth of agony he had just put at risk by taking a chance like that. And for nothing. To avoid picking up some bags, for Christ's sake. He'd known then that he was no longer in control of himself.

Things went from bad to worse after that. Back home in Illinois, he fought with his father. After a few days of dealing with his nerve-wracked son, Marcus Sullivan told Shane the Army had turned him into a psycho. Shane had then stormed out of the house and gone back to Cambridge two weeks before school started.

Once there, he threw the first swim team party of the year in his basement apartment. A party where Marc Brenner—the last year's swim team captain, just come back to Cambridge after claiming homosexuality in front of his Oklahoma draft board—dared Shane to take STP, which turned out to be the street name for a potent combination of LSD and speed.

Marc meant no harm. Probably. STP certainly didn't faze him; he dropped right along with Shane and two of Shane's roommates, who were also on the swim team with Shane. Each of the four of them took turns licking the huge paper tab permeated with dope until, finally, it disintegrated. All the girls left after that little ceremony. They were Cliffies—ugly ones mostly—and they didn't approve of hard drugs.

And then, about an hour into it, Shane freaked out. Objects spun, and then they melted. Soon after the visual experience hit, Shane was crying, puking, you name it. Sometime during all the fuss Shane was making, Marc left the party, disgusted. Leaving Shane's two swim team roomies to bring Shane down, high as they were themselves.

It took them two days to do it. Then Shane went home for another month to try and get back to normal. Missed the beginning of school and a bunch of pre-conditioning the swim coach had ordered up. Scared his Mom shitless when he told her what he'd done. Even worried his Dad. Though, of course, the old man was told nothing of the real truth by anyone.

The rest of 1968 was a struggle. Someone showed Shane an article in a lady's magazine named Redbook about how LSD caused broken chromosomes. The pictures of his supposedly fucked-up blood cells obsessed him. His swimming went to hell, and he was asked to stop attending practice. He did manage to ace the LSAT on pure nervous energy, though, after sleeping less than an hour the night before. He'd stopped sleeping much, period.

Then he broke. Walked into the Harvard ROTC office just before Christmas, completely delusional. Put a hand right on the attending doctor's crotch, telling the old guy he was still fertile. That got the full-bird Colonel that ran Harvard's Army ROTC program on the phone to the Cambridge police in a hurry. The cops took him over to Mass General for observation; two days later, after his parents had parted with the necessary $10,000 down, he was shipped out to McLean, supposedly to be treated with kid gloves while he got better.

But Malcolm didn't wear gloves, and Shane was not getting any better. Not for a long while, anyway.

Chapter Two
Law Offices of Broward, Phillips & Hamburg
San Francisco, CA
{October 1973}

Shane Sullivan's first law job was at Broward, Phillips & Hamburg. The law firm occupied the top four floors of a staid twenty-five-story Montgomery Street sandstone and mortar office building once used as a set in a pre-Code version of the Maltese Falcon. There were about a hundred lawyers employed there.

This made Broward the second-largest law firm in San Francisco, behind Patton, Welts & Sims. Broward was forty years older than PW&S, but PW&S had long since bypassed its more established rival. PW&S had a close association with those two ultimate West Coast robber baron corporations, Standard Oil of California and Union Oil Company, which gushed such a cornucopia of legal fees that Broward's two biggest clients, Southern Pacific and Bank of America, simply paled in comparison.

The first day he showed up at Broward, Shane found himself sitting in a spartanly furnished reception area of the 22nd floor of 111 Montgomery Street, waiting for a Broward partner, one Mr. David Durham, to come out and get him. Shane had never met Dave Durham, knew nothing about him, and, typically, had made no effort to find out anything about him before walking into the lion's den.

Shane had not bothered to look for a law job until the last semester of his third year at Boalt Hall, the University of California's most prestigious law school. Fleeing from the disgrace of his nervous breakdown, Shane had wound up on the West Coast after graduating Harvard a year behind his class.

All the good jobs for third years were usually filled in the fall. But despite his mediocre grades and the lateness of his applications, Shane's aggressive personality got him a surprising number of job offers, Broward's being the most prestigious.

Of course, no one at Broward had explained to him that he was being hired there at the last minute because Gary Lee was threatening to quit, and no one else would go near a partner not-so-affectionately nicknamed Dead End Dave by the Broward associates. Then again, Shane had not felt constrained to explain to Broward that four years ago he'd been locked in seclusion at McLean after a bad acid trip, so candor was not a watch-word on either side of Shane's first job as a lawyer.

Not that Shane saw it that way. While the hiring partner at Broward may have been conscious of having tricked Shane, Shane did not feel he was tricking Broward merely by keeping his nervous breakdown to himself. After all, he'd made it through law school with no problems, and then, just that summer, instead of spending three months studying for the bar like all his goody two-shoes classmates, he'd been drafted, in desperation, by his wife's father to shut down a failing electronics business that threatened to wipe out the man's very substantial net worth.

11

He'd done that, flown all over the world, fired lots of unhappy adults, and saved his wife's family's fortunes in the process. And in the middle of all that, despite virtually no bar-review prep, he'd taken a week off and passed the July bar as well. So, Shane wasn't scared of what might be coming at Broward; he was just looking forward to something new. That was all.

Dave Durham padded silently around a corner. He was slight, ramrod straight, with a grey crew-cut. Bright, look-right-through-you blue eyes. Just what you'd expect of an ex-Marine Lt. Colonel turned lawyer. Even his cheap grey business suit managed to look like a uniform when draped over his spare frame.

Shane didn't know it, couldn't have known it, but Dave was at the lowest rung of partnership at Broward. Someone who'd had to hang on for fifteen years as an associate before being promoted to partner. A guy with no clients and no future beyond biting whomever the higher-ups told him to bite. Despite having the elitist credentials demanded by the firm—in Dave's case Princeton, followed by Stanford Law, along with a Silver Star from Korea—Dave was just an unhappy plodder lost in a field full of charging racehorses.

One indication: in a firm where each of the partners typically had a coterie of from three to as many as six associates, Dave was never assigned more than one at a time. And none of Dead End Dave's associates had made partner in living memory—at least not until Gary Lee had the foresight to resign from Dave's employment, but not the firm, after only a year of servitude, a tactic that ultimately allowed him into the partnership on what had, by then, become the normal nine-year track.

Durham looked at Shane, and Shane looked back at Durham. For an uncomfortably long time, neither said anything. Then Durham spoke:

"You're the new associate. Sullivan, is it?"

"Yes, sir," Shane answered, instinctively falling into military parlance with so obvious an old soldier.

"Well," Durham said, forcing a smile at the word sir, "don't call me that, just plain Dave will do. Glad to meet you, Sullivan."

And he put out his hand, which Shane shook.

"As you'll see, we're badly in need of help around here, so let's get right to work, shall we?"

And that was it. Shane was a lawyer. A very junior lawyer—quite a difference from running a business where he had personally fired fully half the employees on a single day—and expected to know a great deal he didn't actually know about the law. Particularly securities law, which he'd skipped taking in his third year so as to make room for an undergraduate philosophy course.

But Dave never asked Shane about his prior coursework. Just turned to Shane the third day he was there and explained that the

United States was suing an important Broward client on a theory that selling vacation real estate, and then helping the buyers rent their condominiums after purchase, was an illegal sale of securities. Then Dave said he'd be gone three weeks on vacation.

He wanted the hows and whys of the government's case down on paper by the time he returned. He didn't have to say what he'd do to Shane if the job was unsatisfactory. Just scanned him with his baby blues, waiting to see Shane sweat or, worse, dare to ask a question.

Shane just looked back at Dave and said, smiling, "No problem." He was too fearless to sweat, and he didn't know enough to ask a sensible question. There was no "sir" and no "Dave," either, at the end of his sentence. Shane knew when somebody was trying to test him, and he didn't feel obliged to like it.

It was kind of fun, really. There was a luncheon the next day with a Securities and Exchange guy, who was part of the team of government lawyers prosecuting Broward's client, as the featured speaker, and Shane figured a lot of it out just from listening to the guy dodge bullets from the audience. After that he had to teach himself the fundamentals of securities law. Luckily, however, the government theory was so novel that most of the technical stuff was beside the point. The issue which Broward's client was facing was what is it about a security that makes it a security?

The key to that question wound up being a body of Securities and Exchange Commission opinion letters printed on tissue-thin paper by an obscure legal publication. Elaborate dissertations written by SEC staff lawyers that danced around issues similar to the ones Shane was facing, one bureaucrat advancing and another retreating from the main issue, which was how to tell when a buyer was buying something, as opposed to just buying an income stream generated by something? It was an impossibly metaphysical question, but one that was easy to write about. And Shane did so, very well. So well that, when Dave got back, he never asked Shane a single question about the subject. Just read Shane's memo and that was it.

Chapter Three
Boalt Hall School of Law
University of California at Berkeley
Berkeley, CA
{September 1970-June 1971}

Even at a law school where nearly half the first-years were quite extraordinary women, Helen Wilson was hard to miss. Outspokenly brilliant, her Audrey Hepburn good looks and sharp wit had attracted immediate attention—of all kinds—from both classmates and faculty alike.

Take Professor Vett, the randy bachelor contracts professor, who—in sharp contrast to the haughty attitude toward students displayed by Professor Kingsley, his fictional counterpart in The Paper Chase—had shown up on Helen's doorstep with flowers and an impromptu invitation to dinner after the first day of class.

As notorious as his sexual appetites were, Vett usually laid only second and third years. But, as he explained to Helen at Chez Panisse later that evening, she was special, and for her he would make an exception. Helen laughed hard, ate the truly wonderful Alice Waters-prepared food, and didn't let on as to her own intentions for the balance of the evening.

And then, at the end of the night, when Vett grabbed for her on her doorstep, she sidestepped him and went right into her apartment. Before he could follow, she had locked the door. With that obstacle between them, she asked in an agreeable voice whether trying to get into her pants at night while teaching her law during the day should be illegal. An hour-long discussion of applicable precedent ensued, and Vett went home intellectually, if not physically, satisfied.

Smart girl, he thought, reflecting on Helen's keen responses to his descriptions of the first few cases on sexual harassment then creeping into the official reporters. Messing around with her, that's a stupid thing to do, even for somebody with tenure. After that night, like most of her other worshippers, he confined himself to admiring Helen from a distance.

Such were the beginnings of Helen Wilson's romantic life at Boalt. As far as such things went, Helen was neither a nun nor any other kind of plaster saint; she just liked to do the choosing, something her looks and wit had always allowed her the luxury of. Even Vett might have had a chance if he hadn't been so obvious about abusing his authority as her professor, a tactic she'd been brushing off, each time with increasing irritation, since her freshman year of college.

Instead, about two weeks into classes, she settled on Stanley Jacobs, an athletic, sweet-tempered Jewish boy from Cornell, a ladies' man who'd had the kind of experience with women that someone as well-traveled as Helen could appreciate. Their relationship was pleasantly gymnastic, a relief from the intense mental effort she—as opposed to Stan—was pouring into their studies.

While Stan smoked dope and dabbled in the texts, Helen absorbed the course materials with a Germanic attention to detail. She could recite a fair amount of their reading from memory. At the end of the year, Stan's intellect propelled him well into the top third of the class, despite his competing interests in good hash and satisfying his libido; Helen, meanwhile, was third in the class overall, a truly exalted academic achievement. She was on her way at Boalt, automatically assigned to the California Law Review, and her reputation among the faculty as a comer well assured.

That summer she went back home to DC. At the airport she told Stan it was time for him to make other arrangements. It was news he took a lot harder than she would have expected, despite the fact that he'd fucked four or five other women while they'd been a thing. And assumed he'd gotten away with it, too. Which, of course, he hadn't.

Chapter Four
Law Offices of Broward, Phillips & Hamburg
San Francisco, CA
{Fall 1973-Spring 1975}

It only took that first securities-law assignment from Dave Durham to make Shane Sullivan realize his decision to skip nearly all the high-specialty business courses taught at Boalt hadn't given him much in the way of survival skills in his new environment. But, released from the classroom, and even with the hapless Dead End Dave as his taskmaster, Shane thrived.

It was a tribute to his adaptability that, starting with that untutored essay on securities law, and moving on to equally arcane aspects of real estate and bankruptcy law, Dave never figured out that Shane was actually learning on the job.

And quite soon, as the tasks became more repetitive and his knowledge of business law increased, Shane got ahead of the curve to the point that he was routinely able to avoid the gruesome hours being put in by his better-educated fellow associates and their promotion-hungry bosses. Working for Dave, and only for Dave, Shane had settled into something comfortable, albeit professionally unrewarding.

Then came the Shenk scandal. It started simply enough. Hartley Jones, Broward's most senior tax partner and a former general counsel to the IRS, had C. Reynolds Gleason—the man who had brought Volkswagen to the West Coast—as his premier client. And Gleason owned considerable real estate—ownership records for which, it turned out, were poorly kept.

A large tenant had moved out early, leaving a sizable debt behind. Normally this would have been a matter for the Litigation Department, but in this case the transactional Real Estate Department lawyers decided to collect the bill themselves. Tom Shenk, one of Shane's more amiable classmates in the firm, was assigned the task. And Tom, for some reason, made the matter into a crusade, noticing endless depositions, sending the Santa Clara County Sheriff's Department on one trip to the tenant's bank after another to collect small deposits. This went on, without much success in actually collecting money, until Tom suddenly got busy with another, more important real-estate project. Which was when the matter of *Gleason v. Maldonado Corp.* was, at last, kicked over to the Litigation Department, and there assigned to Dave and by Dave to Shane.

Almost immediately, Shane realized that Mr. Gleason no longer owned the building where the Maldonado corporation had formerly been a tenant. Then, simply by running through the deal documents Broward had itself prepared, Shane discovered that the building had been sold without reserving any rights for Mr. Gleason against Maldonado Corp.

This meant Mr. Gleason had never had any business suing Maldonado in the first place, let alone trying to collect what was a bogus judgment. The default was the current owner's problem. Which meant Mr. Gleason, an individual worth tens of millions of

1970s dollars, was not only out the tens of thousands he had paid Broward for all their vain effort on his behalf; he was almost automatically guilty of malicious prosecution as well.

And no one was more likely to sue Gleason for malicious prosecution—and the punitive damages that nearly always went with that tort—than some hard-luck tenant that had never made any money from its actual business, which was importing agricultural products from Mexico. Not to mention that the minority-owned Maldonado Corp. Had been wrongfully sued by Tom Shenk in Santa Clara County. A county which, in those pre-Silicon Valley days, was still heavily agricultural, and thus had a substantial Hispanic population, some of whom actually got on civil juries.

In short, the case against Gleason was any lawyer's wet dream. As soon as he saw the paperwork between Mr. Gleason and the new building owner—which had independently decided that Maldonado Corp. was not worth spending legal fees pursuing—Shane realized how serious the situation was. The plain facts were that Gleason had been victimized by Broward's incompetence.

Shane had watched the Watergate hearings unfold on TV while taking breaks during the Bar Exam. What the Nixon White House did in its scramble for survival, though, seemed mild compared to the self-protective clutch he witnessed once he went in to see Dead End Dave with the news that Tom Shenk needed to be fired. Dave listened to what Shane had to say, looked at the title deed Gleason had given the new buyer, looked at the deal documents, and looked at the judgment that Tom Shenk had obtained against Maldonado Corp. under false pretenses.

"You write this up yet?" he asked Shane.

"No, Dave," Shane said. "I thought I'd pass it by you before I started creating a paper trail."

David Durham looked up at Shane with a start, as if noticing him for the first time. Looking over at his young associate, with whom he was only marginally content, Dave realized that Shane fully understood what the information he had could do to the firm, and even to Dave's tenure at the firm, if it wasn't controlled. And, even as he realized this, Dave intuited two other things: Shane did not like Dave, and Shane did not give a rat's ass what happened to either Dave or Broward.

Moved by what he saw in Shane's face, Dave affected an entirely atypical politeness. "Let me handle this for a few days," he said. "People are bound to have some questions, and you mustn't speak to anyone about it until we get those questions sorted out."

Then, once again disturbed by Shane's increasingly cold appraisal of him, Dave Durham decided he'd better keep the kid off-balance. Throw him a bone, he thought.

"It looks like you've done something useful, Sullivan," he said. "Keep it up and you're likely to make some new friends here."

"No problem, boss," Shane replied, "I'll sit on it for a few days." He paused. "But there's a limit to how long this charade can go on without making it even worse. Assuming I'm right, of course."

It took everything Dave had to resist exploding with rage at Shane's smug and untrustworthy demeanor. Shane's effrontery simply infuriated Dave Durham, as did the fact that Dave had to smile and say nothing in return, all for fear of pushing this ever-volatile youngster in a direction neither he nor his partners would like. As he dismissed him with a friendly wave, he could only think about Shane calling Mr. Gleason and explaining his view of things directly.

With Shane gone, Dave hastened to call Moshe Janofsky, the most senior and fearsome of all Broward's various senior, fearsome partners. And there he reported the sad tale of how Tom Shenk had exposed Hartley Jones to the loss of his best client and Broward to a large malpractice claim—not to mention laughingstock status, if the story of Shenk's complete ineptitude ever got out into the legal community at large. The case of the missing case, the PW&S partners would probably call it, right before they took the unfortunate if hardly impoverished Mr. Gleason in under their protective wing. It would be an all too easy sell, offering to right the various wrongs done to that scion of industry by Broward.

Moshe Janofsky, having listened impatiently to Dave Durham's plodding, repetitive account, cut him off after only a few minutes.

"So, this possibly disloyal Sullivan has caught this idiot Shenk in what you think is probably a bad mistake, is that it?" Moshe said, biting off his words dismissively.

"Long and short, yes, Moshe."

Realizing it would have otherwise taken Durham half an hour to get to the point, Janofsky once again regretted not having blackballed Durham five years before. The by-then-fifteen-year associate had finally been proposed for partnership in 1969, and the war-hero thing, along with the fact that Durham was highly valued by that most mundane of Broward's clients, Bank of America, had managed to stay Janofsky's hand. And so Durham had sneaked into the bottom rung of the partnership by the thinnest of margins, with the result that Janofsky now had to endure his doltish mentality and fawning expressions of respect at every turn, this unwanted call included.

"Well, have Hartley Jones assign a team to grill the shit out of this Sullivan youngster. And if Sullivan's right, tell Hart to be careful with him, keep him in the fold. Hart will know how to handle that. And until I have better visibility here, you go easy on Sullivan. I can tell you don't like him, Dave, but you are officially to lay off him from now on. Check?"

"Of course, Moshe—whatever's best for the firm. You know you can always count on me."

It took two full days of interviews over that weekend, with waves of transactional and litigation lawyers coming in and out of the conference room that Shane never left, except for bathroom and meal breaks, before the firm was convinced that he was right. Tom Shenk, as he'd said, was the villain of the piece. Though Shane had always liked Tom, he understood that at least one of them was bound to go, depending on the outcome of the analysis. So, he was mightily relieved to hear, on returning to his normal duties on the third day following his initial meeting with Dave Durham, that Shenk had been fired the night before—called in from the suburbs and abruptly dismissed. All without any idea of the consternation his handling of *Gleason v. Maldonado Corp.* had caused within the firm.

Shane had not been at work for more than an hour when he was called up to the twenty-fifth floor and into the august presence of Hartley Jones, Esq. A patrician charmer of the first order, Hart Jones was Yale College, Class of 1942; then had put in three years' service as a Marine fighter pilot during WWII; followed by graduation from Yale Law, Class of 1948.

Jones had recently taken leave from the firm to serve as general counsel to the IRS during the first three years of Nixon's initial term; he'd returned to Broward only a few months before Shane had begun work there. The man knew everyone with serious money on the West Coast; was much in demand by most of them; and deservedly so.

It was 10:00 AM Jones was speaking intently into the phone, and gently motioned Shane into one of the commodious leather club chairs in his elaborately paneled office while he continued his conversation. The elegance of the room served to illustrate that, as measured by his comparatively spartan quarters way down on the twenty-second floor, Mr. Dave Durham, Esq., was simply not playing in the same league as Hartley Jones.

About fifteen minutes passed before Jones got disentangled from what appeared to Shane to be very arcane discussion of a tax point on which a great deal of money seemed to be riding. Then, that done, Jones placed the phone back in its cradle and turned up the high beams of his good looks and personality on Shane Sullivan. High beams that Shane Sullivan—after dealing with the dismal welcome to the firm Dave Durham had supplied for nearly a year—found both lustrous and warming.

"So, you're the young guy who saved our asses up here, is that it, then?" Jones said.

Shane smiled. "Nothing to it, Mr. Jones," he said. "I just read the file from top to bottom, that's all. Not that all those goons you sent at me were willing to give me any credit. My God, where do you keep those people? I've never met any of them to have a drink with or anything."

Jones smiled blandly back, his eyes twinkling merrily. This arrogant young fucker is just as dangerous as Dave said he'd be, he thought. Imagine speaking that way to a senior partner you've just met. In Jones's day an impertinent young man like this one would never have been let in the door, let alone allowed to read confidential files. And to then become such a threat, Hart thought, wrenched once again by the realization of what this kid could do to his treasured relationship with Gleason with just one phone call.

But these days, what can you do? With all the protesting and the drugs, not to mention the Christ only knows what kinds of sexual promiscuity, every year we take the best of an increasingly bad lot. But to look at this guy—even by current standards he must have snuck in under the fence. His entirely insolent face reflected that much.

"Feel like a walk?" Hart said, lifting himself out of his deeply piled leather chair and heading for the suit jacket hanging behind the door to his office. Before Shane could respond, Hart was briskly striding down the hall toward the elevator.

With Shane trailing behind in his not inconsiderable wake, Hart glad-handed partners and secretaries alike as he made his way along the twenty-fifth floor's corridor of power. A minute or so later they were out in front of 111 Montgomery, looking up at that imposing structure together while Hart fumbled for his cigarettes. He lit one and offered Shane the pack. Shane declined. Though he did indulge occasionally, to the great dismay of his health-conscious wife, Shane smoked only filters. Hart was a Camel man, yellowed fingers and all.

The two men walked around the corner of Montgomery and Post and headed north, toward Nob Hill. Hart was a master of the art of casual conversation, using the time spent walking to artfully inquire about Shane's commute, his reading habits, his exercise routine, and eventually his family. From all this Hart gleaned that Shane worked at being physically fit, was something of an intellectual, and most importantly—given the money he had married into during law school—didn't need his job at Broward.

As an acute observer of human nature, Hart also saw something in Shane which had entirely escaped Dave Durham. The boy had been traumatized somehow. He was completely vicious. More and more troubling, Hart thought. Why, this kid would ruin me as soon as look at me if he thought it would do him the least amount of good. That fucking insensitive moron Durham has been nurturing a viper. A viper that will wind up biting my titties off, not his, Hart thought.

Like his mentor—that boss of all bosses, Moshe Janofsky—had done just a few days before, Hart took a moment to marvel at the 1965 partnership vote which had allowed Durham to stay on at Broward. We should have kicked that simpleton out right then, Hart thought. Put him in his place over on a collection desk at Bank of America. It's all he was ever good for, anyway. He would have been out of harm's way, waiting for a bank pension—anywhere but inside the firm, overlooking a menace like this Sullivan character. Hart made a mental note to look into who else had been involved in Sullivan's employment. Heads would roll, that was for sure.

Thirty minutes of brisk walking later, they were at Post and Taylor, standing before the august portals of the Bohemian Club. Before showing Shane in, Hart made an effort to explain the place's history to his young companion.

"Olympic, Pacific Union, Family—why clubs like those have nothing on this old place. This is the home of presidents, pal, and right on down from there. Why, Cap Weinberger and Henry Kissinger have lunch here every time they're both in town, and I'm proud to say I've been invited to those lunches more than a few times. Young guy like you, though, you got to sing or dance before you'll get in. And I'm not talking metaphors here, kid—I mean really sing or dance. Somebody's got to get on stage up at the Grove and it can't be an overweight old bum like me, you know? You sing or dance, kid?"

Somehow Shane got the idea that there was more to Hart's question than met the eye. Like Satan showing Christ the whole world if only Christ would fall down and worship him. Something along those lines. But Shane played it straight and gave an honest, if blunt, answer.

"I sing like a frog and I'm clumsy as hell, Mr. Jones. I guess this'll be my one peek inside."

29

Jones hadn't actually meant that much by his question, but once again he was struck by the discordance of Shane's answer. Charmless, he thought. Mean as hell, smart as hell, and totally charmless. With my balls held in a vice. What to do? Why, if I were back in the Pacific, I'd send him to a remote island so fast it would make his head swim.

The two men lunched, and, over lunch, at Hart's lead, discussed whether Nixon would tough Watergate out. Shane's pretense of interest in the subject was as transparent to Hart as the younger man's antipathy for Dave Durham in particular and Broward in general. They took a cab back to the office.

A week later, again without warning, Shane was summoned to Hart Jones's office once more. Once again, the older man was on the phone—this time, as Shane quickly realized, speaking with Mr. C. Reynolds Gleason himself.

"Ray," Hart was saying, "we don't like to let go of a bone any more than you do, but this Maldonado operation is headed for bankruptcy. You can't get blood out of a turnip. Now, look, we just don't want to keep sending you bills, so I've decided we're not going any further. You just pay the last bill and that's the end of the matter."

Shane was shocked. Sitting right there in front of him, Hart Jones was happily lying his ass off to Gleason, telling him nothing about Shenk's fuck-up or Gleason's own exposure. He was even making sure that last bill was paid. It probably included all the time for the internal and entirely self-protective Shenk investigation, for Christ's sake.

But the best thing of all was when old Hart actually winked at Shane as he hung up. "Questions, Sullivan?" was all Hart said, looking right at him. Meaning, 'say the wrong word and you are done here. And think about it before you start fucking with me, pal, because it's all going to happen at once for you if you do.'

Shane was a quick study, and his decision-making process was aided by the fact that he had no more attachment to Gleason than to any other bug that happened to hit his windshield. "No questions, Mr. Jones," he replied, without apparent hesitation. And that was it. Hart Jones dismissively turned his chair around to face a window, and Shane left the senior partner's office without further invitation to go or stay.

After that, Hart Jones never seemed to notice Shane again. The hard feelings Shane had set loose in the upper reaches of Broward remained an opaque mystery to him. Shane never understood how just playing ball wasn't enough for some people. How they wanted you to like it, too.

Chapter Five
Boalt Hall School of Law
University of California at Berkeley
Berkeley, CA
{September 1971-June 1972}

By the time Shane first befriended Helen Wilson, he'd been married for six months. Still, her first casual approach—coming over to him in the middle of the fall semester of their third year, at the end of a four-hour lecture in which Shane had taken no notes—and asking, "So, what are you, a genius or something?" had flummoxed him.

He was no genius at coursework, that was for sure. Instead, as he hastened to tell her, he just couldn't listen and write notes at the same time—he'd lose all track of whatever was said while he was writing. Whatever that meant about his mentality, he had no idea. But, for some reason, his explanation interested Helen, who began loaning him her excellent notes, and eventually invited him into her up-to-that-time all-female study group.

Helen made no effort to socialize with him. She did, however, freely describe her intimacy with Turner Smiley, their common Boalt classmate—whom everyone called TS—in front of Shane and her other study-group partners. Especially the nuances of TS's ability to manipulate nearly everyone, except, according to her own lights, Helen herself.

"That boy could be president," she said to the group one evening, after they'd finished exhausting the possible uses of the federal writ of habeas corpus to free prisoners first convicted in state courts. "He looks it, he feels it, and he's just nasty enough to do what it takes to get it. But you know," and here she looked right over at Shane, "he'd have no idea what to do once he got there. To TS there's really no difference between being president of the class or president of the US. Either one just means lots of people who don't know you love you the most. That's all. The only people who ever get anything good done out of someone like TS's getting what he wants are the people around him. Like me, maybe."

Shane couldn't help himself. Here was his by now dear friend, beautiful and oh-so-brainy Helen, acting like second fiddle to this Smiley character. A guy who, even on a short acquaintance, struck charmless Shane—who was very hard, in his turn, to charm—as nothing more than some kind of Ralph Lauren model.

"Jesus, Helen, what are you doing with that guy?" Shane said. "You don't need whatever it is he's got. You're the feminazi. Act like one."

That got a good laugh from the four women other than Helen in the study group, none of whom would have had a chance with handsome TS, and all of whom thought their sister-in-arms was throwing herself away on an empty moron.

"Even feminazis need love, Shane," Helen said. "And, trust me on this; TS is in touch with his feelings when it comes to women.

Besides, we girls like eye candy just as much as you men do. More, maybe."

"And anyway," she said, laughing now, "one man or another, to a modern woman, what's the difference?"

The truth, of course, was more complex than Helen's braggadocio. Like many of her male counterparts, who preferred good-looking women considerably less intellectually intense than themselves, Helen had no desire to engage emotionally with anyone—Shane being a good example—whose personality would wear on her, rather than allow her to relax.

TS, for all his shortcomings, was courteous to a fault, beautiful, vigorously athletic, and correspondingly wonderful in bed. While he read little, he was bright enough to pass time with while a girl recharged her batteries; hiking in the High Sierra, say. And he had enough charisma to charm birds down from trees and into the mouths of waiting kitties.

A former Dartmouth fraternity boy, TS's social network consisted of a group of similarly-minded beer-swilling-until-dawn touch-football types, all of whom were oddly out of place on the long-haired, dope driven, anti-war Berkeley campus as it existed at the beginning of the 70s. If it weren't for his connection with Helen, Shane would have been invisible to the man.

But the two's contacts were pleasant enough. You couldn't help but feel the heat of TS's charm, no matter who you were. It wasn't until Bill Clinton appeared in the 1991 run-up to the presidential election that Shane ever again saw anything to approach the Cheshire-cat grin TS could bring to bear on any situation. And on a moment's notice, at that.

Chapter Six
Law Offices of Broward, Phillips & Hamburg
San Francisco, CA
{Spring 1975-Spring 1976}

A few weeks after Tom Shenk was fired, Shane got transferred to a new Broward partner, no explanations offered. Shane assumed it was a reward for keeping his mouth shut about the Gleason fiasco. Maybe it was.

In any event, the firm wasn't ready to fire him. Hart Jones valued his relationship with the Volkswagen magnet far too much to have anyone put out on the street with the kind of insider's knowledge Shane had.

Justin Elder, the senior partner Shane was assigned to, already had two junior partners and three younger lawyers working under him—a much more conventional working group within the firm than the one-partner-one-associate mix Shane had been used to. And Elder himself was a true Broward comer.

Only forty-six, Jus had been fronting Broward's defense of Howard Hughes for the previous four years. The billionaire had been sued for dragging out negotiations respecting—and thereby beating down the price of—his purchase of a failing West Coast airline named AirW, which Hughes had bought in late 1970.

Hughes had been a notoriously tough businessman throughout his career, but showing he had broken any laws merely by slow-walking negotiations with the AirW board as the company slid ever closer to a financial meltdown—why, that was a very difficult plaintiff's case indeed.

Defending Hughes presented a special problem, however. Hughes had his personal fingerprints all over the 1970 transaction, and, as would become increasingly obvious as the decade went on, the tycoon had been entirely nuts for many years.

The problem Broward faced was that Hughes would not emerge from whatever bat cave he happened to be holed up in, even if the alternative were his own beheading—let alone just losing a few hundred million dollars in a lawsuit. These circumstances had been explained to Jus Elder and his team when they were first interviewed for the job by Hughes's New York lawyer, Chester Davis, at the latter's Las Vegas hotel suite in February 1971, shortly after the first AirW lawsuits had been filed.

As Jus and his junior partners had studiously tried to ignore an underdressed—and underage—waif that the nearly seventy-year-old Davis was obviously sharing a penthouse hotel suite with, Davis had complained bitterly about the wave of lawsuits the airline transaction was embroiling his most valued client in.

"Jackals," he'd said. "Jackals. After TWA, they're betting that the boss won't answer any questions, at least not in person. All these ridiculous allegations, they know they can't back them up—why, it's all just a bet they can get through a motion to dismiss, and then the boss won't show for questioning. And they're right, you know. Just like those jackals in TWA were right. The boss will never show. Not that they'll ever make any money for being right."

Jus and his colleagues were fully aware of the reference. Hughes Tool was then before the US Supreme Court, seeking to overturn a default judgment in favor of TWA for more than $200,000,000. A default judgment taken at the District Court level because the boss had refused to appear in person and answer any questions about his business. No matter what the financial consequences were for his company.

"So what the Hughes people need here, fellows," Davis had continued, "is a firm with some balls, lawyers who aren't going to melt just because some guinea son of a bitch doesn't like their client."

Again the reference was clear. All the federal securities litigation arising out of the AirW acquisition—which was, as usual, the main attraction in any allegedly crooked business dealing—was likely going to be consolidated before the Honorable Peter Zirponzi.

And Zirp, as he was nicknamed, was the strong-willed son of Italian immigrants, a judge cut out of the same cloth as his more famous countryman, District Judge John J. Sirica of Watergate fame.

Before joining the federal bench in 1961, Zirp had been a long-time Assistant US Attorney. In that capacity, he'd prosecuted many a famous West Coast triggerman, achieving enormous play in the popular press of the time. Jus knew very well that Zirp had always loved the media limelight. And now the old man was clearly embracing the AirW litigation as the capstone of his career as a federal judge.

"Balls," Jus assured, "are something my firm has plenty of."

Chester Davis looked knowingly over at Justin Elder, amused by the younger man's cockiness as well as his obvious ambition.

"You wouldn't be here in my company enjoying this fine air-conditioned desert air, Jus," Davis said quietly, "if that hadn't already been established to my satisfaction. But there's another issue, and it's one that seems to be putting some otherwise qualified firms in your small city off their feed in taking this assignment. You never talk to the boss. You talk to me, I talk to the boss. That's the way it is, that's the way it's always been. Now what do you say about that, my young friend? And I don't want any hesitation here. You got a problem with what I just said, the airport is only five minutes from the Strip. Have a nice day."

Going into the meeting, Jus Elder had figured there was at least $2,000,000 a year in fees on the table. He had assumed Hughes would never show up in person for anything resembling a question-and-answer session. And he had also predicted that Zirp would roast him alive once the judge had figured out that Hughes could care less what any court had to say about anything. Guinea bastard was a very fair description for what Zirp would become once you got on his bad side, a bad side which, throughout his whole career thus far, Jus had more or less successfully avoided.

But Jus had always figured on at least having a real client he could directly advise. And he'd been excited at the prospect of talking to the great Mr. Hughes in person. Now, with Davis's insistence on acting as a cut-out, Jus found himself wondering.

Why, for all Jus knew, Hughes was dead. Or lying somewhere strapped to a bed with an IV in his arm and a sock in his mouth. There was just no way to rationalize the ethics of having Broward do what Davis was asking, which was simply pretend it had a client.

But $2,000,000 a year was $2,000,000 a year. And in the end, the real question was very simple: So what?

Elder looked Davis in the eye.

"Not a problem," he said. "I'll just need the boss's signature on the fee agreement, since he's an individual defendant. After that, you and the boss run your affairs the way you want to. I talk to you, you talk to him. Welcome to Broward."

The conversation then turned to the nature and extent of the charges against Hughes, how Broward would work with both of Hughes's long-term DC and NY firms, and, finally, what needed most attention the soonest.

Hours later, as Elder and his two partners turned to leave, they caught a glimpse through a doorway of a by-then-naked teenager, fifteen at most, sprawled on a round bed, legs akimbo, sleepily waiting for Davis to finish with them and attend to her. Elder swallowed his disgust and walked straight out of the room.

By 1975, the AirW litigation was reaching its inevitable negative climax. Zirp was determined to hang Hughes for failing to appear for questioning. New lawsuits were being filed daily on the same basis. And it wasn't only small-bore plaintiff's firms suing Hughes; the queue included all sorts of mainstream firms as well, all eager to plunder the Hughes baggage train.

In those pre-computer days, it was an exercise just to keep track of each new case as it was served, and the two precise old ladies, who together comprised Broward's entire calendar department, were at their wits' ends. Not that they would consider giving up the reins of power by hiring new help. That intransigence wound up subjecting them to all kinds of unusual reading matter, including one Johnny-come-lately lawsuit attaching a *Playgirl* article speculating Hughes had been kidnapped by space aliens. As unusual as the article was, it had nothing on the full-frontal nude male model splayed out beside the text. Strange days indeed.

As for Shane, he suddenly found himself playing team ball. And the team, particularly the three younger lawyers who were not yet partners, didn't just work together; they socialized as well. Drinks most nights together before going home; all playing on a BP&H sponsored basketball team together; you name it.

Lu Odom was the undoubted fair-haired boy of the group. Only a year ahead of Shane at the firm, Lu's ability and charm had won Justin Elder over completely by the end of Lu's first year. He was sure to make partner at the earliest possible opportunity.

The other two junior lawyers were a big step down the food chain from Lu Odom. Jay Jay Martin and Dan Bowen were classic grinders. Neither particularly able nor at all charming, there was no task too mind numbing as far as either of them was concerned. They were the infantry of the group, the guys who strove to answer the hundreds of repetitive and ultimately meaningless motions, interrogatories and document requests being hurled at Hughes, all the while hurling back hundreds more of the same volleys at their opponents, thereby keeping the rapidly deflating Hughes ball in the air for as long as possible.

Lu, meanwhile, was a true leader. Shane's insensitivity to others would later be diagnosed as symptomatic of Asberger's syndrome; this was one reason that working in isolation for an equally anti-social Dead End Dave had been water off a duck's back for him. But freezing out Lu Odom was another matter. Lu was a genuine prince. His charm was not of the turn-it-on/turn-it-off variety that leaders like Turner Smiley and Hartley Jones possessed in such abundance. Their more common ability to project charm at will was something that a true misanthrope like Shane—who'd been beaten on by every popular kid he'd ever met—couldn't be fooled by.

No, Lu was simply the real deal. His charm came only in the on position, and it was fueled by great affection and real kindness toward others. Any platoon he led would go up the hill, do or die, just because they wanted him to know they loved him back as much as he loved them. And before he knew it, Shane was as much in thrall to Lu as the lowest paralegal, the one who always put a little more swing into her hips anytime she walked past Lu in the hall.

But leadership qualities alone do not a Napoleon make. Conquest against impossible odds takes great imagination, not just a talent for group dynamics. And there is no profession as lacking in imagination as the precedent-revering law business.

So, while Lu had the necessary ability to lead his small group up any hill he chose, he never had a clue as to which hill the platoon should take. And, other than the $2,000,000-in-fees hill he had seen so clearly in Las Vegas, neither did Justin Elder. Churning was the order of the day, and not much else.

Shane had no talent for churn. But almost as soon as he joined their working group, he had a chance to demonstrate his value to Elder and Odom, and thereby elevate himself from grunt work once and for all.

To distract the lawyers who had first closed the AirW deal and then turned around and sued Hughes, Broward had sued them for legal malpractice shortly after taking on Hughes's defense. The very thought of one large firm suing another large firm, even one that, like AirW's lawyers, Martin & Jones, was considered second rate, was serious apostasy. And, as the decision to have a non-client sue an opposing party's counsel was so obviously tactical, many prominent city lawyers began vocally complaining that Justin Elder was a serious menace to the San Francisco Bar Association.

Despite all this, the lawyers working for Elder had diligently tried time and again to dress up Hughes's claims against the Martin firm in enough high-sounding legal language to cause the Superior Court judge sitting in the Law and Motion Department to throw up his hands and allow the case to proceed past the pleading stage. And time and again, the low-rent insurance-defense lawyers who were in charge of protecting the Martin firm from Broward had convinced the law and motion judge that there simply was no such thing in law as allowing Howard Hughes to sue AirW's lawyers for anything. By the time Shane came on board, Elder was getting discouraged.

Lu had a feeling, though. And one day he breezed into Shane's tiny office with a thick file folder under his arm.

"Feel like being a hero?" he said to Shane, who was trying to answer interrogatories on some obscure aspect of the financial end of the AirW transaction. Bored to tears and doing a shitty job of it at that.

"Meaning?" Shane said, smiling back at his already trusted new friend.

44

"Jus is up shit creek and he needs a miracle. No one has a clue how we can keep Hughes in court on this mal claim against Martin & Jones, but if we have to back off they'll sue our firm, for Christ's sake. Probably for malicious prosecution, which is at least a legal theory people have heard of. The goddamn thing is radioactive, and all people want to do is make sure they're not around when the axe falls. But you, pal, you I already know are too stupid to know trouble when you see it. Whether you can figure something out, that I don't know. Not yet, at least. All I know is I don't have any good ideas. And the next best thing I can do for the boss, whom I dearly love, is find him a hero. Fuck up, maybe you get fired. Win, no more interrogs. I personally promise you that. What do you think?"

"I think I'll take a look," said Shane. "When is this masterpiece due?"

"We've got two weeks to file something with the court," Lu shot back. "So,I'll give you a week to come up with something before I tell the boss I've even showed you the file. See, I don't think he likes you very much so far. You don't fit Jus' idea of what a hardworking young guy is supposed to be willing to do to get ahead. Doesn't know you may be a genius, like I do. So, much better for me to tell him you're working on this after you come up with something worth talking about."

In the end it wasn't hard at all. Hughes had gotten a short opinion letter from Martin & Jones as a condition of closing. It said 'Gee, Howard, everything is in order, please close.' Which

Hughes did. Then, the very next day, Joe Martin wrote a very long letter to AirW that said 'Holy shit, you, AirW, have just been suddenly raped by none other than the famous Howard R. Hughes.'

The drones working for Elder had never been able to solve the conundrum presented by the fact that Hughes could not logically attack the accuracy of the short I'm-OK/you're-OK letter, even though Joe Martin had immediately turned around and repudiated that short letter in his much longer you've-been-raped letter. They'd just talked around the situation, never attacking Joe Martin's dishonesty. They were afraid to say the short letter was actually inaccurate.

Shane's approach was to say the short letter, while true, was not an accurate representation of what Joe Martin thought was true. And Joe Martin's state of mind, he argued, was just as important to Hughes as what Joe Martin had put on paper.

Lu Odom bought it. Then Justin Elder bought it. And, finally, Harry Chin, the San Francisco County Superior Court law and motion judge, bought it. Nobody had liked Joe Martin's talking out of both sides of his mouth, but until Shane explained what was wrong with it, nobody had had a clue about what to do about it. Within a month Joe Martin and his firm were no longer counsel to AirW in the case against Hughes, conflicted because they were cross-defendants in the same case.

Never made a bit of difference in the AirW case itself, of course, as AirW had no trouble replacing old Joe and continuing to get Zirp to beat on Hughes for refusing to show up for deposition. Only Hughes's death in April 1976 would change that dynamic.

But Shane's victory sure made an impression on Elder and Odom, and Shane stayed on at Broward for at least a year beyond what would have otherwise been his tenure there because of the special treatment he received from both thereafter. Ultimately, however, people like Shane were useful to a place like Broward only when the firm was in extremis. And as far as Broward was concerned, in extremis came around once in a blue moon. Mainly, Shane was a constant disturbance to his superiors and peers alike, his rapid intuitions, especially when they were correct, an unseemly embarrassment to all those careful lawyers whose own ponderous thought processes rarely led to mistakes.

Chapter Seven
Berkeley, CA
{September 1971-December 1973}

TS had gotten Helen pregnant in the fall of 1971, after she'd had too much cheap red wine at a law-review party. He had taken advantage of the situation by hurriedly taking her once they were home, without putting on the protection she normally insisted on. Helen didn't like how bloated the pill made her feel; just relied on her usual ability to force a condom on the reluctant TS as her first and last line of defense against both stds and unwanted pregnancy.

She'd figured out what had happened by Thanksgiving, and promptly thrown TS out of the apartment they were renting together. Then she made an appointment with a Berkeley abortion clinic with a month-long waiting list for non-emergency cases. But something odd happened after that. When Helen finally came down from the ceiling long enough—out of sheer practical necessity and common interest—to resume speaking to him at all, TS came crawling back to her.

"I've never met anyone like you," he pleaded one evening, late in December, 1971. They were both lingering over cappuccino in an old burger place that had lately been converted by some far-seeing entrepreneur into a high-priced Italian coffee emporium that sat across from the law school at the corner of College and Bancroft Way.

"And I'll never meet anyone like you again. I know that now. Please, Helen, please don't ruin both our lives just because I was such a selfish, stupid jerk that I went in bareback. I was drunk, and you were too. I just wanted you right then. No waiting, that's all. There was nothing sinister in any of it. I swear to God.

"Besides," he went on, "why look at any baby of ours as a bad thing? We're young and healthy. That baby will be great. You want to work, we'll get you all the help you want taking care of it, and you can work as much as you want. You know we're both going to get great jobs. Make money. You know my parents are loaded. And I know you like me. That you're easy in my company."

"So what if you're smarter than me?" TS said next, getting closer to what he knew was the real problem. "So what if it's not love? Who needs a Hollywood romance anyway? This is the real world, not some movie set."

There was a pause. TS let out a long sigh. Then, after Helen remained silent, he resumed speaking. "Please, Helen," he said, "please believe me now. Even if you've never believed a single word I've ever said to you in all the time we've known each other."

He looked right at her then, with all that empathy projecting toward her, his beautiful, sensitive green eyes tearing. "I want this baby. I really do. For both of us."

At bottom, Helen was still a small-town Oregon girl with small-town Oregon moral values. However much she distrusted TS's rhetoric, and she did distrust it, all of it, abortion was an enormous emotional chasm for her. One she knew she'd have trouble dealing with after the fact.

So, Helen cancelled her appointment at the clinic. She and TS got married in February 1972, over at the beautiful, non-denominational Swedenborgian Church in Pacific Heights. TS's parents came out from Boston for the ceremony.

There they first met Helen, and all of Helen's hardscrabble small-town Oregon family. A day later, the main branch of Wells Fargo Bank was put in charge of a seven-figure trust to ensure the well-being of the well-known Smiley family of Boston's first grandchild-to-be.

That spring semester of her second year at Boalt, Helen carried her child to term and a bit beyond. As might be expected with such physically beautiful parents, when the infant finally came—nearly three weeks late—she was heavenly looking. Baby Ellen Smiley was black haired, with deep baby-blue eyes that would never lose their original magical color. She looked wistfully up at her parents from the incubator that first morning of her life and love seemed everywhere. But, as matters would soon develop, Baby Ellen's otherworldly appearance was no coincidence. She never emoted or babbled. And her dreams—for there was never any doubt at all in Helen's mind that this child of her body dreamed wonderful dreams—remained unknowable mysteries.

It was the summer of 1973, and Helen and TS were law school graduates studying for the July Bar, when they got the first intimation of doom from their live-in help, Juanny. It was seventeen-year-old Juanny, an illegal émigré from Salvador, who had taken Baby Ellen to her one-year well-baby exam one sunny June day a few weeks after the Boalt graduation ceremony.

Before Juanny gave her broken-English explanation of what she had been told by an exasperated pediatrician at Alta Bates, neither parent had really noticed how quiet and remote Baby Ellen was. What with the stress of their lives, the fact the child rarely cried and was unresponsive when held had not registered much with either of them.

Helen was alone when Juanny came in with the quiet-as-usual Baby Ellen bundled under her arm. Big tears were falling from Juanny's eyes. She was red in the face, sweating profusely, and appeared to have run all the way home from the hospital, where Dr. Piel had his practice.

It was a sweltering hike of several miles to the Northside of the Berkeley campus, where TS and Helen had their latest apartment, and Juanny had been told to take a cab both ways. Parking at Alta Bates was impossible, and anyway Juanny was a terrible driver, no matter how proud she was of her recently acquired license.

Before Helen could question her appearance, though, Juanny burst into a sobbing explanation of what had happened. "The doctor, Piel, he yell at me, Missus. He say baby sick, he say where the mother? He say, where someone speaking English? He cursing me, Missus, he saying bad words, and he speak so fast."

Juanny was defensive about her English, and she bristled visibly at Doctor Piel's abuse.

"I can speak my English better now, you know, Missus. Much better than before. You know, Missus. You help Juanny all the time with my English. I glad. But that doctor so mad and he just yell at Juanny. I cry when he yell at Juanny."

"Sick," Helen repeated. She was looking askance at both the obviously hysterical Juanny and a badly overheated Baby Ellen.

"Sick? What the hell do you mean, sick?"

Helen was almost shouting now.

"Why, that little girl has never been sick a day in her life. She's the best baby anybody ever heard of! Juanny, this had better be good, with you scaring me this way. I mean, I'm trying to study. You can't just come in here with your hair all on fire like this and upset me so much."

The normally kind-to-a-fault Helen then gave her trembling teenage servant a quite menacing look.

"If I have to tell TS you're acting crazy, he'll fire you."

Both Helen and Juanny knew that TS disliked having Juanny around. Juanny was déclassé. But when Helen had found she couldn't cope with both her third-year studies and a newborn, Juanny had been all that was available. She'd been living at the Old Unitarian Church on College, which provided sanctuary for illegals and tried to find them jobs. And now Juanny was terrified of being fired and put back on the street, where the Immigration would get her and send her back home.

"Missus, please don't scare Juanny. I love baby. I try to do everything for baby. And be help for you. But doctor said baby sick. He told me tell you; baby sick, you must talk him right away. No more send Juanny. Juanny no understand what doctor say. But he do say baby sick. Really, Missus. So, you need talk doctor. Now, Missus, now. You talk doctor. Ok, please. For Juanny."

Juanny had gone from being merely hysterical to the point of despair when she'd been threatened with firing by Helen. In the middle of her speech, she'd collapsed in a heap on the floor of the spacious living room, still holding Baby Ellen under her arm as if she were a throw rug.

And Baby Ellen, as usual, did and said nothing. Not even gurgled.

Helen put them both to bed. Then she went grimly to the telephone.

It took Helen about an hour to get Dr. Piel. When she'd finally succeeded, she'd started by complaining bitterly.

"What do you mean by terrifying my housekeeper, doctor? She barely speaks English, and she came home crying and nearly suffering from heatstroke after running all the way home. With the baby under her arm, for god's sake. How could you possibly speak to her that way?"

Dr. Piel was nearly seventy. He'd been one of East Bay society's leading pediatricians of choice for most of his career. He was quite used to dealing with high-strung young mothers. So, he ignored Helen's tone, ignored her accusations of having abused Juanny—with whom he had indeed lost his legendary temper—and immediately got down to a somber discussion of Baby Ellen's unfortunate condition.

"Your child is not progressing normally, Mrs. Smiley. Haven't you noticed how quiet and, well, unresponsive to stimuli she is?"

Helen felt her heart palpitate with sudden fear. She'd been an only child. And she'd done next to no babysitting as a teenager. The family lived so far outside what passed for a town in central Oregon that it always cost more money in gas than the job would pay. So, she'd had virtually no experience with babies before having Baby Ellen.

"Well, so she's quiet, so what?" Helen said defensively.

"I'm sure you must care deeply about your child, Mrs. Smiley," Dr. Piel said gently.

Helen felt a stab. She knew this Dr. Piel must know something bad, real bad. Why, the fucker had practically slapped Juanny, and yet here he was now, just gentling Helen along. Just a month after she'd married TS, Helen's own mother had been diagnosed with cervical cancer. Helen had gone up to Oregon in late May 1972, and when she got there she'd heard that same sorrowful tone in their small-town G.P.'s voice when he'd sat down with her family to tell them the facts about Martha Wilson's tenuous lease on life. Martha Wilson who was now six months in the grave.

"Just stop playing with me, doctor," she said, bravely. "And tell me what's on your mind."

Dr. Piel refused to be definite, but the word autism was mentioned in that first telephone call, as well as the immediate need for extensive testing. Two months later, the final, horrifying results were in. There was an autism present in Baby Ellen so severe that the child would likely be vegetative her entire life. A life that was just as likely to extend for its full natural course of seventy or eighty years as that of any normal child her age. Especially with a large trust fund already in place to pay for Baby Ellen's care.

As soon as she'd looked up the condition in a medical dictionary, Helen had stopped preparing for the Bar and begun staying home full-time with her daughter, studying her intently for signs that Dr. Piel's initial off-the-cuff diagnosis might be inaccurate. Scheming how she'd sue that know-it-all son of a bitch for all he was worth if he'd been wrong and frightened her needlessly.

TS, too, had refused to believe anything until it was confirmed by testing, and he particularly refused to read any of the massive amounts of printed materials Helen rapidly accumulated on autism. Instead he just kept working toward his Bar passage, spending as little time as he could at the apartment with his increasingly depressed, obsessive wife. Some nights he didn't come home at all, and Helen was sure he'd gone off and fucked some bimbo or other, as TS didn't like being deprived of regular sex.

When she thought about TS having sex with someone else, the-by-now frantic Helen told herself she just didn't care. She certainly wasn't in the mood to blow off any steam herself, not with an ominously silent baby lying in a crib set up beside her bed, eating and breathing, eating and breathing.

By the time there was no doubt about the hopelessness of Baby Ellen's condition, TS had taken the Bar. He had also moved out of their Scenic Way apartment and into a bachelor flat with two fraternity brothers from Dartmouth, both recently arrived in the Bay Area and working for investment banks. Once he had spoken with the doctors, TS wanted nothing further to do with what he had begun to think of as 'the problem.'

To his parents and the others who expressed sympathy, he would say stolidly that it was just "one of those things people have to get through." And when he spoke to Helen, which, as time went on, was not often, he would remind her that his parents had already provided for the child.

And every time he would add, "What more can anyone do? You won't starve, and neither will she." That was it. 'The problem' was solved.

By the end of 1974, TS and Helen were in the divorce courts. No-fault divorce, the brainchild of a radical feminist Boalt professor, was the order of the day. It had been a short-term marriage, and TS had no money of his own, so it was a clean split. No alimony, and, because of the trust fund, no child support, either. In and out, one life never really begun, one life wrecked, and TS off to bigger and better things.

Chapter Eight
Law Offices of Broward, Phillips & Hamburg
San Francisco, CA
{Fall 1976}

The end for Shane came unexpectedly. Elder, trying to keep Shane busy and out of his own hair, began lending his young associate out to other partners who had brush fires burning out of control. Few of these partners were grateful for Shane's assistance, since Shane's brashness, as Hart Jones had bitterly observed firsthand, was entirely jarring in a firm as hierarchal as Broward.

One of these partners was the younger son of Herman Phillips, one Hillsborough Phillips, known as Hills. He was the Broward representative on the board of Bank of America, Chairman of the Board of the San Francisco Opera Company, and a member of the Bohemian Club since he was fourteen. Stanford Law graduate, Class of 1958. He'd been hooked on prescription painkillers ever since he'd suffered a devastating Squaw Valley ski injury in 1971, one that had left him in a wheelchair.

Moshe Janofsky, who was then more or less successfully defending Westinghouse from an outraged citizenry's entirely accurate claims that the BART system was a cluster fuck of monumental proportions, had used his very considerable influence with the board of Westinghouse back in Pittsburgh, Pennsylvania to pressure management into stripping a condemnation case—then being prosecuted by the State of California against a Westinghouse real-estate division—away from the local dean of the condemnation bar and over to Broward. Once that was done, Moshe had allowed Hills to handle the matter, again playing politics, this time the politics of allowing Hills the illusion the firm still valued him as a lawyer, rather than simply for his many social connections both in San Francisco and among the old money families of the Peninsula.

While Hills accepted the compliment greedily, the fact was he had long since stopped functioning as anything but a pretty face, and was clueless as to how to actually litigate his new case. It would take a State Bar investigation some five years later—itself precipitated by Hills's attending an annual Bank of America shareholders meeting wearing only Bermuda shorts and sneakers, and loudly cursing a female board member who dared to publicly question Hills's sartorial choices—to bring Hills's drug problems to the official attention of the firm.

When the Westinghouse case first arrived on Hills's plate, Hills's associate, an Order of the Coif graduate from Shane's own Class of 1973 at Boalt named Ed Rust, had tried to run the case on his own, filing pleadings and taking discovery with next to no input from Hills. But then Rust had been offered a job with the US Attorney's Office. He took it and ran. Rather than tell Moshe he knew next to nothing about a case he was supposed to be responsible for, Hills had instead gone down to Justin Elder's office and asked Elder for his help.

Shortly after Hills left, Elder had called Shane into his modest office.

"You busy?" Elder said.

"I'm working on stuff, but I'm always interested in something new," Shane had replied, trying to get along with Elder, whom Lu was constantly telling him was an OK guy.

Elder looked at him hard.

"Well, Shane, I already know from Hart Jones that you're no stranger to the fact that sometimes we have things go wrong at this firm. I mean, we're not perfect, and some of the people who work here are not perfect. And sometimes some of those people need help. Now, this firm is not an easy place to get ahead. And you may or may not have what it takes. But you've got something. Lu and I both see that in you. If you're going to make it here, we have to put whatever it is you have to work pulling this firm's sleigh."

At this point Shane figured there was some new kind of scandal brewing, and he was being set up to take a fall if he couldn't put it to rest without a fuss. So, he was actually relieved to hear what came next.

"One of our partners is Hills Phillips, old Herman Phillips's son. You know that, right?"

"Sure, boss. Ed Rust was my Boalt classmate, and Rust worked for that guy before he left us and went public. I don't think Ed liked Phillips very much, but Ed was real closed mouthed about it, so maybe I'm wrong."

"Hills is an arrogant prick, Shane, and working for him had to have been a misery for Rust. You understand me. I'm not hiding anything here."

Shane said nothing, amazed at Elder's candor.

"But Hills has as big a book of business as any partner in this firm, and he has a shitload of personal money that he got from Herman as well. The only person in the firm who can touch him is Moshe Janofsky, whom Hills knows absolutely can't stand him. So, about a half an hour ago Hills came in here and asked me to bail him out of having to tell Moshe that he's been off playing hooky while your pal Rust tried to learn condemnation law on the job. And what's worse, now that Rust is gone, Hills is afraid to pick up the case and do his own work for a change. So, he says he wants me to help him, meaning he wants me to see that someone else gets assigned to do his work while he takes all the credit. And, mainly, he doesn't want a word of any of this breathed to another living soul but me, and now you. You understand what I'm telling you?"

Shane said nothing.

"You do want me to be your friend, like I'm already Lu's friend? Right? So, you do this and maybe we start to be friends."

Shane again said nothing.

Elder looked at him. "Is there a problem here, Mister Sullivan?"

"Naw, boss, there's no problem. I'm not even worried about the work. But what Ed Rust actually says about Phillips is that the guy is a head case. And you know I lack bedside manner. So, how do I get along with him?"

Elder was not sympathetic.

"That's your problem. This here is a hard place for non-conformists, and you're just going to have to figure out how to fit in. You do your best and you keep your mouth shut and your head down. Good luck. With Hills as a boss, you're going to need it."

At first, Hills was all upper-class charm and appreciation for Shane's 'stepping in' to replace Ed Rust, a non-person whom Hills clearly regarded as a traitorous betrayer. It was clear the case had driven Rust out of the firm; Ed's ignorance of the subject matter and his inability to get help from other partners without embarrassing Hills had driven the highly regimented, responsible-to-a-fault Navy veteran simply crazy.

But Shane Sullivan was no Ed Rust. He simply called Broward's predecessor counsel, Burton Goldsmith, Esq., eminent author of the leading text on condemnation law and hapless victim of Moshe Janofsky's power politics at the Westinghouse board level, and told him the truth. Without asking anybody at Broward for permission, that was for sure.

Goldsmith was sufficiently intrigued by the strange call for help from deep within the bowels of Broward that he immediately invited Shane over to his opulent office at San Francisco's old-timey Russ Building, just up the street from the slightly newer but still '30s-vintage office building occupied by Broward. Once in Goldsmith's presence, Shane did not mince words.

"The way I see it, they pulled the case from you using politics and then turned it over to a nincompoop, again for politics' sake. And now someone has to pay the piper when this blows up in their faces, and very likely that's going to be me. So, fuck it," Shane said harshly, "you're the only possible friend I got here. Because I need help, and I know you know this case, and I'm not afraid to tell you the truth about that."

Goldsmith loved it. And he loved the fact that Shane had read his text cover to cover and actually had some nuanced questions to ask. And some ideas of his own, too, though it was apparent Shane was a generalist, with no particular love for condemnation law as a specialty field in and of itself.

Their first meeting lasted three hours. It was a masterful seminar on both the case itself and what was hidden between the lines of Goldsmith's condemnation text. After that, Goldsmith acted as Shane's sounding board every step of the way. Hills, meanwhile, just stayed out of Shane's way.

But Shane's old boogeyman, his lack of interpersonal skills, eventually became a problem. The crisis came when Shane, with

Burt Goldsmith's full support, questioned the State of California's theory that the land it was condemning at Half Moon Bay was severed by Highway 1 from the uplands owned by Westinghouse. If true, it meant that the state only had to pay for the beach property it wanted, leaving Westinghouse holding the bag on the rest.

Shane figured out that the State of California likely had to pay what were called severance damages on all of Westinghouse's lands because Highway 1 actually ran over an easement which the state had acquired from a defunct railroad. Or so said some nineteenth-century condemnation cases Shane had dug up, all with an increasing sense of excitement once Burt had confirmed his radical approach had potential.

Hills was less impressed. What he knew was that this kid lawyer had gotten way too big for his britches, marching into his office with some claim that there was an important issue in the case that Hills had never thought of. At least Ed Rust would have had the tact to let Hills think it was Hills's input that had somehow led Ed to make such an important discovery. But here was Shane, knocking at the door with a memo that, velobound with a great deal in the way of back-up materials, left no doubt who had first thought of what.

Not knowing what else to do, and acting out of sheer frustration, Hills had physically ripped the velobinding of the memo apart while Shane watched in quiet disbelief. What came next very much surprised Hills. Shane didn't say a word. Just stared at the mess Hills had created by spilling the long memo onto the floor, then turned on his heels, went down to Justin Elder's office, and quit Broward on the spot. He made a point of telling the young partner Moshe Janofsky sent to do an exit interview with him later that day that Hills had seemed doped up. Half-crazy, anyway. And that was it. Shane was allowed to go.

Chapter Nine
Howard University School of Law
Howard University
Washington DC
{September 1973-June 1974}

Leticia Madison was a thirty-year-old single mother with a thirteen-year-old child by the time she became a 1L at Howard Law School in the fall of 1973. Her climb—from ground zero as a fifteen-year-old heroin-snorting prostitute working the mean streets of Washington DC's infamous Northeast quadrangle up to a Howard law school applicant—had been the subject of an admissions essay so moving it had induced Howard to make her an offer despite a 470 LSAT and a formal education that had stopped at the sixth grade.

The story was more or less true, but Leticia—like her later mentee, TS—had quietly employed outside assistance in its telling. What she hadn't needed any help with, professional or otherwise, was charming the all-male panel that constituted the ad hoc Howard faculty committee charged with considering hardship cases such as hers. That process was part of Howard's self-conscious efforts to remember its roots in the poor black community, now that seats in its law school were so prized amongst the progeny of the many middle- and upper-class black families a Howard degree had lifted up from poverty in generations past.

The same animal magnetism Leticia once employed to lure men into the back of abandoned automobiles or vacant lots—places where, as often as not, she would rob them without letting them lay a finger on her, fucking only those who genuinely seemed too rough to disappoint—she had happily used to seduce the more genteel male audience present at her admit interview.

What attracted all these men to her, professors and johns alike, had nothing to do with her looks. She was plain almost to the point of ugliness, and her sexual allure had long since been used up. Rather, it was her empathy—quite false, but utterly compelling—that left the men on the receiving end of it with the conviction that here was a person who understood them, who would be there for them if ever the need arose. A hooker with a heart of gold.

Her admit essay described how she'd become pregnant in 1959, at sixteen, with what turned out to be a white john's child. How the man, a truck driver far too burly to assault, had paid an extra $12 not to wear a condom. How she had refused an abortion and stopped taking drugs so as not to harm her child. How she had then gone on AFDC, eventually taking mail-order secretarial courses in an effort to improve herself. And how, at age twenty-three, the year her daughter turned seven, Leticia had first embarked on a secretarial career at a large, prestigious DC firm.

What the essay didn't describe was what she had learned there. Not grammar and spelling. Only the blackest of skin colors and her oft repeated up-from-the-ghetto life story had kept her from being fired on account of her utter lackof those skills. But she did swiftly learn the personal dynamics of the firm, consistently sorting out, well in advance of actual developments, who was winning the ever-present struggle for money and influence. And why the winners won.

For an ex-hooker with only six years of the poorest kind of classroom education, Leticia acquired an insight into the methods and psyches of the lily-white partners at Holland & Harper that would have made Dale Carnegie blush with envy. She had used that insight to transfer out of the secretarial pool and into an assistant's position within H&H's rapidly expanding Human Resources Department.

At that time, HR primarily involved dealing with the nuances of DC's increasingly Byzantine labor laws, in an effort to keep the firm itself from becoming the subject of various types of litigation. Once she arrived, Leticia's people skills with the largely minority, often disgruntled, staff made her a much valued addition.

At Howard Law, however, her first year was nearly her last. It was one thing to have H&H's head of HR translate Leticia's admit essay into a reasonable approximation of American English. It was quite another to pass a law school exam with no editor along to ghostwrite.

Howard's December exams were given to the 1Ls as an exercise; their grades would be based solely on a set of finals given in May. The writing contained in Leticia's blue books was so untutored that it was apparent to her professors that, without some special consideration, she would never pass a course at Howard. And using any sort of affirmative-action rationale to keep Leticia from flunking out was an exquisitely sensitive subject at a black university that prided itself on the renown that its graduates had carved out for themselves and their law school in the face of the most blatant racial prejudice.

Leticia came to the same realization. And understanding that her poor performance on the December practice exams had put her on what amounted to a faculty death watch, she decided to find an edge.

Merely being a poor, uneducated, older black woman wasn't going to cut it at Howard—at least not the way it would have at Yale or Berkeley, where many of the faculty were so committed to the civil rights struggle that no black student, once admitted, would ever have been permitted to fail out. So, it was back to Ellen Silverstein, head of HR at H&H—the George Washington University graduate who had so convincingly elevated Leticia's casual decision at sixteen to accept that extra $12 from the merely banal into a rousing tale of redemption. A task which Ellen had taken on because, in the increasingly race-sensitive capital city, the woman had the good sense to see Leticia as an eventual threat to Ellen's own job as head of HR.

But now Leticia had something on Ellen. Any involvement with plagiarism was a major sin at H&H, and Ellen's ghostwriting an admissions essay for Leticia was enough to finish her career for good and all. So, when Leticia called on a busy Christmas Eve afternoon, Ellen had been immediately responsive. The two women made arrangements to meet for drinks at Wisconsin and M Street later that evening.

Ellen found Leticia sitting at Georgetown's tony Rive Gauche bar when she arrived, a bit past six. "Hello, darling," the older woman began, as she approached her former protégée. Even when she saw the fury in Leticia's demeanor, she struggled on, trying to diffuse matters. "You sounded so upset, Letty, honey, so now you tell your momma Ellen all about what the bad men are trying to do to my sweetie."

Ellen had been using this faux-maternal routine on Leticia from the first moment she had been forced to work with a person whom she truly considered a viper. Ellen, a stout Jewish woman of sixty-five, had an ailing husband. There was nothing more than his small university pension and her salary to support them both. She had not gotten ahead at a DC firm—owned and operated by members of the WASP establishment who still basically, if quite guardedly, regarded Jews, Catholics, and blacks alike with equal disdain—by being any less canny or vicious than her younger black counterpart.

Leticia hated Ellen's baby talk almost as much as she hated the anglicized nickname, Letty, that Ellen had tagged her with on the day the two first began working together. But she had never complained. Just watched and learned, and in the process of watching and learning, came to admire the manipulative qualities

70

of her fat-assed Jew lady boss, a woman whom she considered, like herself, a survivor of the first order.

"I'm flunking, momma Ellen, and all the black mens have suddenly figured out that maybe a sixth-grade education and a law degree don't go together so easy. And just being black, that ain't no good when everybody else be black too. So, I need a fix, and it better be good, momma Ellen, because them same black mens may start asking a lot of questions about how good that first essay was once I be gone. And if I can't get what I want, I just may start blabbing about how I got me some white friends who were soooo glad when I wanted to be a lawyer, they decided to help me out a little, you know?"

Ellen Silverstein was quite shocked by Leticia's sudden lapse into Ebonics, something she had never heard her former colleague—who normally did not even speak with a Southern accent—indulge in before. And she took it for exactly the hostile threat it was meant to be. If I go down here, Jew lady, so do you. Simple as that. And no exaggeration.

Ellen cursed herself for thinking that once Letty—or whatever the hell her real name was—left the firm she'd be done with her. Who'd ever heard of anyone flunking out of a Shwarzers' college, for god's sake? But this crack whore was managing it, and threatening to destroy Ellen if she didn't help keep the girl in school.

But Ellen was no pushover, and, after a few panicked moments, she realized there was a ready answer to Leticia's dilemma. Dyslexia. That all-purpose remedy for failing at practically any white-collar occupation, most specifically being a student. Easy to fake and so *au courant*.

Since passage of the federal Rehabilitation Act the January before, Ellen had been plagued by H&H staffers conveniently diagnosed as dyslexic, thus requiring that H&H give them impossible amounts of extra time to complete projects. All of which mishigas was supported by dubiously credentialed psychologists, who used a limitless number of mumbo-jumbo categories to diagnose their patients. Ellen looked over at Leticia.

"Why threaten me, Letty?" she said. "There's no need. Your momma Ellen won't let you down, not ever. You are going to get that degree, and you are going to be a lawyer. Not stuck in the back like me. I promise."

Leticia was shocked by the immediacy and coolness of Ellen's response. She realized, once again, how smart her old boss was. She must have already figured out an angle, and a good one, too, to be so relaxed. After all, her own ass was so clearly on the line. But despite Leticia's earnest questioning over the next hour, as they both got increasingly drunk, Ellen refused to share any more information. Just told Leticia to be patient. She'd get back to her right after the New Year.

Chapter Ten
Law Offices of Broward, Phillips & Hamburg
San Francisco, CA
{Winter 1980}

Helen Wilson stayed a full-time mother with Ellen Smiley at home until the girl was six years of age. This was long after it was obvious that only an institution could adequately care for the person that her still outwardly beautiful child had become. Over those five long years since the diagnosis, Helen had stoically endured Ellen's lack of toilet training, her unpredictable screams, and her habit of running up to friends and strangers alike and furiously striking at whatever body parts she could reach. Always hoping for some sign of grace.

Helen's breaking point came the evening Ellen broke the cat's neck. The cat, a Tom of no particular breed, had been the only living thing—aside from Helen herself—able to tolerate living with Ellen in Helen's ground-floor Berkeley flat. A flat with bars on its windows that Helen had rented to keep her daughter from accidentally falling out of anything higher up, even though being higher up would have minimized the little family's ever-present risk of being robbed by the growing number of meth freaks and crackheads then roaming the university town at will.

Helen had heard the Tom scream, and, as she rushed toward the living room, she'd also heard the awful suddenness with which her much-beloved Pus had stopped screaming. Entering the room,

Helen found Ellen sitting quietly on the sofa, her face in shreds, her dreamy blue eyes awash in the fresh blood that Pus's dying attempts to scratch out her eyes had drawn.

Ellen had not screamed, and she was oblivious to her many frightful wounds. She was equally oblivious to the presence in the far end of the room of one very dead cat, whose twisted corpse was lying against the wall. Ellen had tossed it into the corner, much like a spoiled but normal child might have thrown away an unwanted rag doll, always intending to retrieve it if things got dull later on.

Helen did not stop loving Ellen because of the dead cat. She never stopped loving Ellen her whole life long. But Pus's death finally made Helen see what a menace Ellen had become to herself. For one thing—as Dr. Piel made quite clear during the office visit following Helen's frantic trip to the Alta Bates Emergency Room—it was a miracle Ellen had not been blinded by the pet's efforts to keep Ellen from killing it.

After all, Pus had survived nearly ten years of frequent back-alley fights, usually emerging much more intact than his opponents. A murderous six-year-old child, no matter how oblivious to pain, had neither claws nor the same will to live as an old battered tomcat that found itself facing sudden and painful strangulation. So, Pus had instinctively set out to blind Ellen, and it was just dumb luck Ellen had broken Pus's neck before Pus had successfully clawed out both her eyes.

Helen cremated her Pus. Then she took what was left of the trust fund the Smiley family had set up at Ellen's birth and used it to buy an annuity sufficient to support Ellen at Heartspring School, a residential autism program located in Kansas, famous throughout the country both for its expertise and for the expense of maintaining a loved one there.

Once Ellen was packed off to Wichita, Helen borrowed more money from her dad and went to work preparing for the California Bar Exam, which she had never wound up taking. She failed. She took it again, and she failed again. By her third attempt the money from home had run out. She was reduced to waitressing while studying law at night, trying to reconstruct a legal education she had largely forgotten. The third time she took the exam, more than a year after losing Ellen to the hospital—which is how she thought of Heartspring, call it a school or whatever else they wanted to call it—she passed.

The night she found out she was finally a lawyer, she went out and got quietly and very sincerely drunk. Then she allowed herself to be picked up by the roughest trade she could stomach, intending to have as much down-low, penetrating sex as she could tolerate, with what would be her first man since TS. Her eventual date turned out to be a farm boy from Clovis. A guy who played second-string forward on the Cal Rugby team, who merely looked rough because he was constantly being beaten to a pulp by the first string. He wound up satisfying Helen very well, though she'd left her apartment that evening thinking she'd lay a Hell's Angel, not some randy college kid.

She tossed the young man out of her apartment early the next morning, never to be seen again. Then, after a few more hours of beauty sleep, she went to work finding a job. That project turned out to be a lot easier than either passing the Bar or picking up a biker for immoral purposes.

By 1980, even the stuffiest San Francisco firms were hiring for brains, regardless of sex. And what was then coming out of the most competitive law schools were hundreds of women lawyers whose intellectual quality could not be denied. Besides which, California labor law—traditionally the sole province of classic labor-management contracts arrived at by collective bargaining in earlier decades—had by then deteriorated into a swollen mass of common-law torts, many founded upon the previously absurd notion that sexual harassment allowed working women access to the courts in order to sue for practices previously thought to be as sacrosanct as *droit de seigneur*.

To defend themselves against such lawsuits, major firms were adopting protective coloration, sometimes quite literally. If the lead plaintiff's trial lawyer was a fat thirty-something black woman, suddenly the corporate defense team would consist of an even more overweight Hispanic female in a wheelchair, backed up by a handsome black male associate.

Helen—whose working-class background gave her the common touch—was an ideal candidate for this out-woman, out-minority, out-disability-the-enemy approach to labor litigation. And so she'd wound up at Broward, one of the first large firms to cynically embrace this practical approach to keeping its wealthy establishment clients safe from the counter-culture.

In the four short years since Shane had left, Broward had already become a radically different firm. For one thing, a by-then-seventy-year-old Moshe Janofsky, who would practice another twenty years, had grown tired of the administrative problems the firm's growth, from one hundred to two hundred lawyers, was thrusting on him. Before the new decade began he had stormed off with his core group of anti-trust lawyers and associates.

Hills, meanwhile, seldom went to the office; he was no longer a Bank of America director, and had managed to keep his seat on the Opera board only by dint of his increasingly large annual contributions. He had acquired a new trophy wife, but his increasing dependence on prescription painkillers made him a less than ideal lover for the gorgeous twenty-nine-year-old dental hygienist who had latched onto him when gum troubles led him to the Hillsborough dentist's office where she worked.

And Dead End Dave was dead, the victim of a stroke during his daily exercise routine. The pathologist who laid open Dave's mortal remains commented that he had never seen a healthier corpse. Aside from his very social-register wife, Winnie, and his gentle black lab, Tuffy, no one much mourned the childless Dead End's passage across the Styx. His legend lived on only in apocryphal tales told to firm youngsters about the bad old frontier days before Broward had moved from 111 Montgomery to One Market.

The labor group Helen went to work for was a true bright spot within the new Broward. Its leaders were Don Connolly and Bailey Shea, both then near sixty, each of whom had been strikebreaking since the early 1950s. The two men were both long divorced, their family lives swallowed up by their striving at work. Their striving days were over now as well. They would start drinking at lunch, and were both routinely plastered—after a short break for any unavoidable work—by late afternoon.

Helen became their particular pet within weeks of her arrival at the firm. They were fond of young people in general and beautiful women in particular, and Helen was both. This meant immediate jury-trial experience, and plenty of it. First-chair stuff, too, if only in the smaller cases. Which was something only real Broward comers like Lu Odom—still on the business-lit side of the firm, which remained the true center of gravity for Broward—otherwise got.

There was a negative attached to being assigned to the labor group, however. Compared to business lit, labor lit was plebian. Ultimately, the labor group was just a high-turnover shock troop, useful enough for disposing of troublesome, lower-management types and bullying fanny-pinched secretaries into cheap settlements. But if a real boss quit or ever got into any other kind of beef with a real company, why, that was different. That was business lit, not labor lit, at least the way Broward management saw it. And two old rummies and their merry band of women and minorities weren't ever going to be allowed anywhere near that kind of hallowed ground.

So, as the 1980s began, Broward left upper-management disputes exclusively in the hands of its white male partners. Typically graduates of Harvard or Stanford law schools. With club memberships that included both the Bohemian and P.U. Who commuted home each night to Presidio Heights, Hillsborough, or Ross. Of which rarefied types Broward would always have plenty. Right to the end.

Chapter Eleven
Superior Court in and for the
City and County of San Francisco
{Morning, Tuesday, February 12, 1985}

Judge Joan Marie looked out over her courtroom, barely able to
conceal a conspiratorial glint in her eye. Slouching in the open
doorway leading to her chambers, visible to her but well out of
sight of the various participants in the *Sugarman v. Siamak* matter
then arguing post-trial motions, stood the Honorable Fran Meyer, a
recently retired Superior Court judge. He winked broadly at his old
friend and protégé, Judge Marie. Who very nearly winked back.

Shane had hit a home run against Broward in the Sugarman
case. Up against Lu Odom, he had ridden roughshod over his old
pal, doing things like waiving the attorney-client privilege in the
middle of trial. An act so surprising it had drawn an objection from
Lu—and the riposte "Aren't you interested in the truth?" from
Shane—all before Judge Marie had a chance to figure out what
was going on.

Not that it would have mattered anyway. Judge Marie, a
sixtyish former divorce lawyer, well-known for her eccentricities,
had seemed bemused by Shane's theatrics during the trial. She'd
sourly rejected nearly all of the objections to evidence incessantly
argued by Lu and his stout, severely dressed, female associate,
Sara MacCarty. As Shane, arguing for Sugarman, never objected to
anything, the whole trial had looked like a disorganized retreat

from reality by the Siamak interests, landlords of a massive Ocean Beach amusement park who were being sued by a group of their concessionaires over improper efforts to drive them from the site in order to make way for a pricey residential development.

Nor did it help that the Siamaks were wealthy Iranian immigrants. Not only did they look foreign, they'd also obviously retained the more cutthroat attitudes of the bazaar from whence they'd come, fleeing the Ayatollahs. Overt racism was beyond the pale, even for Shane, but he had let the other side self-destruct on that score, hardly bothering to cross-examine any of the three Siamak brothers as they used the witness box to loudly protest their good intentions towards their tenants.

At the end, Shane had been so confident of a big win that he'd had a bus standing by to whisk the jury to a private reception in order to celebrate his victory. And he let Lu know it by showing him the bus and inviting him along. All before the jury came back.

After a six-week trial, the bus only had to wait two days. Lu cursed Shane and the jury in an audible whisper as each part of the long verdict form was read out by Judge Marie. Ten of the twelve jurors were then very glad to get on Shane's bus.

The one person he didn't account for was Sara MacCarty. Lu's associate, little did he know, claimed as her great uncle none other than the legendary Herman Phillips himself, Hills's father. Herman, in his late eighties, was a semi-retired but quite vital curmudgeon of a man. He had built Broward from the ground up.

Herman had first come to the firm in the early 1920s, back when Silas Broward III was the only name partner, and the whole firm consisted of only four lawyers. Silas—whose own father, Abraham Broward, had arrived on the West Coast during the gold rush, a pick axe in one hand and a Harvard L.L.B. in the other—was strictly an estates and trusts man. A careful advisor to wealthy widows and their spoiled children. The City's corporate work, oil and real estate and some banking, was over at upstart PW&S, which was first formed late in the Gay '90s. No one in the Broward firm went to court back then. Cases that required trials were referred to the thugs who routinely dealt with such matters. Who knew the judges, and whom the judges knew.

Herman changed all that, starting with a raid on a PW&S banking client, the Bank of Italy, in 1930. Mr. Giannini's little bank was a litigation client if ever there was one, especially as the Depression got under way. And if radically changing the nature of Broward's practice, so as to focus it on litigation, meant buying and selling judges, then Herman not only did what had to be done, he did it even more effectively than any of his rivals. Neither the federal nor the state benches were immune to Herman's many blandishments, ranging the gamut from 9th Circuit promotions to the more traditional bags of cash.

The raw nature of corporate litigation practice changed over the years, of course, and by the mid-1980s neither Broward nor its rivals competed quite so infamously for judicial favors. But, one weekend evening late in the Sugarman trial, as Herman listened to his favorite grand-niece—whose homeliness mimicked his own—describe her outrage at Shane's behavior and Judge Marie's tolerance of it, the old man began to think, as he often did, that the old ways were still the best ways. He said nothing to Sara, of course; young people didn't understand how things really worked; of that much he was quite sure. And besides, he thought, let her believe she really won. That would build up her confidence no end.

It didn't take much doing, as things turned out. Certainly no need to pay anybody anything, something even Herman now thought of as a messy business in the priggish new world his firm and his grand-niece now found themselves in. No, this Joan Marie woman turned out to be just some lady-in-a-big-hat type, who had squeaked onto the bench in the late '70s without a gubernatorial endorsement, taking advantage of the feminist wave then sweeping through the San Francisco electorate.

Once on the bench, however, she had proved so inept that both the district attorney and the public defender had banished her from the criminal courts, taking turns challenging her without cause—a prerogative limited to one judge per case per side, and aptly called a bullet. All the civil litigants soon began bulleting Marie as well, to the point where she was now spending days and even weeks sitting idly in her courtroom at City Hall.

Shane, though, had tried a small non-jury trial in front of her, won it hands down, and thought he could handle her. He had taunted Lu into not filing a challenge, snidely remarking that it wasn't Judge Marie that Lu was afraid of, but Shane. Lu's temper was legendary, and it sometimes overcame his ordinarily very good judgment.

And so it was that within an hour of looking into matters early the Monday morning after Sara had sounded the alarm, Herman realized that Judge Marie was about to face her second election. Her first six-year term was due to expire that June. While no one had yet challenged for her seat, anyone who wished to do so still had nearly sixty days to make themselves known. Herman immediately called Fran Meyer.

Fran had started life as a hack P.I. lawyer with a night-school degree from lowly USF Law. In 1954, though, on Herman's recommendation, Governor Knight nominated him to the San Francisco Municipal Court bench. Fran had gone on to serve on the Muni Court for twenty years. For the last ten years of his entirely uninspired tenure, he had achieved his life-long dream of a seat on the Superior Court bench.

Fran, in other words, was an old creature of Herman's. Even more happily, he had also acted as a mentor to Joan. And Fran assured Herman that Joan would be quite reasonable about listening to any friendly advice Fran might have to offer—especially about how to avoid having Broward run a well-financed candidate against her.

"And you tell her we'll do it, too. Even if we have to find a goddamn lesbian to run against her, just to make sure we get her out," Herman had growled into the phone.

Something which, Fran explained to Joan in her chambers later that day, was sure to put her back into a small-time family-law practice for good. Joan had to realize that there were a lot of lawyers out to get her already, Fran said, without her needing to piss off old Herman Phillips. And for what? To reward some kid lawyer who—based on Fran's observation of the closing arguments that afternoon from the gallery—was clearly abusing Joan, Broward, and the judicial system. All for no good reason.

"Why, you can't allow a bunch of carney operators," Fran concluded, "to just come into a court of laws, your court of laws, and assault legitimate business people by taking advantage of their unfortunate national origin, for god's sake."

The fact that Shane had never said anything about anybody's race, whether in closing or at any other time during the trial—and that the jury was as racially diverse as San Francisco itself—none of that detracted from the force of Fran's argument to her Honor Joan Marie. She barely paid any mind to any of the increasingly few cases that came before her. Just sat there. Let it all in. Let the Court of Appeal worry about it later.

So, for her it was like hearing the case for the first time when Fran went into his shtick. And while Joan did not know much about this man Herman Phillips, she knew Fran was her friend, and that when he said someone important was out to get her, she could trust him to tell her when to worry.

That was how Shane became a problem for Joan Marie. As for Sara MacCarty, whom the judge—a very thin, elegant woman, who, whatever her emotional and intellectual failings, always dressed with exquisite taste—had disliked as an irritating troll, that same trollish Sara now became Judge Marie's imaginary sister-in-arms, someone whose favor must be curried, whatever the risk to the judge's own reputation that any complete turnabout so late in the Sugarman case would represent.

A day later the word came down, first from Herman to Elder and then from Elder to Lu, that Lu should turn the case over to Sara. Let her brief the standard motions for judgment notwithstanding the verdict and a new trial, and let her argue those motions as well. Lu was to keep the shellshocked clients in line. He didn't get why the firm wanted to stick his turd in his young associate's pocket, especially considering who she was. And he hated not getting to vent his spleen on Shane, though the chances of gaining any traction with this idiot judge, who had been no help at trial, seemed unlikely. But he went along.

Sara was thrilled. She was far too young to be cynical about anything, and she was sure Judge Marie was still open-minded about correcting the miscarriage of justice that this beastly Sullivan fellow, who had insulted her Uncle Hills, and been fired for doing so, had brought down on his old friend Lu and his old firm Broward. Her brief was a model of intemperance. It accused Shane of every possible kind of misconduct before the jury, the most fanciful of which was the claim that he had been secretly communicating with the jurors about the Iranian hostage crisis, speaking too softly for the judge or Sara herself to hear. This last tactic, Sara said, was apparent from the fact that the verdicts were so ridiculously large.

Lu would have pulled that last punch, but he had been told by Elder to let it all go. Sara's brief, approved by Herman, and only by Herman, went in more or less as written. Shane laughed the whole thing off, of course. These post-trial motions were always filed, never granted. The system didn't have time to retry jury cases every time somebody took a chance at a trial and got screwed. There were too many other suckers waiting to get their tickets punched to allow for it. Why, even if Joan Marie wanted to do such a ridiculous thing, the Presiding Judge would talk her out of it, threatening to banish her to traffic court if she ignored him. So, Shane had written a very sober, restrained opposition and gone on a three-week vacation to Italy.

That day in February, when Fran stood winking just out of sight was Shane's first day back. Sara spoke first, with Lu sitting sphinx-like next to her. Incredibly, she led with the race issue, and even reiterated the *sotto voce* argument. Joan Marie sat impassively, just as she had every other time the squeaky-voiced Sara had raised one fanatic objection or another. Then Shane stood. Before he could say a word, the judge looked hard at him.

"How could you, Mr. Sullivan?" she said. "How could you use race to win a case in my courtroom? What is wrong with you? How could you expect to get away with such a thing? You're lucky

I don't report you to the State Bar. If my court reporter was any good, and I had a decent transcript to work with here, that's exactly what I would do. All I can really say is that Ms. MacCarty here has been far too kind in her argument today in describing your misconduct and the travesty this case represents."

Shane had never seen a fix in operation before, and that was not his first interpretation of what he had just heard. His first reaction was to start believing all the stories about what an airhead Joan Marie was. He actually tried to talk her down, reason with her. That lasted no more than four or five minutes. When he saw that her mind really was made up, he just shut up in mid-sentence and sat down, glaring.

Lu looked over at Shane, who had an expression akin to a man just hit in the face by a rake, and grinned broadly. Under the table he flipped Shane the bird. The judge promised a formal written decision within a few days. The hearing was over.

As Shane got up to leave, the court reporter, an elderly grey-haired lady, married to a long-time DA, followed him out into the hallway, loudly asking if he wanted today's transcript.

Then, making sure Lu and Sara had turned a corner and that the coast was clear, she said, softly:

"You poor dear. Well, she is flighty. So, you never know with her. But look, Mr. Sullivan," Megan Norman said then, lowering her head, speaking ever more softly, "there is something else you need to know here. May not help you very much to know it, but you should know it anyway. So, you call me, in the evening, at my home number on the back of this card. Don't call me here. Give me a few days. I want to talk to my husband Bill about what went on here this morning before I talk to you. He'll know what to do, my Bill will. You call me then, OK?"

Shane was too beat up to know or care what all the intrigue was about. He assumed the court reporter was just pissed at Joan Marie for questioning her competence. So, he'd ordered the transcript and humored the old lady by saying he'd call her.

Then Shane went home and actually wept.

Chapter Twelve
Superior Court in and for the
City and County of San Francisco
{Morning, Wednesday, March 18, 1992}

Lu Odom sat familiarly in the front of the Presiding Judge's cavernous City Hall courtroom, dealing with an endless list of the dead and dying. The merely dying—their lives shortened by decades due to asbestos exposure—had a procedural right to immediate trials. Trials which, when they went to verdict while the plaintiffs still lived, carried with them a right to massive pain and suffering damages against what was euphemistically referred to as the Asbestos Claims Facility.

That loose amalgam of corporate asbestos defendants had hired Lu and his team of lawyers to keep as many defendants from reaching trial as they could. The idea was to stall until their emphysemas, their cancers, or their damaged hearts had killed them off, and thereby cut the damages down to making up for the loss of projected blue-collar wages.

Various plaintiffs' lawyers' earnest efforts to use class-action mechanisms to deal with the asbestos crisis had failed. The circumstances of each pathetic worker's life were too individualized. Who was out on the line, making fireproof roof shingles, or in a WWII Liberty ship, spraying the evil stuff all over the vessel's narrow corridors? Who had just worked in a Maxcon shipyard office, or even just served hamburgers at the Maxcon cafeteria to guys covered in asbestos dust? Who, most of all, gave the ACF a delicious "blame the victim" quandary to exploit by having smoked cigarettes and thereby compounding the problems of asbestos exposure?

Everybody was different, and there were as many fakers as real victims. Once the first appellate cases had come down recognizing asbestosis as a mass tort that was exempt from coverage under niggardly workmen's compensation laws, Bay Area trial courts had quickly become boas with pigs stuck in their collective guts.

If you were truly cynical, though, and, like Shane, had other business in the courts on a given day, it was a show worth watching. There was old Lu, deliberately alone at the counsel table, with not another ACF lawyer in sight, facing his nemesis, the San Francisco Presiding Judge, the Honorable John Bensen. Bensen was an extraordinarily able jurist, and determined to get some of these asbestosis cases tried in the hope that large adverse verdicts against the ACF would frighten them into making mass settlements. And thus give him back command of his trial courts.

Judge Bensen knew Lu had numerous lawyers helping him, but even he would never have guessed that the actual number, spread out across Broward and other, lesser, firms, was literally in the hundreds. And under rules of procedure never designed to handle the phenomenon of mass tort claims, Judge Bensen was forced to discuss each case and its readiness for trial with Lu and only Lu. As if there was no forest of the injured, but only an infinity of single cases for the two of them to contemplate together.

Lu had it down. Mostly he could credibly say that ACF's necessary trial preparation was not done, that the relevant medical or economic expert needed to prepare the ACF defense case was testifying in some other part of the state, or was on vacation, or had just retired, or was only recently dead. The truth being that the raw number of such disclosed experts was deliberately kept down to an absolute minimum in order to facilitate such claims of needful delay. Equally qualified but undisclosed MD- and PhD-credentialed consultants were, of course, legion. And always available in a pinch.

Sometimes, if Lu perceived that Judge Bensen had grown truly furious, he would retreat by allowing a case to go to trial—but only where the ACF medicos had confirmed the particular plaintiff was unlikely to survive the six to nine months of actual trial that would precede any verdict. Otherwise, nothing was too low in the cause of delay, right down to frequently spilling water on his papers and business suit, then retreating to the men's room to escape the judge. Day after day. While more and more asbestosis victims dropped, dropped, and dropped again.

Shane no longer spoke to Lu. Not after Megan Norman had clued him into what Fran Meyer's role had been in turning Judge Marie against Shane and his clients in the Sugarman case. Something Megan Norman had overheard Fran do the very day it happened, while she worked on overdue appellate transcripts in an otherwise empty courtroom. Due to a peculiarity in the acoustics of the City Hall courtroom where Judge Marie then sat, Megan could always overhear whatever went on in her judge's supposedly private chambers. When she placed her chair just so, of course.

Over Megan's objection, and despite her refusal to cooperate, Shane had complained about both judges to the Commission on Judicial Performance, which was supposed to discipline judicial officers. Just as Megan and her DA husband Bill had feared, however, all the resulting contretemps had achieved was to get Megan fired by Joan Marie. The Sugarman case itself had been appealed, reversed, and then won again after a second jury trial. But all by another lawyer, a lawyer who got Shane's people much less money the second time around.

And while Shane eventually figured out just who it was that Sara MacCarty was related to, and thus why there was so much juice employed to fuck him, he never found out—and would never have believed, anyway—that Lu was not also a part of the fix. No, as far as Shane was concerned, he had stuck a sharp stick in Lu's eye during the Sugarman trial—on the up and up, but a sharp stick for all that—and Lu had retaliated by means of criminal misconduct. Not the guy he thought he knew, but a guy Shane thought he now saw for what he must have been all along. A pious fraud—this son of Midwest German Protestants, who had named him for Martin Luther—and one who was now fronting yet another abuse of the justice system.

Even more upsetting to Shane than Lu's by-now-predictable role in forcing a breakdown on the San Francisco courts was his inspired use of Broward's first woman partner, Helen Wilson, to try the few deathwatch cases that actually made it to court. When the first wave of asbestos litigation had hit the Bay Area in the mid-1980s, Helen had still been a senior associate in labor lit. At that point, she could have counted on one hand the number of conversations she'd had with Lu or any of the other Brahmins over in business lit. And that included the only woman associate assigned over there, the plug-ugly Sara MacCarty, who'd joined Broward out of Stanford Law in 1984 and landed that high-profile trial as second chair to Lu against Shane in February of the next year.

Then one day, late in the fall of 1985, while she sat quietly in her small office preparing for a trial the next day, in came one of her two bosses, big, gruff Don Connolly. Don's liver was acting up. He'd be dead from cirrhosis within the year, though he didn't know it yet. Both he and Bailey had grown more and more attached to Helen as time passed, and both were determined to bust her out of the no-future ghetto which the labor-lit field had become. Which meant business lit.

Between Bailey and Don, Don fancied himself as the expert at getting things done within the firm. In fact, Don had once helped Justin Elder emerge out of the younger man's beginning specialty of maritime law and into the business lit department, in the same way he and Bailey had now told each other they must aid their latest protégé.

"Helen," Don began, while squeezing himself into the one guest chair Helen's tiny office contained, "I don't know how well

94

you know these two fellows," gesturing over to Jus Elder and Lu Odom, who had entered Helen's office behind him, closed her door, and now stood leaning against the side wall, blocking her exit given the narrowness of the place.

Helen did not rise to greet any of her visitors, mainly out of confusion about what the proper etiquette was when three large men suddenly crammed into her closet of an office, shut her door, and demanded her attention. Instead she studied Jus and Lu intently, trying to figure out what the hell was going on.

Jus was the more well-known to her of the two. Late fifties. As thin and wiry as any marathon runner, though obviously a smoker, given the bad breath and yellowed teeth which Helen couldn't help but notice. On the seven-man management committee ever since Moshe Janofsky had left the firm, and the one guy, according to the whispers that she'd heard, that anyone who wanted a partnership at the firm had to win over.

Lu she knew less about, but both by reputation and appearances he was mister charm and personality. The Stanford Law version of TS, but considerably brainier. According to his Broward bio—which Helen struggled to recall as she sat looking at him—Lu had been both editor in chief of the Stanford Law Review as well as Order of the Coif when he graduated from the Farm in 1972. He'd made partner in 1979, a full four years ahead of the rest of his hiring class.

The year Lu made partner happened to be the same year Moshe abandoned the firm—otherwise, many said, Moshe would never have stood for such a break in the Broward tradition of waiting at least eleven years before making anyone a partner, no matter how talented they might be. But, under the circumstances, the senior partners were unwilling to deny Jus Elder anything he wanted, out of fear Jus might up and leave along with Moshe. And, as matters had turned out, Lu's early partnership had brought the average wait for partnership down for everyone that followed to a mere nine years.

It was only six years later, again at Jus Elder's insistence, that Lu had been put on the Broward management committee. He was the youngest member there by fifteen years. Lu was simply light years ahead of Helen at the firm, though, at thirty-nine, he was only a year her senior in age.

He spoke next. "Ms. Wilson, may I call you Helen?"

Helen nodded.

"Jus and I have a problem. According to Don here, he thinks you may have one, too. So, Don invited Jus and me down here to have a little get-to-know-you session before we all decide whether we can help each other out here or not."

Helen didn't focus on Lu's suggestion that he and Elder had a problem. That went right over her head. What she heard was that she had a problem. Don had never told Helen that she had anything of the sort, let alone that it had somehow become a matter of attention at the senior management level.

It seemed obvious, though, that these men could have her out on the street with a word, so her immediate assumption, reflected in her furious expression, was that Don was using these two management Nazis to give her the axe. Her opinion of male trustworthiness had not improved much since TS had walked out on her and Baby Ellen. Even so, the possibility of some sudden betrayal by her kind old supervisor hadn't even been on her radar screen.

Don's hound-dog reaction to the fury in Helen's face made both Jus and Lu laugh out loud. "Jesus, Helen," said Jus, "we're not here to fire you. And certainly not because of anything Don has ever said about you. He and Bailey would both like to marry you, far as I can see, if you were dumb enough to have either of them for the few remaining years they've got. Lu here has a proposition for you, that's all."

Still flustered, Helen looked over at Lu sardonically.

"A proposition? Isn't there a more delicate way to phrase that kind of query, Mr. Odom?"

This time Don—immensely glad to be out of the glare of Helen's misplaced ire, a glare which he had never experienced before—intervened, intending to deflect any resentment Jus might have on account of Helen smart-assing in front of him, something

Don knew very well was not healthy behavior for any Broward junior.

"Helen, now, you stop talking back to your betters," Don said peremptorily, more for Jus's benefit than hers. "You were raised better than that, young lady. And I didn't drag these two important personages down from the twenty-fifth floor, where you and I never go, not to mention call in every favor I'm owed by Mr. Justin Elder, Esquire, here, to have you blow this wonderful opportunity by feigning offense."

Don turned to Jus and Lu.

"Hell, gentlemen, she's propositioned about three times a day down here, and that's just by the lesbians she has to try most of her cases against. I'm not even accounting for the number of other indecencies that may be suggested by normal people who should know better."

He turned back to Helen.

"Am I right, my darling girl?"

At this point Helen stood. She looked right at Jus and Lu. She gave them both the smile she knew lit up every room she chose to display it in. Then she said:

"So, let's start over, shall we? Helen Wilson, six years at Broward, no prospects of partnership. Made some good friends, though, maybe better friends than even I know." She glanced fondly at Don, who blushed in return. "And who is now ready to listen politely to any reasonable proposition," she added, grinning for all she was worth.

It was close to 11:00 AM, so the three of them took her to Sam's. To one of the private booths way in the back where—despite the clamor of the always busy lunchtime crowd—you could always hear yourself think. And, what's more, where it was always so noisy outside your booth that you could speak candidly without fear of being overheard.

Don had a vodka martini. Out of solidarity with his old mentor, so did Jus. Lu and Helen settled for white wine. Over the sand dabs they all shared, Lu explained his dilemma.

"Look Helen, there's something coming into this office that's going to top anything we've ever seen before, more than AirW and all that NFL and C&H Sugar anti-trust stuff combined," he said, naming some of the biggest-buck cases that had come into Broward over the last ten years. All of them, needless to say, business-lit stuff Helen had never been allowed near, and all of it, except AirW, initially attracted by Moshe Janofsky and nobody but Moshe Janofsky.

"This new stuff that's coming is going to bring us to, I don't know" —Lu glanced over at his boss—" what, Jus? Four hundred lawyers by the time it's over? Maybe even more than that."

Broward had grown from 200 lawyers to 250 in Helen's time there. Projected growth of more than 50 percent caught Helen's attention, though "when this is over" was more than a little vague to her.

Lu was talking with his mouth full. Jus ignored his gaucherie, said nothing, and just kept digging into the sand dabs the ancient waiter kept replenishing. After a moment, he poured himself a glass of the Napa Chardonnay he'd bought for the table,once that first round of drinks had been consumed. Don was on his third martini, barely tasting his food. The conversation was all between the two youngsters.

"OK, OK, Mr. Odom, Lu, whatever," Helen stumbled as she tried to resist both her companion's enthusiasm and his all but overwhelming charisma. What 'stuff' is coming, and why am I suddenly so popular?"

"You know what black lung is?" Lu shot back.

"I'm from Oregon. Lot of people up there work in the mills. They tend to get sawdust in their lungs. Sort of the same idea, I think, only miners get it from breathing in the coal, right?"

"Sure, sure. All the same. Real bad for your health. But not as bad as asbestos. You know," Lu said, assuming Helen had never heard the word asbestos, or at least didn't know much about it, "the stuff they use to make stuff fireproof, spray it everywhere. Use it and you get the Good Housekeeping Seal of Approval from your local fire department. Only it turns out, this stuff is worse for your lungs than just about anything. Coats your lungs so they can't absorb oxygen, gives you cancer, especially if you smoke, even causes heart attacks. They're still figuring out all the bad stuff it does, but just based on what is now more or less provable, it stands to ruin companies like Johns Manville, W.R. Grace & Company, and our old client Maxcon here in the Bay Area, which built all the WWII Liberty ships in Richmond using this stuff, and which has the largest roofing business in the country. Every damn shingle manufactured with asbestos."

Lu's assumption that Helen was entirely ignorant of the threat asbestos posed to corporate America was incorrect. Always a compulsive reader, Helen had kept abreast of newly published appellate cases in all areas of the law, even criminal stuff. So, she'd already seen the spate of recent judicial decisions exempting asbestos-affected workers from the notoriously penurious California Workmen's Compensation laws normally applicable to on-the-job injuries, on the grounds that the companies involved, like their contemporaries in the tobacco industry, had been less than candid about the early research—some going back to the 1930s—demonstrating the hazards of exposing human beings to asbestos.

But what Helen hadn't seen, had no way of seeing, was the panic overwhelming entities like Maxcon at the prospect of the thousands and tens of thousands of P.I. cases these few appellate decisions were likely to bring down. Entities that controlled seemingly limitless assets, and which had never encountered anything on the scale of this disaster.

Lu had stopped eating. "So, what we have is an odd sort of cross-over here. The individual cases, against the poor mopes who got sick, those are standard P.I. defense cases, even lower down the trial food chain than the stuff Don's been feeding you the whole time you've been here with us. But unlike regular down-and-dirty P.I. defense work, here every case is a crown jewel. It cannot be lost, at least not for big money, because it sets a price for all the other cases to come. Now, this is not an assignment for the faint of heart, Ms. Wilson." Lu hesitated, obviously once again sizing her up, before going on.

"It's not a job for someone who wants to do justice, or who roots for the common man. Or the common woman. Or the common child, come to that. No. We are going to bust our butts—I am personally going to bust my butt—to keep as many asbestos cases from ever being assigned to trial as I can. And, along the way, I am only going to settle cheap, and then usually after the plaintiff has died and we're out of the woods pain-and-suffering-wise. But I need a trial partner on this team. Someone to gentle the plaintiffs—just the ones who somehow get through all the pre-trial traps I am going to set for them—down, down, down. Until, hopefully, they all drop dead before verdict. Or, if, for Christ's sweet sake, that isn't going to work in some oddball case, a trial partner who can still make a deal that won't kill the goose that lays the golden eggs for this firm. Or a trial partner who can even *win a trial*, in the right case. Long and short, I need somebody who may look like she's all sweetness and light, but who really has balls the size of an elephant, Ms. Wilson. And

I'm even willing to take on somebody who wears a skirt to work for this project, if that's the person who has what I need. Which is who Don tells Jus you are. Just the person I need."

Three years later, Helen was Broward's first woman partner, beating Sara MacCarty to that honor by a full two years. In that time Helen had assumed management of more than a hundred cases Lu had been unable to settle. Only three had gone to successful plaintiffs' verdicts, and even those three—benefitting from Helen's entirely remarkable trial skills—had resulted in remarkably low pain-and-suffering awards. Under her supervision, Broward had defensed ten others, and settled the rest—typically after a death occurred during the usual nine or ten months it took to try each case.

By 1992, even Shane had to admit it looked like Helen's instincts about where her future lay had been right. She had asked for, and received, his advice about going to Broward back in 1980, though she had ignored him when he said to forget it, and instead join him in his then recently begun sole practice. And she had come back to Shane for more advice, again disregarded, about accepting the devil's bargain Lu had offered her over sand dabs at Sam's.

As Broward's prominence had grown, so too had Helen's status in the San Francisco Bar. Not only had she been selected as president of the Queen's Bench, the Bar organization for women lawyers, she was on the ballot that fall of 1992 for president of the San Francisco Bar Association itself. And some, particularly the senior partners at most of the established downtown San Francisco firms, thought she was a shoo-in for the job.

But Bar politics, like any politics, can bring unwanted attention to private lives. There were persistent rumors, both at Broward and within the stereotypically gossipy membership of Queen's Bench, that Helen and Lu's relationship was more than professional. Lu Odom was a married man living in Ross with his wife and three children. Lu's wife—whom he had married in 1969, the year they had both graduated from St. Olaf's College—was a largish woman with little apparent interest in anything beside her young children. That fact also did little to dampen suspicions about his relations with Helen.

These rumors led to a backlash of opposition to Helen's candidacy among her sister lawyers. Many of them balked at giving the Bar Presidency to someone who appeared to have slept her way to a partnership at such a large, reprehensible,firm as Broward. Helen's candidacy, they argued privately, was hardly the way to change common perceptions of the role of women lawyers at the Bar. In the end, however, none of their petty resentments mattered, and Helen won in a walk.

Chapter Thirteen
Main Dining Room, Pacific Union Club
San Francisco, CA
{Evening, Tuesday, October 6, 1998}

TS sat beaming as Steve Boothe, the retiring Broward, Phillips & Hamburg Chairman, wrapped up his remarks. Boothe thanked the partners for all their support during his two consecutive three-year terms, and praised their selection of TS as his replacement. Particularly admirable, he said, was the firm's willingness to not hold TS's arrival at the firm only eighteen months ago against him.

"Broward is a great place. And it's been a great place for more than a hundred and thirty-five years," Boothe said. "But to keep up with the times and grow, Broward needs new faces and new ideas. TS has come back to his roots here in the Bay Area, after many successful experiences on Wall Street, ready to rumble with our East Coast competition. And we are here tonight to tell him we are with him 110 percent. Am I right, gentlemen?"

One hundred and fifty-three Broward partners—all but three of them white men—were gathered in the main dining room of the Pacific Union Club, high atop Nob Hill. They stood in unison and cheered wildly as Steve Boothe sat down and TS took the podium.

TS's overall appearance was indistinguishable from that of any TV anchorman in a major media market. Perfect height, perfect weight, perfect face, and perfect hair. Who cared that he had been an entirely undistinguished law student? Who cared that, from a strictly professional standpoint, TS was just another securities defense litigator who had personally taken only one jury case to verdict, and then lost the case big-time at that?

"This firm is special," he began, once he had taken Boothe's place at the podium and succeeded in quieting his colleagues down. "Special to me and special to you. But we are not special because we are elite, though we are elite. And we are not special because we are an institution, though we are an institution. We are special because we are the future. And the future is coming, every day, down in Silicon Valley and everywhere else on the West Coast, where we are already the dominant force in the venture capital markets. Our competitors have stagnated, stuck with the oil and gas work that used to be the top of the market. Their days are done."

Every partner in the dining room knew that this was a direct slap in the face of PW&S. The cheering started up again.

TS smiled indulgently, waited for order to be restored, and then went on.

"There is going to be a great battle fought out here on the West Coast," he said. "New York will try and co-opt our future, steal our clients, and stifle our growth. And we will have to outwit them and outfight them and outgrow them just to survive. Never forget, we have what they want—the future. And tonight, my friends, I am here to tell you one thing and one thing only: the future is ours, not

New York's. And now I thank you, most humbly, for the chance to lead this firm into that bright future, which belongs to us and only to us."

It was a great, mercifully short speech, and the crowd, as usual, loved it. Which was just as it should have been, given that it was written, at a cost of $10,000, by speechwriters who also routinely worked for the Clintons. TS had been paying out of his own pocket for such professional help with all his public speaking engagements over the past year, beginning as soon as he'd been inside Broward long enough to figure out that the firm was ripe for a change in management.

Chapter Fourteen
Law Offices of Broward LLP
San Francisco, CA
{December 1998}

TS had been running things for less than a month when he hired Leticia Madison to run HR at Broward. Their paths had first crossed the year before, when he'd seen her lecture on the finer points of taming senior partners with a history of sexually harassing staff. The setting was a highly confidential management conference attended by various New York and Washington DC managing partners in the aftermath of the California Court of Appeal's public affirmance of the multi-million dollar *Weeks v. Baker & McKenzie* sexual harassment verdict.

By then, TS was running the Manhattan branch of the San Francisco firm where he'd started his career. He'd been on the East Coast for the last six years, and he had felt privileged to finally be invited to rub shoulders with his more upscale brethren at places like Sklar, Ark, Slapp, Mead & Flood, Crowden, Peabody & Moore, Debevoise & Plimpton, and similar luminaries of the East Coast Bar. Even given the sordidness of the subject matter, this was heady company indeed.

Like nearly everyone else in the room, TS had assumed the conference's first speaker, a marginally credentialed, rough spoken, and physically unattractive black woman from Washington DC's Holland & Harper, was some kind of token Negro. But, as rapidly became apparent to all concerned, Leticia Madison was nobody's fool. Moreover, the advice she gave was eminently practical; if implemented as forcefully as it was presented, it was more likely to have an impact on the financial bottom line than all the nonsense presented afterward by the various social science PhDs who spoke to an increasingly restive group of partners. Many of whom soon realized that they might as well have just gone home after Leticia had finished speaking.

Two weeks after the seminar, Leticia had a new job: second in command of HR operations for Sklar, officed out of that behemoth's New York City headquarters. TS had an eye for winners, and once Leticia was ensconced in a Park Slope apartment over in Brooklyn, he had immediately begun courting her. Taking his new friend to the Manhattan jazz clubs she already knew and loved, introducing her to the Opera, and generally spending all the time he thought necessary to figure her out. Even slept with her once, just to show he wasn't bigoted. Against blacks. Or even against ugly people. Whatever.

Not that he wanted to recruit her to his present firm, Ludwig Smith. TS knew very well that Ludwig was quite properly viewed by everyone knowledgeable about such things as a pedestrian public-finance firm. Fine as far as it went—certainly within the first tier of San Francisco's backwater corporate bar—and with a national reputation in its core specialization that had allowed it to accomplish a moderate expansion into both the Chicago and New York legal markets.

TS, however, already had designs on something larger than Ludwig. Maybe a New York firm, maybe back to California, but something much, much better than the kind of firm his marginal record at that barely first-tier law school had earned him coming out of the gate. And TS had known intuitively that to do what needed doing he would need troops.

On graduation from Howard, Leticia had used her hold on Ellen to get her to persuade Holland & Harper that HR had become such a hotbed of liability that it should be run not by some fat Jew lady with a BA from George Washington, but by one very tough black lady, who had a far more relevant JD from Howard. A tough black lady who had worked her way up through the ranks at H&H, and whom everyone knew understood the workings of the firm, inside and out.

Ellen hated it, of course, but she also knew, or thought she did, what her other choice was. Leticia had made that very clear to Ellen over dinner at Ellen's home the day after Leticia had graduated from Howard. The younger woman wasn't going into some easily arranged, made-for-Shwarzers, civil service job, where nothing ever happened and no one ever noticed.

Instead, Leticia told Ellen, if Ellen didn't make room, she'd blow up both of their careers. Expose the plagiarized application essay and the dyslexia fraud, both. Looking at Leticia's angry, intense face, Ellen had believed it. Even though, in truth, Leticia herself had not fully made up her mind about what to do if Ellen showed some backbone.

Fortunately for Leticia, Ellen's husband was dying. Her old boss was not in a mood to take risks, not with so much depending on her at home. As her cancer-ridden husband moaned in the next room, his morphine drip no doubt run low, Ellen decided life would be much easier if Leticia were placated. She bowed her head and, taking her clue from Chamberlain at Munich, gave in to Leticia's superior force of personality. From now on it would be Ellen who worked for Leticia.

And that had been the way it had been for nearly three years, until Ellen's Mort finally died. After that Ellen retired and moved to Sun City, where she tried to forget what a nightmare it had been keeping up with Leticia's endless appetite for stirring intrigue within the firm.

A nightmare that numerous generations of young people, nearly always women playing Eve to Leticia's Margo, would then inherit over the next two decades. And all the while, Leticia's influence at H&H was growing by leaps and bounds. By the early 1990s, no personnel decisions were made without her input, H&H partnerships included.

Still, first Sklar had pulled her away from H&H and then TS had pulled her away from Sklar. And now here they both were, together on the West Coast, with TS in his early fifties and Leticia some five years older. Both at the top of their game. The question of what to do next was really no question at all.

111

TS would deal with the lawyers. Always a suspicious lot, and very resistant to change, however much they cheered at the P.U. Club. Leticia would build bridges to the staff, the ones who really ran things in any large organization. A senior partner will think twice about disturbing the pecking order if the admin he relies on is content. He will remain lulled by a false sense of security until the moment he's called in and fired. In the end, Rommel's spring 1940 blitzkrieg into hapless France had nothing on TS's and Leticia's takeover at Broward.

Chapter Fifteen
Law Offices of Broward LLP
San Francisco, CA
{1999}

They shortened the firm's name to Broward LLP within a month of TS's becoming Chairman. It was part of adopting what TS liked to call "top-down law management" in the new limited liability partnership agreement—meaning TS and a group of five other partners, all hand-picked by TS, were the top and everybody else was the down.

This was made necessary, as TS had explained at the December 1998 all-hands meeting of the partnership, by the realities of the legal marketplace. A legal marketplace where there was no longer anything like tenure, no matter how prominent a partner might once have been. A legal marketplace where somebody had to quickly make hard decisions about hiring and firing, all without being subjected to the sentimental lobbying that kept so many lesser firms moss bound.

Life was good under TS's not-so-benevolent dictatorship during 1999. As of January 1, Broward had nearly six hundred lawyers spread out over seven offices, one hundred and seventy two of whom were partners, which meant that those partners had what firm business analysts euphemized as proper New York leverage—the ability to mainly earn their daily bread off the sweaty backs of their young associates. Antebellum plantations in the Deep South were once operated on much the same business principles.

Because the firm had pushed into the Silicon Valley legal marketplace back when mainframe computers were the state of the art—opening a Palo Alto office in the late 1970s, at a time when the only local competition was from unknown homegrown firms—Broward's roots went deep into the soil of hi-tech commerce by the time the internet boom hit the Valley in the mid-1990s. The firm's Valley practice was built on Broward's recognized ability to introduce startup entrepreneurs to venture capital, and by 1999 Broward's famous Paly reception area had become the hi-tech businessman-on-the-make's equivalent of a 1970s fern bar.

So, important was the aura of that Paly office, that many a career-making attorney-client relationship began with a chance encounter between a Broward junior partner working the ballroom-sized reception area and a budding entrepreneur hoping to waylay any stray vencap on the premises. A cynical counter-point to all the bonhomie was the urban legend, circulating on www.greedyassociates.com, that no junior Broward associates were allowed to set foot in the Paly reception area—an injunction designed to prevent twentyish attorneys from sucking blood only their thirtyish betters were meant to enjoy.

The office—which occupied the whole of an enormous low-rise building on Sand Hill Road—held fully three hundred of Broward's lawyers, and more than five hundred separate support staff. There were just two hundred lawyers, plus three hundred more staff, at the firm's San Francisco headquarters.

A typical P.R. photo from this period showed TS dressed in jeans and an open-collared shirt, peering thoughtfully at the San Francisco Bay through a fragile looking floor-to-ceiling glass wall. This Shangri-la formed the outer skin of a massively ugly, big-box waterfront high-rise building—a building which, as a perfect metaphor for Broward's use of proper New York leverage to drive its profits, had sixteen windowless work spaces for every private office with a view of anything at all, let alone the pristine waters of the San Francisco Bay.

The rest of Broward's staff was scattered across high-tech office parks in San Diego, Los Angeles, Seattle, and Austin. Minor outposts all. The real money all came from Paly—a Paly which, for all its commercial dynamism, and despite the august presence of Leland Stanford Junior University within its borders, was nothing more than a bland Peninsula suburb where the arts, the private schools, and the restaurants were all quite inferior to what could be had in the City. Which was the place where TS, and TS's most cosseted senior colleagues, all chose to live and work.

Chapter Sixteen
Fleur de Lys Restaurant
San Francisco, CA
{Evening, Wednesday, March 3, 1999}

TS, Leticia, Lu, and Helen were seated comfortably in a curtained-off section of San Francisco's best French restaurant. Even though the old place had its usual heavy traffic, no one else had been seated at the remaining tables around them. Which was the second thing that made Lu and Helen sure they were about to be fucked by their dinner companions, whom they had openly taken to calling Batman and Robin within their asbestos-litigation group. The first sure sign of trouble had been the invitation to dinner itself.

The minute Lu had gotten off the phone after accepting TS's peremptory summons to dine that same evening, he'd called Helen into his office. The two of them had then called Steve Boothe at the latter's Berkeley home, all in an effort to try to scope out what was coming. Boothe—who'd taken early retirement after he'd stepped down as chairman—had been saying for the past several months what a disappointment TS was to him. How TS was too radical a reformer. That he was much too insensitive to the traditions of the firm and the partners' historical prerogatives. How people shouldn't have to sweat blood to make partner, and then be treated like office boys by a guy who hadn't even grown up in the firm.

116

"What the hell does the boy wonder want with me and Helen, Steve?" Lu had demanded. "I mean, our group is profitable and it's still growing. This asbestos work was what built this firm into a major player, and it's good for another decade at least. So, who the hell is this guy, calls me up, says you and Helen both be at dinner tonight? Not even, 'can you make it'? Not even 'is Helen available'? No nothing. Just join me and my Nazi H.R. woman I've got going around chopping heads off all over the place. See you there. The only god-damn sign of any respect is at least the dinner is at the Fleur, and he must know I love the Fleur. Everybody knows that much about me, right? Even you, right?"

This last was an attempt at humor. Steve Boothe had brought a brown bag lunch to work every day he'd worked at Broward. He had dinner out at restaurants twice a year at most. He couldn't pronounce Fleur de Lys, let alone order from its elaborate French-language menu.

What Steve wanted to say, though he knew nothing for sure, was that the fact that Lu had been discretely fucking Helen for years might be proving more controversial under the new administration than it had been when he was running things. Especially since Lu had hung on to his first wife long after her natural expiration date, being too cheap to face up to the financial consequences of a divorce. Not to mention that Helen was TS's ex-wife.

Besides, Boothe had been studying TS too carefully to believe he would use sex as anything other than an excuse to demote or fire the two litigators he had now so ominously called onto the carpet. No, the problem wasn't sex. If they were profitable enough, Lu and Helen could fuck on their secretaries' desks in full view of reception. But while the number of asbestos deaths was endless, membership in the Asbestos Claims Facility was shrinking. Bankruptcy had killed off one major player after another.

Hourly rates were a problem, too. The competition was charging insurance defense rates that Broward wasn't interested in matching. And the logic of clients paying Broward top dollar to implement Lu's plan of never losing a big case had been largely mooted by several huge verdicts against asbestos mines, though no asbestos mines had ever been members of the ACF.

So, Steve thought he saw what was going on. TS wanted out of the asbestos business, and he was going to explain the facts of life to Lu and Helen on that score. Probably reassign Lu to Paly to do securities and IP litigation, where Lu's Stanford connections would fit him into a burgeoning field.

As for Helen, who knew? No one understood what was going on between TS and Helen, not with all that history of a brief early marriage that had produced a kid who should have been aborted. One thing was for sure, TS hated being around people he couldn't charm, and he surely couldn't charm her. A real witches' brew.

With all this in mind, what Steve actually said back to Lu was, "You know I'm not a restaurant guy, Lu. But why ask you both to such a nice place if he wants to hurt you? I mean, why even go anywhere for that kind of rough stuff? For that he'd just call you into his office, or maybe send you a letter. So, my advice is to take it as it comes. Keep your guard up, but take it as it comes. Going after your group this soon after he's been put in charge, that's more than I see TS and his lady friend wanting to bite off."

In the event, Lu had ordered a martini. No one else ordered alcohol. There was a stony silence as Lu downed his drink, staring bellicosely at TS. The hostility in Lu's attitude toward her sponsor at Broward motivated Leticia to speak first, though that wasn't how she and TS had rehearsed what would go down at this meeting. A dinner where it was planned, just as Steve Boothe had anticipated, that TS would announce his intentions to shut down Broward's asbestos practice. Send Lu to Paly to do other kinds of business lit. And toss Helen on the rubbish heap.

"Who you think you are, Mr. Odom?" Leticia said in the flattest possible manner. "Who you think he is?" she said, gesturing at TS. "Well, I guess you must be some kind of ignorant, is all. So, I'll tell you who is who, so we all get off on the right foot here. And the only reason I'm being so nice about it is, if you act nice, then maybe you're not another middle-aged white man looking for a job. You see?"

Helen might as well have been invisible to Leticia. But Helen knew immediately that, with Lu in such jeopardy, she was certainly toast. That she'd been invited to dinner just so TS could have the pleasure of seeing her shocked at being summarily dispatched.

Since Boothe hadn't chosen to warn them off, Lu was flabbergasted by Leticia's manner and horrified by her blunt message. Still, he was a survivor. So, for starters, he affected a deep calm. Then he spoke, not to TS but back to Leticia.

"I know the score, Ms. Madison. Why, I put TS up for chairman along with Steve Boothe, so I know what he can do and what he can't do. And I also know that what he can't do isn't very much. So, let's just say I didn't see this was such a serious thing, and I thought I had the luxury of showing a little pique at being dragged here on such short notice. And let's also say I'm not stupid. I never pick fights I can't win. So, as of right now, we're all on the same page as to who is who here."

It didn't take long to get it all out on the table. Lu was still in. Helen was out, though they'd give her a couple of months to sort through finding another job, and she was welcome to the ACF if she wanted to move that client to another firm as a way of getting her foot in the door. She could have her pick of the junior associates whom Broward would otherwise be letting go.

They were done before the main course arrived, and Helen then excused herself, rather than share a meal with TS and her former friend Lu. A Lu who had made not one protest at her firing. A Lu who'd followed her outside on that rainy San Francisco evening and tried to justify what he'd done.

"Jesus, Helen, don't be mad. They'd just have dumped me too, if I'd fought back. And two of the kids are in private college, plus that goddamn Faye takes it all out on me by spending me to death. I'm in hock up to my ass. So, I can't lose this job. I just can't. Please forgive me," he'd pleaded, clumsily trying to embrace her.

"Please," he'd repeated, after she'd pushed him away with a look that said their days of lovemaking in the early afternoons at the Park Hyatt were over.

Then, finally, it came, that last pathetic whine. "You know I love you. I do. I really do."

She'd laughed at him then. Really laughed.

"What you love is your dick," she'd said. "And so did I, for quite a while, anyway. But don't flatter yourself with all this 'I love you so you must love me' nonsense. You're not a real man. My dad, now he was a real man. See, he stuck with the people he said he loved right through to the end. But bastards like TS and you, why, you're not real men, and you never will be. All you ever were to me was a matter of convenience. Remember that, pretty boy, 'cause that's all there ever was between us. Just convenience."

Chapter Seventeen
Law Offices of Broward LLP
San Francisco, CA
{Afternoon, Wednesday, March 10, 1999}

Salvaging a law practice after her sudden firing had not proven easy for Helen. TS's perception that the ACF lacked any long-term future had turned into a self-fulfilling prophecy. Once word was out about Lu's reassignment and Helen's lost partnership, all of the ACF's remaining members—except Maxcon—were quickly gobbled up by conventional insurance-defense firms. Helen was reduced to taking three Broward trial associates and going in-house at Maxcon as an Assistant General Counsel. Both her salary and her prestige had suffered badly as a result.

The only mercy was that the need to linger at Broward had been brief. Only a week had passed between the abortive dinner at the Fleur and her moving day.

It was on that last day that, on impulse, just before she walked away, she stormed past TS's P.A. and into TS's office, rather than depart Broward without incident. She found the great man conferring with Lu and several partners up from the Paly office. Lu turned pale, expecting a scene he had no wish to be present for. The other men, knowing little about Helen and TS's history, assumed a routine goodbye was all that was in order.

TS knew Helen better than to think that. He saw the storm warnings in her eyes. He was, however, as usual, the master of any difficult situation. Without hesitation, he walked through a private door and over to an adjoining space he kept for the break-out meetings that often occurred when tempers flared between contending sides. And Helen quietly followed him.

"You coward," she began, once they were both inside the large, imposing, very well soundproofed conference room. "You didn't really think I'd leave without saying a word, did you? What is it with you, Turner? I mean, why pick on me? Fuck me with no protection when I had four glasses of bad red wine; leave me alone with that poor disabled baby; then, when even I can see there's nothing anyone can do for her outside of a hospital—when I finally get my career going, when my life is maybe going to be OK, when I can finally make time to go see our daughter every couple of months, when I can finally feel like I'm somebody at my work—in you come and out I go. I'd like to murder you," she said then, looking like she meant it, too. "Just get out my Dad's old Remington and shoot you in the gut, like some polecat that's been out eating the stock. Watch you bleed out, you asshole."

She looked at him more carefully then, noticing something in his expression, something she didn't like.

"Wipe that look off your face. The one that says security is on the way."

TS hadn't said anything, nor did he intend to. Nor did he change his expression. There was another door into the conference room. It led to the freight elevators where Helen would be loaded aboard, taken down to street level, and told quite firmly never to return to One Market Street. Security, TS knew, would indeed be along, and quickly. His only real concern in letting Helen into his private conference room had been the possibility of a concealed handgun, so Helen's reference to her dad's Remington—a long-barreled shotgun with which TS had seen the older Wilson shoot skeet—had actually calmed him.

Helen was down on Mission Street fifteen minutes after she'd first confronted TS. A junior Broward associate from the employment law section was there with her, explaining that the firm would be appearing at 9:00 AMin San Francisco Superior Court the next day to seek an harassment order preventing her from coming within 300 yards of any of the firm's offices and making a public record of her ill-considered death threat to her senior partner.

"Everything in that conference room is recorded, Ms. Wilson," the steely-eyed associate said. "The area is clearly posted to permit such recording. Most people ask to have the recording devices turned off, but that apparently didn't happen here. So, you can see, you've really put yourself in a real bad way."

Then the little snot wound himself up and delivered the coup de grace to Helen's career.

"I assume you must know," he said, "that since Broward still acts as Maxcon's outside counsel, this unfortunate incident will have to be reported to Maxcon's senior management as well as to the courts. Good day to you."

Chapter Eighteen
Napa State Hospital
Napa, CA
{Afternoon, Friday, November 26, 1999}

It gave Shane the creeps every time he visited Napa State. The way things were organized, they let you right onto what was an otherwise locked-down ward to see whoever it was you wanted to see. So, you got the whole experience the minute you walked in. The acting out by the crazies who were clearly never going home. The stench of the always-clogged toilets that Freud had somehow missed in his various treatises on the most common symptoms of mental illness. And of course, the all-too-familiar seclusion room.

And in the midst of this all chaos, there was Helen. Sullen. Downcast. A deep scar on her left wrist. The last showing she had not been kidding when she'd tried to do herself in the evening Broward had her served with its anti-harassment papers. Papers which contained sufficient accusations of mental instability to finish her professionally.

The only thing that had saved her was the scream she'd let out when she'd cut herself. A neighbor in her Pacific Heights apartment house had been out walking his dog. The man was on his way back to his place on the same floor as Helen's when he heard her wail. He'd tried Helen's door, and found it locked, before rushing back home and dialing 911. His subsequent efforts to break down Helen's heavy door while he waited for the police to come proved unavailing. By the time the cops arrived, she had very nearly died.

For Shane, an attempted suicide by anyone even marginally close to him was quite traumatic. Two of his uncles had passed that way, and when Shane was eighteen, just weeks away from college, his older brother Jim had hung himself in their shared bathroom. Shane's parents were away on vacation. Jim had come home from summer school at UI Springfield to do it, on the point of academic suspension as matters would turn out.

Shane had found Jim with his neck broken by the short jump he had made off the ledge in the shower. Stayed by the body for an hour or more before having the presence of mind to call the cops. He'd wet himself when he realized what he was seeing. Later, during his worst moments at McLean, Shane had spent quite a lot of time shouting about how Jim had died. So,when Helen's story began making its rounds through the San Francisco legal community, Shane had gotten on his white horse and immediately ridden to the rescue. Nobody else he cared about was going to off themselves. Not on his watch.

It normally took a great deal more by way of bizarre behavior to get yourself locked up at Napa State in 1999 than it had to land oneself in McLean some thirty years before. Part of what had gone on, of course, was influence peddling by the lawyer Shane had hired to see to it his old friend was not dumped out of the system and put in a position to finish what she'd started. Like every other nook and cranny of the law, there was always somebody who really did what needed doing for a living.

By the time of Shane's latest visit, Helen had been locked up for more than seven months. In that time she'd stopped eating to the point of being force-fed through a tube on several occasions. She weighed barely ninety pounds, and had weighed even less than that before the force-feedings began. One of her recent, increasingly imaginative suicide attempts had cost her three front teeth.She'd leapt from a top bunk intending to crack her skull open. That exercise had also entirely flattened the previously delicate shape of her small nose. So, her looks were shot, at least until a dentist and a plastic surgeon could get to work on her. However, Shane knew, being a toothless skinny hag had certain advantages in a place with so many incidences of forced sex between staff and patients.

What to do? Shane thought. He'd tried to save Helen by sticking her up here. Instead, it seemed, all he'd done was prolong the agony. He, of all people, knew she wasn't crazy. Not schizophrenic, and not bi-polar either. Not in any ordinary sense. She'd been badly crapped on, and she was so furious at the situation that she wanted out.

You couldn't medicate that kind of thinking, Shane believed, and you couldn't psychoanalyze somebody that tough-minded either. All you could do was use facts and logic to try and reach them, to persuade them life was worth living. That was what he'd been trying to do, visit after visit, mainly using Baby Ellen's continuing need for a protector against the vagaries of her long-term future as his principal argument against Helen's single-minded determination to destroy herself. That and her hatred for TS.

As for TS, Shane kept telling his old friend, killing yourself was letting him win. And of all the people she had ever known, letting that individual dictate what she did next with her life had to be wrong.

Today, they took up the second theme first.

"Look, Helen, you've never been disciplined. And, come on, you know as well as I do that just saying you'd like to murder a bastard like TS isn't really something the San Francisco DA would ever prosecute, even if you did say it on tape. Now, I admit, you may have some trouble with the State Bar after being in a place like this, especially given how long you've been in here, but that's nothing I can't get somebody good to handle for you. Why, Elias wouldn't even break a sweat dealing with that."

Shane's old friend, Elias Borah, was by far the best State Bar lawyer there was. Though putting it that way was a form of condemnation by faint praise. Elias was a lot more than just a creature of the State Bar courts—he was also a criminal defense lawyer of enormous renown, and a wizened, physically tiny, very Jewish man of great intellect who had been particularly fascinated by the mob his whole career. A guy who'd had more than his share of success in his fifty-plus years in practice keeping the

Sicilians—as he fondly called them—out of jail and happily killing each other out in the world.

Shane and Helen were on a plastic couch, in a dayroom where the wall-mounted TV blared and several unsupervised occupants screamed at each over which channel they should watch. A shopping-channel program contending with a soap opera, back and forth, back and forth.

Shane well understood why places like McLean and Napa State were necessary, despite the fact that what sensitives like Helen needed most once they'd hit emotional rock bottom, was calm, quiet, and order. Despite the fact that throwing such persons into the cesspool of angst present on every psych ward was the most exquisitely wrong way to treat them imaginable. That is, except for everything else. The street being one example.

So, he ignored his surroundings, concentrated on Helen. Who, whatever else was wrong with her, seemed unfazed by the place. Just carried on a conversation as if she was having lunch in the cafeteria before making her way to class with Professor Mishkin thirty years before.

"Come on, Shane," she said. "Don't act like I'm suddenly stupid, OK. Smarts are about all I've got left in here. What the hell good is a law license with no job and no prospect of a job? And, what kind of a job am I going to get, looking this way, and as whacked out as I've been?"

Shane was quite startled. All he'd ever gotten from Helen before this were complaints about Napa State. Complaints that clearly assumed she was a lifer there. Not to mention a number of very violent statements about who the hell did he think he was putting her up there in the first place. It hadn't taken Helen long to intuit that simple fact, though Shane had steadfastly denied it, thinking a lie might serve him better in the end in dealing with her, earning her trust.

Now, though, if he'd been a Doberman, his ears would have stood on end. "What," he said, "do you think I am, some kind of a potted plant?"

Helen got the reference. It was a remark made famous by a Williams & Connolly lawyer who had stood up for Ollie North before the House committee investigating Iran Contra when taunted by a Chair who had thundered down at him that counsel had no role to play when a witness testified before Congress.

The mere fact that she suddenly found herself able to focus on such an oblique reference, to act like what she was, the brilliant woman he'd always known and admired, nearly brought Shane to tears right there. And Helen saw that too. And smiled. Missing teeth and all.

"Are you proposing, Shane?" she said, despite knowing full well Shane had a wife, six kids, and two dogs.

"Funny," he'd snapped back. "No, Helen, not a proposal. It's not even a proposition, at least not until you see a dentist, get your nose put back in the middle of your face, and put some pounds on your skinny ass. But a job, that you can have. And a salary. And health benefits. And the whole shtick. You know all the shit Bondoc got me in at my old place. But my new firm's up to four lawyers, and I decide who works there. No decisions by committee at Sullivan LLP. No mental health exams, either. Otherwise they'd have to fire me, and I own the damn place. No kidding. Ask around, Pal."

He'd been using that last phrase on large-firm opponents for ten years, just as a tune-up. His way of saying "Don't even think you can scare me off."

Helen had always said the phrase was too much. Silly. Juvenile. Macho. That Shane was too much of a nerd to play tough guy the way he did.

But now she wasn't complaining. She knew Shane meant what he said, and what's more she knew that he must think that she could do the job, even with all that had happened. Shane was no bleeding heart when it came to job performance. She knew that.

She'd started crying in earnest then, sobbing so uncontrollably that, after a few minutes, a burly attendant arrived, glaring at Shane. At which point Shane was asked to leave and the guy proceeded to grab Helen. Shane left, but only after coming within inches of trying to tear Helen from the grip of her keeper. That luminary swiftly led the by-then-even-more-hysterical Helen off.

Probably going to stick her in seclusion just to get her out of his hair, Shane thought.

Chapter Nineteen
Law Offices of Broward LLP
Worldwide
{January 2000-March 2001}

Though TS wasn't cultural, he'd been the lead in several student-run Shakespeare productions in college. He kept a large bronze of the regicide Brutus on his desk. Brutus's famous, and fatally accepted, urgings to Cassius that they should immediately attack the forces of Octavius and Marc Antony at Philippi, stood emblazoned on its base: *There is a tide in the affairs of men which, taken at the flood, leads on to fortune.*

The important personages who came to see TS all loved the bronze. So, much so that copies of it became a regular Christmas offering to Broward's best clients. Some of these recipients were techies who had never read their Shakespeare; they mainly assumed the bronzed sentiment was some over-the-top homage from TS to himself. As did many classically educated persons who instantly recognized the line from *Julius Caesar*.

TS took Brutus's sense of how to best utilize a flood tide fully to heart as the old millennium came to a close in 2000. The dot-com boom was in full swing, and the future seemed limitless from where TS sat. Broward clients like Cisco Systems, E-Trade, AOL, and Yahoo, none of which had existed five years before, now had market caps greater than GM and Ford, and their earnings per share consistently outpaced those of Exxon and Chevron. Even better than that, these young companies—particularly Cisco, which made the hardware and wrote the basic software supporting the infrastructure of the internet as a whole—were gobbling up other even younger companies so quickly that Broward could hardly hire laterals and first-years quickly enough to keep the paperwork flowing and get the deals done.

Broward had gone from a headcount of six hundred lawyers in January 1999 to nearly a thousand in the spring of 2000. As a result, its Paly office was bursting at the seams. Plans were afoot to take an enormous new space in a spec office park just off Highway 280 in East Palo Alto. The new East Paly office had a Taj Mahal quality to its interior design, even when judged by prevailing Sand Hill investment-bank standards. Shown the architectural drawings, a Recorder editor immediately coined what turned out to be the prophetic phrase "real expensive" in one of the many news pieces the move into the new space generated.

To TS's delight, all this left coast activity was driving New York nuts. Only Los Angeles-based Latham was close to being as well-positioned as Broward, tech-wise. That is, if you didn't count Tandini Sandino.

Tandini Sandino was a first-generation Sicilian immigrant. He had come to the US in the 1950s with his family, fleeing threatened Mafia violence against Tandini's father, who had been a minor government official. Tandini had been fifteen when he arrived in the Bay Area, not knowing a word of English. After attending public high school in Martinez, he had attended St.

Mary's College in Moraga, and then gone on to graduate from Boalt Hall in 1962. His still-accented English had put off the corporate law firm employers he interviewed with at Boalt; so, despite his high class ranking, he drew no respectable offers anywhere. Right out of law school, he had wound up starting his own Paly firm.

And there he was, thirty-eight years later, the most ubiquitous face on Silicon Valley start-up boards imaginable. But Tandini's firm, though grown to six hundred lawyers by 2000, was still only a one-office shop. And try as Tandini might to fight his hometown image, Sandino LLP was widely thought to be a good fit only for founder-managed startups. Not a suitable representative for those few success stories that prospered to the point where they had acquired professional management. When you got that far, the conventional wisdom said, what you needed to be taken seriously in the capital markets was a Broward or a Latham—or, as the New York firms all claimed, one or more of them.

TS had met Tandini numerous times prior to his 1998 election as Broward's Chairman. Once in that role, however, TS made a point of avoiding public contact with Tandini, in particular avoiding sharing any of the same podiums with the man. All as TS's way of emphasizing the to-him-all-too-obvious gulf that lay between the lawyers for mighty Cisco and Tandini's down-market Paly firm.

Tandini, who had always been on good terms with Steve Boothe and his various predecessors, could not help but notice the snub. He bore it lightly, however. In stark contrast to TS, Tandini's leadership role at his firm wasn't based on the results of any election. As he personally held 60 percent of the firm's equity, no one else had ever had to elect Tandini to anything. He had built his own firm, brick by brick, sharing ownership with his partners only sparingly.

Now he looked on Broward's headlong growth under TS with amazement, wondering how the old, gray Broward he had been competing with his whole legal career had ever wound up in thrall to a 1960s-era flower child, whose leadership position appeared to be based on good looks and fancy speechmaking. Having seen, and survived, many down business cycles, Tandini also wondered how many heads would wind up on pikes over at his kinetic competition when the inevitable bust came.

And, mainly, Tandini wondered where Cisco would eventually wind up if Broward—having risen up so high and so fast on the back of this once-in-a-life-time wunderkind of a client—came crashing down for good and all. Tandini, after all, was not merely an advanced thinker of great intuition; he was also possessed of an over-abundance of killer instinct.

But such negativity was nowhere to be seen at Broward. There, every day began with a 7:00 AM breakfast meeting between TS and Leticia, held in the same conference room in which Helen's fury had been caught on tape. The recording capacity of the room was still made good use of. Their early morning meetings were recorded, then fully transcribed; all so as to allow Leticia to keep

137

track of and implement the multiple, rapid-fire decisions made at each session.

By 2000, TS had determined that the most effective way to build Broward's prestige was to expand Broward's up-to-then exclusively West Coast presence into every major center of finance there was. In the US, this meant New York and Washington DC. Internationally, it meant, just for starters, London, Paris, Frankfurt, Zurich, Shanghai, Singapore, Hong Kong, and Tokyo. All of which had enormously insular legal communities, and all of which were very expensive to operate in.

On tape Leticia and TS made a pretense of reviewing the various budgets and consultant's reports that were provided them as aids to their decision making. But a spirit of manifest destiny was what really prevailed in that room. All they really knew was that no one ever said no, least of all the hired management consultants whose fees depended on it.

Buried in all the cheerleading language of the expansionary management reports, however, were budget projections exclusively built on financial results that were themselves exclusively a product of the dot-com boom that began in 1999. Nothing mentioned what would happen to Broward's finances in a slump.

This didn't bother TS and Leticia. It didn't bother the few Broward partners senior enough to get a look at the memoranda which set forth the basis for each expansion. And, most importantly, it didn't bother Bank of America, which lent Broward any amount it requested.

As one more extravagant credit request followed another, Broward's credit officer would simply point out to his credit-review committee that Broward had been with the bank all the way back to when A.P. Giannini was running things. It had never been a day late in repaying any money borrowed, plus a healthy rate of interest. Now it was simply financing a major, and obviously very healthy, world-wide expansion.

Broward was counting on the bank, the credit V.P. said, and it had every right to. And if the bank, in turn, couldn't count on Broward, then who could it count on?

Using equal measures of Bank of America's money and Cisco's credibility, TS and Leticia had one amazing ride. Each new office had to be staffed, mainly with high-powered lateral partners lured away from the best firms in the US, Britain, and Europe. Japan and China did not have well-developed legal communities, so there the big-name laterals had to come not from the native population but from those international lawyers who were long resident in both countries.

Nobody and nothing came cheap. Books of business were not nearly as portable overseas as they were in the US at the end of the millennium. In many cases, what Broward bought with its banker's money were expensive leaseholds and even more expensive partners, but not any expanded client base. Build it and they will come, as long as it's shiny and new—that was TS's philosophy. To the extent that there was any actual philosophy behind any of it, that is.

The truth was closer to a manic episode. Even for someone as relatively well-balanced and calculating as TS, the combined psychological effect of too many hours at work and too much sycophantism on the part of his partners and the legal press were having their predictably noxious effect. Eighteen-hour days when at the San Francisco office, combined with the brutal travel schedule necessary to negotiate opening one high-profile new-money law office after another—all these things had put TS into such a state of mental turmoil that he required sedatives to get to sleep.

As any psychologist will tell you, no REM sleep—and sedatives rarely get you REM—equals no judgment. This truism, well known to military experts who attempt to allow for its effects by using sleep-deprivation training to insulate their officer corps from its short-term effects, has no long-term solution other than complete removal from command.

Except for the occasional lucky escape, what usually follows lack of REM sleep in any high-pressure situation is some sort of otherwise avoidable disaster. Not that TS had any great well of business judgment to draw from to begin with. The Smiley family's wealth dated back to the Civil War, when TS's ancestors had taken advantage of the Union embargo on Southern ports to ship large quantities of contraband raw cotton from Boston to

Liverpool. The profits, while short-lived, had been truly extraordinary, and were wisely reinvested in Back Bay real estate.

From then on, hardly a one of what became an ever-larger Smiley clan ever did a day's work in any common business endeavor, concentrating instead on the kind of volunteerism that sometimes passes for an occupation in good society, with an occasional clergyman, doctor, or lawyer thrown in for good measure.

For three generations after the Smiley family had first become wealthy, its men had been routinely accepted at Harvard College. There they married their sisters' friends at Radcliffe, Wellesley, Mt. Holyoke, and Smith, more for their good looks than any perceived excess of brains. The resulting lack of both high intellect and practical business acumen had to come to a bad end. And, in TS, it did.

By the time TS had graduated in the lower third of his class in Exeter's Class of 1966, the rules for how one got into Harvard had changed significantly. Although preppy legacies still made up a good part of the Harvard Class of 1970, WASPS from the provinces, not to mention Jews, Asians, Blacks, Catholics and you name it—all with impossible-to-ignore records of achievement—were also being accommodated at the Big H in large numbers.

Given his marginal grades and only average SATS, the best college the Smiley family's money could arrange for TS had been

Dartmouth, not Harvard. Dartmouth, an isolated, ice-bound fortress of Ivy League traditionalism, stuck in the same nowheresville State of New Hampshire, from which every senior at Exeter was desperate to escape after four years of forced residence there.

As TS had been only too well aware from the sniggers of his more successful classmates, Dartmouth was second tier, lumped together with Penn and Columbia, and only marginally above the barely-Ivy-at-all-Brown. But TS had not let being exiled to Dartmouth get him down. With women only a once-or-twice-a-month possibility, he had buckled down and gotten good grades. Not top of his class, and not in some impossible major like Chemistry or Biology. But he achieved a very high grade point in his Political Science major, and he did well enough on the LSATS, scoring in the low 600s.

Despite these achievements, Harvard Law eluded him. The baby boom had hit its admissions desk with full force in the fall of 1969, and a left-leaning agenda at the faculty level demanded an extraordinary number of placements be reserved for otherwise underqualified minorities. That same left-leaning agenda meant being the scion of a family long identified with Harvard College—especially one which had an undergraduate hall named to commemorate its past financial generosity to the University—was not the gilt-edged guaranty of admission it had once been. Harvard Law rejected him out of hand at its first opportunity.

He hadn't applied anywhere else. And so, when the surprise rejection was delivered to his Hanover mailbox the morning of one very cold, snowy, and depressing New England day in January 1970, he cut class and went running across the quad to Dartmouth's academic counseling office. Admissions were already closed at every good law school, he learned, but UC Berkeley often took late applications from disappointed Ivy League applicants. Their admissions people were anxious to shed that institution's public-school reputation, and also wanted to achieve the kind of national standing that Stanford Law, alone among West Coast law schools, already had.

TS had been dubious. But he went to down to BOS by train the next day and flew from there into SFO that evening. He interviewed at Berkeley the morning after he arrived on the West Coast. He learned from his interview with a spinsterish woman who served as an assistant dean of admissions that Berkeley's law school went by the name of Boalt Hall, and that it was named for a turn-of-the-century Grande Dame named Elizabeth Josselyn Boalt, an early feminist as well as a large donor to a then-nascent jurisprudence department at a Berkeley campus which had admitted co-eds from its very beginnings.

In response to this pious pronouncement, TS had immediately professed his own long-standing belief in the importance of equality in educational opportunities for women, passionately criticizing Dartmouth for its tradition of excluding women from its student body—though not, perhaps, out of the selfless motivations his interviewer perceived.

TS left the interview to learn that the weather in Berkeley was always great. And, even better, that there were wonderful-looking women everywhere, both in and out of the law school classes. As far as he was concerned, once Harvard had said no, any other school would just be school, wherever you went. So, he asked Boalt to take him. And, with the enthusiastic support of his thoroughly charmed interviewer, Boalt did. All on that same bright California day in January 1970.

That was always the way for TS. One door shut and another door opened. Harvard had said no twice. And yet here he was, a mere Dartmouth and Boalt grad, running the New York bar absolutely ragged down in Silicon Valley, from a Yale Law dominated Crowden to a Harvard Law led Sklar. And everybody in between, including all the newly prominent Jewish firms, like Wachtell and Weil Gotshall.

All this with no experience in running any sort of a business. All this without ever having done anything but get elected to run a Broward firm that had been around even longer than the Smiley family money had existed. Most importantly, all this without ever once having been really kicked in the balls by life. An experience much more valued by those who eventually and truly succeeded in any endeavor than any early successes they might otherwise have had. You never learn anything valuable from success.

Leticia was no help. Rather than dampening TS's increasingly irrational exuberance, she fed it. She got high from king-making, after all, and, by the beginning of 2001, Broward was shaping up into a kingdom over which any potentate and his consort might wish to possess absolute power.

And absolute was a good word for the power she and TS wielded at Broward as the new millennium began. Just to make her own status in the new hierarchy clear, Leticia had single-handedly exercised her prerogative as the attorney heading up Broward's HR department to summarily fire two otherwise well-entrenched partners on New Year's Day. Those firings came in response to Leticia's overhearing the two men make loud jokes to their wives about the extravagance of the fixtures at the new East Paly office during a drunken New Year's Eve party the firm had hosted to show off its new digs. Leticia's show of force had sure shut people up when work had resumed on January 2, 2001, as she told TS with great satisfaction.

What Leticia did worry about that early winter of 2001 was the fact that TS's sex life seemed non-existent. After his disastrous first marriage to Helen, he had contented himself with a string of short-term affairs, usually with junior women associates employed by other firms. With his present schedule, however, he had no time for even the minimal amount of effort that bedding those usually very pliable persons took. Leticia knew that TS's using call girls as outlets for his libido could easily bring down scandal on the firm.

She also knew that any such scandal would certainly hamper Broward's furious expansion efforts.

In reaction to this perceived problem, she did what she considered to be the simplest thing. One night in Zurich, after the two of them had returned to their hotel well after 11:00 PMand had a quiet drink together in the hotel bar, she had quietly followed him into his room. Once in, she pushed him back onto the bed and efficiently unzipped his trousers. TS had no time to react to this unexpected intrusion into his personal space; she found his penis quite flaccid to the touch. Undeterred, and without uttering a word of explanation, she grabbed his scrotum, hard, thereby provoking a true erection. She then performed an hour or so of professional—and, for the sex-starved TS, quite exhilarating—fellatio on the Broward Chairman. After which TS slept like a baby, feeling no need for his usual sleeping draft. While Leticia had long since determined she preferred women—pretty young black women if it came to that—she was no slouch when it came to fellatio.

After Zurich, TS soon resumed his by-now-compulsive pill-taking, obtaining only fitful sleep in exchange. One result of which was that he was too exhausted to do anything but lie down passively when Leticia serviced him as opportunity presented.

Chapter Twenty
Law Offices of Broward LLP
San Francisco, CA
{Morning, Monday, March 12, 2001}

TS and Leticia could see that Whit Lambert, Broward's credit officer at Bank of America, was uncharacteristically glum. The three of them were alone in Broward's grandest conference room, having their annual, albeit long delayed, discussion about Broward's year-end financial results; with 2000 profits at a record breaking $1.17 million per equity partner, the firm's recent earnings could not be the cause of Whit's obvious discomfiture.

Nor, since the last planned office expansion—Hong Kong—had just closed at the end of February 2001, was the Bank then being asked to fund anything new. So, both TS and Leticia were very curious as to what was on Whit's mind.

"Out with it, Whit," TS said. "Golf game off? Wife left you? What's with this black cloud you dragged in here with you?"

Whit looked over at TS, whose firm's meteorically growing business had greatly benefited Whit's own standing as a mover and a shaker within the bank. He frowned even more deeply, and then spoke.

"New people are coming into the San Francisco headquarters, TS."

TS knew Bank of America had been bought by NationsBank in 1998, but he also knew that the very profitable California Bank of America operation had been left entirely alone up until then by the Charlotte, North Carolina based-entity which now owned it. What Whit was saying disturbed him greatly.

"Deep south people, with their own ideas about how important lending algorithms are. And these are people who don't care how long Broward's been a bank customer or what its track record is. With them, it's just assets and liabilities, is all. Show us a balance sheet and we'll tell you how much we'll lend you. And, shit sakes, TS, Leticia, I know last year was great. But the stock market is getting more nervous by the day about start-up internet companies. And half your firm's balance sheet net worth is tied up in equity positions in some of the most volatile dot coms around. So, bottom line is, last week they up and tell me I'm now off this account. No discussion. Just here's a ticket to Charlotte and, if you don't like the idea of moving to North Carolina, then it's time for you to start looking for other employment. Your next credit officer, I find out, is some twenty-eight-year-old woman from Georgia, a computer whiz, educated at MIT and Harvard Business School. She takes me to lunch. Where she makes it clear she hates relying on intuition and that she never saw a lending algorithm she didn't like. I'm not supposed to tell you any of this. Some high mucky muck from headquarters is supposed to fly out, drop in, and break the news.

"But you guys have been good to me, and you're entitled to know when trouble may be coming your way. Unless you can liquidate most of those dot com positions you're using to pump up the asset side of your balance sheet, last year's earnings aren't going to satisfy Ms. Hadley Bennett's computer model of what your credit line should look like. So, there it is. I'm fucked. And I'm very much afraid you are, too. And all for no good reason, other than the bastards just changed the rules on us, both of us."

Chapter Twenty One
Law Offices of Sklar, Ark, Slapp, Mead& Flood LLP
New York, NY
{Morning, Tuesday, July 24, 2001}

Hadley Bennett had proven more of a nightmare than even Whit Lambert had predicted. During her first visit to Broward, she had coolly informed TS and Leticia that the firm's one-hundred-million-dollar line had to be reduced by half within six weeks.

"None of these privately held dot com stocks can be counted as part of your firm's net worth, Mr. Smiley," she'd told them. "Not only is there no way to sell them in the short term, there's also no way to value them. Not with a bankruptcy rate of more than 50 percent."

TS had tried the familiar litany of Silicon Valley rationales on his new credit officer, a Southern belle. Ash blonde hair, pixyish face and figure, unreconstructed Deep South accent. All accompanied by a truly impassive demeanor.

He'd explained how just one hit made up for a hundred misses. How Broward's approach to fees with start-ups had always been more profitable for the firm than charging even its highest hourly rates, which these types of clients couldn't pay anyway.

Ms. Bennett had retorted by quietly reminding TS that Bank of America also banked Sandino LLP. Which supposedly peer firm, she said, had taken a much more moderate approach to accepting stock in lieu of hourly legal fees. As a result, she'd said, Sandino LLP had passed its recent financial review with flying colors.

TS winced. Hadley Bennett just didn't get it, he realized. That had become apparent when she'd pointed out that Broward could bring its line of credit back into line with her lending algorithm just by withholding partnership draws for 60 to 90 days. Redirecting that cash flow to Bank of America would satisfy everyone, she'd blithely asserted, and thereby keep the firm's relationship with the bank on friendly terms.

She made this entirely stupid point, accurate as it was from a numbers perspective, with zero knowledge of the one true thing about Broward's new go-go business model. The day Broward declared a temporary moratorium on payment of its partnership draws, would be the same day every lateral-staffed, recently opened office would collapse. Every worthwhile hire at the home offices would be out looking for a job, leaving only the Old Broward hands—guys like Gary Lee, Lu Odom, and Jay Jay Martin, who had spent their whole careers at Broward—to be counted on to stick around and try and make things work.

Explaining this reality to her, however, had dangers of its own. The bank had not yet imposed any covenant regarding the number of partners necessary to avoid breach of its lending facility. Suggesting that mighty Broward's ability to retain partners was at all questionable—though the fact should have been obvious, since Broward had based its recent growth on its cannibalizing partners from other well-regarded firms—that would just make things worse.

So, TS and Leticia were caught. If the bank would just ride it out, not insist on removing working capital, they'd be ok. But here was this Scarlett O'Hara type, saying pay down half the line. Right now.

The first thing TS had done after meeting Ms. Bennett was to try and get her fired. He reached as high into Bank of America as Broward's dual status as West Coast outside counsel and large borrower could take him. Which wasn't very far, as it turned out. Bank of America was still NationsBank by another name. By that institution's standards, a hundred million dollars was not a large debt. It was mid-market. A large debt, one that brought you attention from real management, was one with ten figures, not nine.

Nor did Broward's long-standing position as Bank of America's outside counsel buy TS any airtime with anyone that mattered. Sklar was the bank's real corporate counsel. Broward was just another local counsel, and the people it had access to all reported to Charlotte, and through Charlotte to Sklar. Which had been told by Charlotte and Ms. Bennett both that Broward was on a credit watch list, since TS and Leticia showed no signs of responding to Ms. Bennett's far from subtle demand that Broward reduce the bank's exposure.

Sklar was a phenomenon in its own right. Founded just after WWII, it had wedged its way into the very top tier of the New York legal market by handling hostile take-overs well before its more established rivals would consider accepting such work. Then, imitating its corporate raider clients, it had assumed the role of buccaneer in the law business itself, poaching whole departments—tax, insurance regulation, power, lobbying—from other New York and DC based firms. Earning equal measures of hatred and grudging respect from its competition, and enthusiastic approval from a client base that was increasingly interested in results and results only.

While Bank of America was naïve about how deep Broward's problems went, Ken Smythe, the lead partner assigned to the Bank of America account at Sklar, was not. He understood perfectly the fluid dynamic that was causing TS to frantically attempt to terminate the very junior and ultimately insignificant Ms. Bennett as his firm's Bank of America credit officer.

Rather than share his well-honed perception of Broward's dot com related crisis with his client, however, he alerted Lewis Flood, the last original Sklar partner still practicing at the firm, to Broward's plight.

"Interesting play, Lew," Smythe said. "They're a dead man walking unless they merge with someone more stable, but this guy Smiley is an ego-maniac. So, all he's trying to do is fire some young woman at the bank for saying no more money. And, the funny thing is, all that internet craziness on the West Coast has thrown off some real companies. At least a handful of them are really going to last. And somehow, this bunch of amateurs has got more than its fair share of them."

"You mean Cisco, right?" Lew Flood responded. "Hell, even I've heard of Cisco. Bought quite a lot of it four years ago. Best damn stock I ever owned. But so what? Broward, or whatever it's called, goes down. We pick up the pieces."

Smythe took a chance and contradicted his famously short-tempered boss and mentor.

"Not likely, Lew. Our Menlo Park office is a bust. The New York partners we sent out to manage it can't relate to these California types, and so they scare off the laterals we bring in. And this Tandini Sandino guy, he's the real competition. As smart and tough as we've seen anywhere. If he knew what we know now, he'd have Cisco in house at his shop already, even if he had to put cement shoes on Mr. Smiley to do it. What we have here is a situation where we can probably buy Broward for nothing, get Cisco safely landed in our shop, and then just wrap the Broward bank line into ours to keep the client happy. Our line is a hell of a lot more than any hundred million, and it's not even drawn. Win win win."

Lew Flood was ninety-one. He had been at Sklar since its 1945 founding. Then he was its youngest name partner, only thirty-five. He had always been a natural administrator, more businessman than lawyer. And it had been Lew's business acumen, even more than the spectacular legal abilities of his senior partners, that had made Sklar what it was by 2001—the most feared competitor in the Wall Street legal community.

Flood listened to Ken Smythe's description of the Broward situation with keen interest. He knew he himself had to go sometime. Not this year, not next year. Not while he was still healthy and alert. Flood loved the adrenalin of what he did too much to leave Sklar without good reason, and he was long past thinking of mere age as any kind of good reason to do or not do anything.

But Flood was also deeply concerned with what the future held for the institution he had built, once he was gone. And he had long been thinking Ken might be the right guy to step into the firm's chief-executive-officer-style management structure when Lew did go.   Dead or retired.

As good a litigator as Ken was, and he was a great one, everyone said so, Ken had so much more to him than just that. He was diplomatic, a rare quality in people so intense. And he could count, meaning he understood what was economic for a client and what wasn't. So, many otherwise exceptional lawyers had no sense of the impact on either the firm or the client of what they did. Those people, you just armed them, and then off to war—either in the conference room or the courtroom—they went.

What fun, he found himself thinking, midway through his discussion with Ken about Broward. A nice low-down dirty deal.

One where I get a real look at Ken before finally deciding what to do with him here. And one where Sklar acquires a substantial West Coast practice, paying nothing in the process.

The fact that the information about Broward's distress came from inside the bank meant nothing to Flood. Information had to come from somewhere, didn't it? And squeezing the hell out of these Broward deadbeats is something we'd do anyway. The bank won't complain if, after we ruin Broward, we see the bank gets paid back without a fuss. Why, they'll love us for it, he thought, smiling to himself.

The hardball squeeze on Broward's credit line which Ken Smythe had implemented on Bank of America's behalf following his discussion with Lew Flood was what had brought TS, Leticia—and, in a major reshuffling of the pecking order within Broward, the head of Broward's bankruptcy department, Gary Lee—to New York that July 21, 2001. Broward's management had asked to meet in person with Smythe, hoping they would be permitted to do so without Hadley Bennett's annoying presence. They had come to Sklar's lower Manhattan world headquarters, which occupied the top thirty floors of 2 World Financial Center, directly across West Street from the World Trade Center.

TS, Leticia, and the newly informed Gary Lee had plenty to worry about by mid-July 2001. Not only was the bank refusing to extend Broward's hundred million dollar line for much longer, but Hadley Bennett, acting pursuant to Smythe's instructions, had formally threatened to call the line entirely and then notify Broward's clients to pay their fees to the bank and not Broward.

There was also a class of nearly two hundred law grads scheduled to arrive in September. All at the $145,000 a year which Broward, as a supposedly top-tier law firm, had agreed to pay to meet New York starting salaries. Another, even larger class of law students was drawing $40,000 per for the summer. If offers were rescinded to the new associates or not extended to the Class of 2002, the word would be out that Broward was not immune to the malaise the dot bust was causing in the San Francisco legal community.

On top of all that, the East Paly office was now fully ready for occupancy. Rental obligations had commenced, and Broward's existing building could not be subleased at any reasonable price. The dot bust had hit the market for office space on the Peninsula like a tsunami.

TS and Leticia weren't much at figures. But as Gary Lee explained, it was just common sense that, despite all the bad news, a law firm with Broward's still substantial revenues couldn't really go broke. Even now, apart from partnership draws, costs were not more than 50 percent of present gross. As long as the partners didn't insist on drawing down all of the 50 percent in profits, there was always going to be something significant left over to cover the entity's debt repayment problems in a downturn.

So, it wasn't necessarily the economics of the crisis that frightened TS. He was a people person; it was the potential for mass partnership defections that had his attention. TS knew that his charisma was a sufficient glue to hold the firm together only as long as there was no public humiliation of Broward. If, for example, the bank seized Broward's receivables—which Gary Lee said the bank had every legal right to do—then the resulting bad press would halve the partnership ranks in a matter of weeks. And it was any type of massive partnership defections that would kill Broward. No matter how many years it had been on the scene.

TS, Leticia, and Gary had arrived at Sklar promptly at the appointed hour of 10:00 AM.   They were shown into a conference room that had a view not of the Hudson River, which lay to the immediate west of the World Financial Center, but of the truly ugly Twin Towers to the east. The two behemoths seemed to blot out the sky. Their combined presence made the very small, otherwise windowless conference room the Californians had been stuck in seem very dark, even on what was a clear and sunny day in lower Manhattan.

Gary Lee understood the idea. He had used it himself numerous times when negotiating with distressed borrowers. You are shit, the room said. We own you. We'll deal with you how and when we feel like it. Smythe had put his head in at 10:30 AMand said he'd try to join them soon, but that he was still getting his marching orders. Gary Lee's reaction was deep suspicion of Smythe. He did not know the man well, but he had studied his background carefully. Like most second-generation Sklar partners, Smythe was both Harvard College and Harvard Law—in his case, Harvard Law class of 1968. A Sklar partner since 1973, he had been the very first guy to make partner in his entering class.

Smythe was a generalist, but had nonetheless appeared in a number of the largest bankruptcy cases filed in the Southern District of New York, where Gary had played minor roles for West Coast clients caught up in the notorious forum shopping that went on in large bankruptcy cases. While Lester Swartz actually ran Sklar's top-echelon bankruptcy practice, when Smythe said jump Gary had seen the great Lester Swartz humbly ask Smythe how high. Right there at the Bowling Green bankruptcy court, in front of god and Judge Gonzalez both. And this more than once.

So, the idea some diminutive woman credit officer in a sundress was off giving Smythe any sort of marching orders was absurd on its face. But what excited Gary's suspicions even more was that Smythe would bother to tell such an obvious lie by way of making up any explanation at all for his obvious rudeness in standing the three of them up. The normal dance was to arrive several hours late and make no excuses whatsoever. Just start asking where the money was and explaining what the immediate consequences of a bad answer to that question were bound to be.

For the first time since TS and Leticia had come to his Pacific Heights home and let him in on the secret of how difficult a time the firm was having as a result of the dot bust, Gary sensed that the bank's unusual aggressiveness toward such an old client as

Broward might have unusual origins. Maybe Sklar enjoys killing off competition, he thought, and this guy is using this Hadley Bennett woman as his beard.

TS has sure insulted enough of these New York firms on the lecture circuit and in the legal press, Gary Lee thought. And they're animals, really—there's nothing to compare with the New York legal culture on the West Coast. Even the worst of the worst Hollywood lawyers are pussies next to the people they have running around this skyscraper. And around Crowden. And around Wachtell. And around maybe a dozen more like the first three. Jesus Christ, he thought, how did my lightweight firm get caught up in a thing like this, with lawyers like this holding our balls in their hands? Gary had never liked TS, but now he decided he hated the naïve, overblown SOB.

And, he raged inside, this fucking hatchet woman of TS's—what in the fuck, fuck, triple fuck was she doing in a meeting like this? She can't read a balance sheet or even write a coherent sentence, so what's the idea? Does TS think Smythe cares that Broward is an equal opportunity employer? Ship of fools, Gary thought glumly, just as Smythe, at 11:15 AM, finally entered the room with the legendary but seldom seen Lew Flood in tow.

"Hello, Leticia," Flood said.

Leticia stared at Lew Flood open-mouthed, at first saying nothing in return. Then she managed to squeak out a response.

"Lew, I—I never thought I'd see you in as little a room as the one you've stuck us in."

Not knowing what to say, and absolutely flabbergasted by the great man's presence, she went on less good-humoredly, saying:

"I mean, what is this to you?"

During her employment with Sklar, it had been Lew Flood to whom Leticia had mainly reported. And Lew Flood, unlike any boss she'd ever had before or since, had used Leticia as an instrument of his will, not vice versa. Lew had appreciated her strengths, not the least of which was her acute ability to unscramble internal office intrigues and spare him the trouble. But as she'd soon discovered, practicing intrigue on Lew Flood himself always found him waiting at the end of the trail, three steps ahead, with a warning not to keep trying or face the consequences.

Her frustration with her inability to outwit Flood had led her to accept TS's 1998 job offer and move out to the West Coast, where she had hoped to never have to deal with Flood again, at least not from an inferior position. Now there he was, right in the room, and Leticia—more than her naïve boss TS, and even more than the already suspicious Gary—knew right then, right from that first hello, that something very, very no good was in the works for Broward. Something no one could stop. Because Lew never showed up until the dirty deed was done, whatever it was. Well and truly done.

Bad Law

Chapter Twenty Two
Ground Zero
New York, NY
{Morning, Tuesday, September 11, 2001}

TS, Leticia, and Gary Lee cooled their heels in Sklar's vast penthouse reception area. Lew Flood and Ken Smythe were in the firm's largest conference room, meeting with Sklar's Executive Committee. The members of that committee, some fifty-three strong, had gathered from the four points of the compass—not because this meeting couldn't be done by teleconference or because there was any doubt that Lew would get the yes vote on the Broward acquisition he wanted—but rather as an homage to Lew's still marvelous business acumen, as well as to his sheer devotion to the firm. It was 8:30 AM.

In the conference room Ken recounted how, back in July, Lew Flood had trailed after him into the firm's smallest, worst-lit conference room. How Flood had explained to Leticia, hardly glancing at TS or Gary Lee, what Sklar would see to it Bank of America did to Broward before the day was over if there was even one peep of resistance to what he was about to propose. How seizing accounts receivable would be just the beginning. How every Broward dollar in any Bank of America account would be frozen. How every case in which Broward was local counsel for Bank of America would be immediately assigned elsewhere, with

162

the bank paying Broward nothing for any work in progress. And how every Broward partner foolish enough to have ever borrowed money personally from Bank of America would have his or her banking relationship cancelled and demands for loan repayment made.

Ken cackled about how TS had simply gone into shock when confronted with Lew's ferocity, not to mention the old man's undisguised contempt for him. How Lew had made it so simple. Broward was dead. The only thing its management could do was turn over what Broward clients Sklar might want, what Broward partners Sklar might wish to employ, and what office leases Sklar might choose to accept. All for nothing. Nothing, that was, except that Sklar would then pay off Bank of America, and thereby prevent Broward's disappearance into Sklar's maw from raising any eyebrows at the bank.

Finally, Ken explained how, under the guise of Sklar's performing diligence for the bank, Lew had required Broward to open its records to Sklar. Completely. How Lew had insisted that, after a review of those files, and within sixty days, Sklar would unilaterally dictate the terms of an arrangement of some kind with Broward. In the meantime, Sklar would recommend the bank keep Broward alive, using Sklar's own investigation of Broward's affairs as an excuse. An investigation Sklar would charge the bank to conduct.

The real genius of what had been pulled off, Ken said, was that there was never more than a minimal risk that anyone would ever believe that Lew—a former President of the Bar Association of the City of New York, not to mention the longest-serving member of the Harvard Law School Board of Visitors—had said a single word of what he had actually said. If anybody at Broward ever went running to the bank, or even to the US Attorney, it would be explained as just another case of some desperate borrower making up lies rather than paying back their debt. And it would be the end for Broward all the same.

"All roads lead to Rome," Ken concluded, using the same words Lew had finished up by saying to TS. As nice a way to announce someone's demise while they sat right there in front of you as anyone at Sklar had ever heard.

There hadn't been much said after that, back in July. After taking a short break downstairs, TS had gone back up to see Ken Smythe by himself. He had then faithfully promised Ken that he personally would go along with whatever Lew Flood wanted of him. In particular, he had promised that he would immediately and completely open up Broward's affairs to Sklar, and that he, Leticia, and Gary Lee would never discuss the true reasons for Sklar's upcoming review. These promises had been kept.

Ken was just finishing his admiring description of Lew's negotiating prowess when the first plane struck the North Tower of the World Trade Center at 8:46 AM. While you could see the flames from the east side of 2 World Financial Center, no one dared interrupt the meeting going on in the conference room on the west side of the penthouse, the one that had a view solely of the

Hudson. The one where Lew, Ken, and all their most senior colleagues were in session.

When a different plane then hit the South Tower at 9:03 AM, though, that was a different story. At that point, Lew Flood's longtime admin, Rhea Green, ran from her east-side office and burst into the meeting, insisting that her boss just had to look at what was happening across West Street. When he tried to put her off, she threatened to scream. Flood looked at her carefully then, and realized that something truly extraordinary must have happened.

"Ok, Rhea, ok," he said. "Don't get excited. I'm coming. I'm coming."

By the time he and his fifty-two colleagues had streamed over to the east side of the top floor of 2 World Financial Center, where they all pressed up against the windows, right along with TS, Leticia, and Gary Lee, everyone else was already there, craning to get as good a look as possible.

Someone thought he saw a jumper. Then another. People so frightened by the heat, flames, and smoke emanating from both towers that they thought launching themselves out into space was a far better alternative than waiting for a rescue no one believed could reach them. No matter that the planes had flown into the building just within the last half hour.

During WWII, Lew Flood had served as a Marine captain on Guadalcanal. There, the use of flamethrowers to kill Japs hiding in

165

caves had been a commonplace. But this was different. This was New York City, his New York City, for Christ's sake, not some barren rock on the way to conquering somebody else's sorry excuse for a country.

Those were Americans being burned to death across the way. His stockbroker worked over there. So, did his dentist. So, did his oldest child, or at least he thought she might. They had been estranged for so many years, he didn't keep up with her career.

But he knew she had worked pretty high up in the North Tower at some point. Jesus, he thought, maybe even above the point where the first jet had plowed into that now extremely sorry-looking building.

He asked Rhea to get his ex-wife on the phone, make sure his daughter Katie was safe. It didn't take long for Rhea to report back the obvious, that everybody in Manhattan and its environs was trying to use the phone at once. And so no one could get through, not for love or money. It was on the radio, Rhea said, that the fire department couldn't even talk to the police helicopters circling the two burning buildings. Chaos. Unbelievable chaos.

Lew Flood didn't exactly have a heart condition. He just got winded easily, and took a bunch of different pills for high blood pressure. He'd never had a heart attack, and so he didn't recognize the first symptoms. By the time he knew he was in trouble, he was already on the floor, gasping for air and clutching at his chest.

Sklar had an in-house doctor, one Mohammed Chowdry, a Pakistani-trained and US-qualified MD, on its permanent headquarters staff. His normal duties mainly involved advising partners on diet and exercise. He arrived quickly, and did what he could for Lew on the spot. Then, using two associates as stretcher-bearers, Dr. Chowdry had ordered Lew moved down from the penthouse reception area, which was bubbling with panic on account of the scene playing out outside its windows, to the quiet interior medical office on the forty-first floor. A place where Dr. Chowdry could constantly monitor Lew's blood pressure, and where there was a working EKG machine to measure the regularity of Lew's heartbeat.

It could wind up very bad, the harried physician told Ken Smythe, once he'd settled the barely conscious Lew onto a cot he had for such emergencies and run preliminary tests on his first-responder equipment. Lew needed the type of immediate post-seizure diagnostic care only a good hospital could give him. And he needed that type of help right now, not in several hours.

The man emphasized that Lew could easily wind up dead if he wasn't treated more thoroughly. Mainly, the terrified doctor wanted it very clearly understood that he could not be held responsible for the outcome if the patient was left in his hands. He had worked too hard to get qualified in the US to want any sort of trouble over this impossible situation.

Ken thought. The news reports made it clear that every building anywhere in the vicinity of the burning World Trade

Center was being evacuated, and that the crowds teeming out of those buildings were all being directed south, down to Battery Park at the tip of Manhattan. Many of those fleeing the relative safety of their offices were afraid there were more rogue jets ready to strike, questioning why the terrorists, or whoever they were, would stop at just the World Trade Center if what they wanted to do was knock down New York skyscrapers.

Sklar, though, had a fleet of helicopters used to ferry partners and clients to various regional airports and, in the summer, out to the Hamptons and up to Martha's Vineyard. These aircraft were based near JFK, and could be reached by Sklar's own emergency communications system, which was based in Newark and accessible by a hard-wired direct connection from any Sklar headquarters telephone, if one had the appropriate dial-in code.

Ken made the necessary call, and was answered on the first ring.

"Sklar Communications, Newark," the woman who answered the call said.

"Who is this," Ken demanded.

"Martha Wright," intoned the surprised voice of the fifty-five-year-old African American woman who had been answering this line for the last fifteen years. In all that time no one had ever asked her to personally identify herself.

"Now you listen to me, Ms. Wright, I am Kenneth Smythe, and I practically run Sklar, New York, do you know that?"

"No sir," the woman replied. "They don't tell us nothing over here about who is who in New York. They just tell us to be as polite and helpful as possible to everyone who calls."

Ken felt his impatience rising.

"This is either going to be very bad for you or maybe very good. Do you read me? Even you must know who Lew Flood is? Right?"

Martha Wright did know who Lew Flood was. She had read about him in a community newsletter run off on a Xerox machine at her church, about how he had once brought some civil rights case against Jersey City slumlords, and about how important he was.

"Lew Flood is sick. A doctor here in the New York headquarters thinks it's a heart attack. And the goddamn buildings next door are both on fire, it's chaos outside and I can't get him a ground ambulance."

Martha interrupted him.

"My goodness, Mr. Smythe, how terrible. Everything's terrible. I can't believe the pictures on TV I'm seeing."

Ken lost it at that point. He shouted back at her. "Shut up, you dumb bitch. Stop watching the TV and help me. If you don't get on the ball, I won't just fire your sorry ass. I'll have you killed!"

While Martha didn't like being called a bitch, let alone being threatened, she had lived with a husband who drank—and then got ugly afterward—for long enough not to be intimidated by some white man who worked in an office. Besides, she felt sorry for him.

"Just tell me what you want me to do, Mr. Smythe. Please, just tell me and I'll do it."

Ken Smythe had Martha direct two of the Sklar helicopters sitting near Kennedy into lower Manhattan. Flight plans and regulations be damned, he said. One copter was to attempt a landing at the regular helipad, which lay moored out over the Hudson, just west of 4 World Financial Center. The other copter was to land right on West Street, between 2 World Financial Center and 1 World Financial Center. From what Ken could see from his forty-first-floor perch, no one was on West Street north of the South Tower. The jumpers had scared the crowds off. So, that location looked like much the best alternative landing site for a Sklar helicopter if the regular Hudson River helipad was somehow blocked. It was 9:10 AM.

While Ken had been working out the details for Lew's rescue with Martha Wright, Dr. Chowdry had taken advantage of his distraction and snuck away. Ken and the two associates he had dragooned into staying with him put Lew back on a stretcher and carried him down to the lobby of 2 World Financial Center on a freight elevator. It was 9:30 AMwhen the four men first arrived on the Hudson River side of that building.

As Ken had feared, however, the waterfront path south to the regular Sklar helipad was blocked by thousands of milling people. Such obviously panicked proles couldn't be trusted not to force their way onto any aircraft foolish enough to attempt a landing there. The helipad was clearly out.

So, at Ken's barked order of command, the four of them walked quickly back into the 2 World Financial Center lobby and emerged out on the other side of the building, on West Street, with a full ground view of the carnage. Falling bodies were still coming down. Contact with any one of those dead weights meant instant oblivion.

But there, miraculously, just a few hundred feet down West Street, just a bit north of the South Tower—the last tower to be hit—was the largest Sklar helicopter in the fleet. The one designed to hold twelve passengers. Patiently waiting as instructed. It was 9:55 AM.

They reached the waiting aircraft in less than a minute, Ken sacrificing the need to keep Lew quiet and still to the need to keep himself, the two young men with him, and Lew, most of all Lew, ultimately safe. Their party, which by now totaled eight—including the gasping Lew, Ken, the two Sklar associates plus two pilots and two well-trained paramedics—was in the air a minute or so before 10:00 AM.

Which is when the last to be hit South Tower wound up coming down first. The Sklar chopper, caught in a hail of debris thrown off by the collapsing behemoth, crashed to the ground and exploded. DNA techniques were all that eventually allowed authorities to identify the seven brave souls who died attempting to get the ninety-one-year-old Lew Flood to a hospital.

Chapter Twenty Three
Law Offices of Herbert Chambers, LLP
City of London, UK
{Morning, Monday, November 5, 2001}

TS, Leticia, and Gary Lee had survived 9/11 just by staying put at 2 World Financial Center, hunkering down in an interior Sklar office, listening to a radio scrounged from a break area. They were evacuated some two days after the attack by a search team that came looking for people who hadn't made it out of surrounding buildings. There had been bottled water and some junk food available, so the three of them were not really the worse for wear.

Leticia had taken the train out of Grand Central down to Washington DC, where she planned on staying with her married daughter until the shock of the past few months had time to wear off. Gary Lee had taken AMTRAK clear across country to San Francisco. Even without knowing for sure that Lew and Ken were dead, he'd been sufficiently shaken up by events that he had decided it was time to tell the old Broward partners what TS and Leticia had really been up to since March.

TS took a suite at the Hotel Pierre, paying twice the ordinary rack rate. Once settled in and comfortable, he had started making discreet calls to various headhunting firms and other legal-consulting types concerning his own personal future. He was sure Broward was done. If nothing else, the economic calamity which was sure to follow 9/11 would finish what the dot bust had begun. But the enormity of the 9/11 catastrophe also presented an opportunity for him to blame something besides his own idiocy for killing cock robin.

After all, the immediate aftermath of 9/11 brought all kinds of prognostications that the attack would wreck the US economy. Everybody—the Wall Street Journal, the New York Times, the Economist, the Financial Times of London—thought so. Why, all US air traffic had been stopped, and no one knew when or under what circumstances it would resume. And that was just for starters.

His pitch was simple. Sklar had been hot for a merger. He had personally been in their offices when the attack came, working on the deal. But 9/11 had killed off Sklar's top management. How terrible. This had plunged Sklar into chaos, and that firm was no longer a player in any Broward merger. Life must go on, however, and, after all, anything Sklar wanted was obviously worth having. TS could deliver the core of Broward, including its best client, Cisco, to whomever he wanted. So, were you interested?

No one outside Sklar knew how viciously Lew Flood had manipulated TS, for obvious reasons; but as TS claimed, it had been consistently rumored before 9/11 that Sklar was on the point of taking Broward over. And it was also widely thought that both Lew Flood and Ken Smythe were among 9/11's fallen, as no trace of either man had surfaced since that awful day. So, TS's story was accepted, and TS's calls were returned. And now here he was, without ever having returned to California, sitting in the City of London headquarters of Herbert Chambers, LLP. A more than 200 year old law firm that was 1,800 lawyers strong and was considered among the most charmed members of the so-called London Magic Circle, a grouping of City of London law firms which dominated both British and international law practice.

What had been agreed to by the Brits and TS was simple enough. In the roughly two months since 9/11, TS had enlisted around sixty loyalist partners within Broward's California offices, typically laterals of one stripe or another. Acting with his usual chutzpah—and while ostensibly working out of Broward's largely empty New York offices on firm business—he had hired the headhunters at Abman Weilt to solicit these sixty partners to make a move with him out of Broward. Hardly anyone Abman Weilt approached on TS's behalf had said no.

These sixty men and women were intended to start up a West Coast practice for the Herbert Chambers firm, whose only existing US presence was in New York. Herbert Chambers would invest not less than £10,000,000 to get the new operation off the ground. The key article of faith was that Cisco would become a Herbert Chambers client once Herbert Chambers' arrangement with TS and his group of Broward defectors was formalized—something TS had gotten a letter from Cisco's general counsel promising would happen. It was a real letter, and the Brits had verified that fact in a lab before accepting it as genuine. Mad Yanks like this TS fellow weren't to be trusted. They knew that much in London.

TS felt very lucky to have escaped Broward more or less intact. And, having finally been kicked around by life in the way true survivors usually are, he was resolved not to make the same mistakes again. Such as binding himself to an aide de camp like Leticia. That woman's skill set was primitive, he thought, remembering with disgust their mercifully infrequent sexual encounters. She was simply not a professional in any sense, TS told himself, pompously allowing his well-developed sense of classism, if not an overt racism, to allow him to look down his nose at Leticia, despite all her previous loyalty and service. He had cut her off by then, not returning her calls and e-mail. Just cut her dead.

For her part, once she'd figured out TS had abandoned her, Leticia was furious. What fed her sense of outrage more than anything else was the fact that, in the wake of Broward's very public collapse, she was both unemployed and likely unemployable, certainly at anywhere near the level she had grown comfortable. So, despite her considerable savings—as well as her equally substantial 401(k)—she hated her former mentor for every success he had apparently salvaged from the wreckage of their former firm.

Chapter Twenty Four
Hyatt Regency Hotel
Paseo del Alamo
San Antonio, TX
{Morning, Wednesday, February 6, 2002}

Broward shut down by mid-December 2001. Not filed bankruptcy. Just passed a resolution dissolving the partnership, then fired its employees and stopped paying its bills. Its only ongoing business operation was using a collection agency to try and recover what it could on its receivables, and to pay down the Bank of America line of credit.

The very public TS-led defection of some sixty partners to Herbert Chambers the previous November had been the last straw. Those left behind took some small satisfaction from the fact that—despite the reassuring letter Cisco's general counsel had provided—Broward's prize client, in the event, had actually gone over to Sandino LLP. As for Link Cutter—the young Cisco general counsel who had been so presumptuous as to write Herbert Chambers and assure them as to what his board would do with Cisco's legal business once Broward fell apart—well that young man was out looking for a new job himself.

All this was prologue to the meeting the three members of Broward's Liquidation Committee had scheduled with Joe Wood on the morning of February 6. That, and what Gary Lee had first freely—and Leticia Madison had next grudgingly—confessed to their colleagues. It was now known that Sklar had abused its relationship with Bank of America to squeeze Broward in Broward's time of greatest financial need, and that only the 9/11 attack had kept TS from handing the firm over to Sklar for nothing. It was quite a story. And hearing that Gary Lee, an Old Broward hand if there ever was one, had been in on it—that, in particular, had been a difficult thing to accept.

There had been an all-hands meeting at Broward—excluding, at Gary Lee's insistence, those partners thought to be loyal to TS—the day after Gary got off the AMTRAK in Oakland, following a torturous five-day journey across the US on that farcical excuse for a passenger railroad.

"By the time I got wind of this disaster last spring," Gary had told his Old Broward partners, "every bad thing had already happened. We owed the bank the $100 million, fair and square. Our so-called Management Committee—none of whom are going to stick around now that the shit has hit the fan, of that I'm sure—had properly rubber-stamped all of the borrowing TS did to finance his nutty, unbelievably expensive expansion. None of the people who have been with this firm for their whole careers, including me up to that point, were in the loop. All I thought at first was that what I would be doing was attempting a work-out with the bank, using the downturn as a reason for them to work with us until the economy normalized. A very quiet work-out, one that would let the firm survive. They'd done it for other people, so why not for us? I'm good at this stuff, guys, you know that."

His partners all nodded agreement. Gary Lee was both well-liked and well-respected.

"But when this Lew Flood guy walks in the room and announces it's Sklar that actually owns us, not the bank, well, by then I knew we were up such a shit creek of bad financial planning, I thought 'So, what's the difference?' Worst case, the firm's gone, we all need a new job. We're almost certainly there anyway. TS had already killed us. There's no way we can pay the bank, let alone the overhead for all these fucking fancy offices with nobody worth a shit in them. So, assuming Sklar calls it a merger for P.R. reasons, it's less embarrassing all around. In fact, it's a real face-saver."

The story had fascinated Steve Boothe in particular. Gary Lee practiced only bankruptcy law, a field where dead bodies were buried before they began to stink. In contrast, Steve Boothe was a business litigator. Business litigation involving failed companies was a field where dead bodies were never buried. Instead, likely-looking corpses were mummified, and each well-preserved body part was lovingly examined and re-examined for as many years of civil discovery as it took to adduce enough evidence to convince some jury that a wrongful death had taken place. And that some deep-pocket killer had to pay for its egregious malfeasance in allowing the dearly departed to pass on.

As far as Steve Boothe was concerned, Lew Flood and Ken Smythe's conduct—first pressuring Broward financially and then co-opting Broward's management into agreeing to a lopsided merger—presented a near-perfect chance to pick Sklar's enormously deep pockets. The facts were so opprobrious, Steve was convinced, that no jury would care about whose fault it was that Broward had gotten into financial trouble to begin with. Nor would any jury care what would have happened to Broward if Sklar had acted ethically.

Steve knew his own limitations, however. He understood that he wasn't capable of bringing down mighty Sklar in any civil courtroom on his own. Steve was a defense lawyer—a very good one, but even the best defense lawyers of his stripe were a dime a dozen. Their main qualities were the ability to see the train wrecks that might await a case they were handling, before such things had a chance to happen, and the strength to convince their own clients to pay off when necessary.

But Steve had seen—and occasionally been victimized by—enough charismatics to know that the right lawyer could make the case. So, that had become the Old Broward plan. First, confirm Gary Lee's story through Leticia Madison, something Steve had reached out to Kroc Associates to do. Next, a nationwide talent search for someone with the chops, resources, and willingness to sue Sklar for ruining Broward's long-standing business relationship with Bank of America, in the course of abusing its own fiduciary relationship with that important-even-to-Sklar client. A case that would literally be brought, Steve thought to himself, right over Lew Flood and Ken Smythe's dead bodies. Fuckers that they were.

Steve, Jay Jay, and Lu had gathered for breakfast in the vast atrium of the San Antonio Hyatt Regency. The San Antonio River had been diverted right through this atrium, and they were seated at the river's edge, drinking black coffee and watching a multitude of tourists float by on flatboats and even a gondola or two. None of them had ever met Joe Wood, whose solo practice was located way to the east, on the Gulf Coast, in Corpus Christi. Where Joe also led services at some born-again mega-church every Sunday that he was in town.

Aware that Steve Boothe was looking for a plaintiff's lawyer to sue Sklar, Kroc Associates had sent along an American Lawyer article on Wood, along with a VHS tape of one of the man's sermons. The operative who'd sent Steve the materials included a personal note saying the Kroc firm had worked with Wood, and that he thought Steve should interview him for the job.

The article detailed Joe Wood's increasingly important verdicts, each one coming against larger and larger companies, represented by better and better defense firms. He had recently brought down State Farm in a billion-dollar fight over the low quality of replacement parts it had encouraged body shops to put in damaged cars it insured.

In that case, Joe had not only beaten Crowden's David Boisan, he had done it right in a Bloomington, Indiana courtroom, where State Farm had owned the local judiciary for the past hundred years, minimum.

But it hadn't been the list of victories that had focused Steve Boothe on the need to bring Wood on board. Or even the fact that Kroc Associates vouched for him. It was the VHS tape. That's where he saw it. That certain something. You couldn't miss it, even though it came complete with Joe leading his flock while they all spoke in tongues and he closed his eyes and handled the random snakes brought to him that day.

Joe Wood had obtained his law degree from the University of Texas at Austin, but that highly secular experience had little to do with who Joe Wood really was. Rather, Joe Wood was the impossibly small, redneck East Texas town of Lufkin, where he had grown up. Joe was Texas Bible College, where his mother Olive worked in the cafeteria and where, as an undergraduate, Joe had most sincerely trained as a lay minister. In the end, Joe was the sum of his mother's most fervent Pentecostal beliefs, beliefs that had pulled Joe and his younger two siblings through the fright and impoverishment of having their father shipped off to Texas State Prison when Joe Junior was eight. That was when Joe Senior was convicted of accidentally killing a filling-station attendant by backing over the man during a botched stick-up. Thirty years later, Joe Junior still visited his daddy in jail, bringing in Camel cigarettes and the good news of Jesus's love every time he saw the man.

And now, while the three Broward partners were bemusing themselves about what types of snakes were actually employed at the services conducted in Joe Wood's church, the renowned plaintiff's lawyer himself appeared at their table, obviously having overheard their laughing conversation. Not an auspicious beginning, Steve thought.

"Depends," Wood had drawled. "All depends on what kinds of snakes folks turn up with in their baskets that Sunday. Come one, come all, that's the motto of the Corpus Free Pentecostal Church. That includes snakes. And Yankees." Wood winked broadly at Boothe, whom he had spoken with repeatedly before this meeting. "Which is why even you heathens are invited to come along as well."

It was not a straight answer. Nor a particularly friendly one. But it had wit, and it broke the ice.

Wood had read Kroc Associates' report of its agent's interview with Leticia Madison, as well as Gary Lee's detailed summary of the same events. While he had never sued any kind of law firm before, he had acquired a real distaste for Big Law culture. Particularly of the virulent New York strain. During the State Farm trial, Crowden had sunk so low as to have an easily corrupted sub-warden stick an elderly, chronically ill Joe Wood Senior in solitary, thereby hoping to drag Wood away from the Indiana trial and down to Texas for a few days in order to straighten the matter out.

Hadn't worked. Wood's prominence on the religious right and his large campaign contributions had made him many friends in high places within the Republican-dominated Austin statehouse and Joe wasn't above pulling such strings. But it had sure bothered him that these remote, apparently effete New Yorkers would dare fool with him in his own backyard that way.

So, Joe Wood had come ready to accept the opportunity to punch one of those big Manhattan law firms in the nose. As far as Steve Boothe was concerned, anybody who could reach into a big pile of random snakes every few weeks and live was a perfect candidate to sue TS and Sklar before a San Francisco jury. A deal was struck.

Chapter Twenty Five
Office of the US Trustee
San Francisco, CA
{Morning, Wednesday, June 12, 2002}

Locked down in the stocks. That was how it looked to Gary Lee, as he watched his three ex-law partners squirm under questioning at the Broward firm's first meeting of creditors. And next thing, the crowd will start pelting them with lit dog shit.

Gary Lee himself had narrowly escaped being among those hustled to the front of the room to account for his firm's financial sins. That was a humiliation he'd skipped only by virtue of being too savvy to accept appointment to Broward's Liquidation Committee, a group elected by the Broward partners some seven months earlier, in a last futile effort to avoid a bankruptcy filing by the firm. Instead, he'd agreed only to a consulting role, informally assisting his three now very glum-looking friends of thirty years: Steve Boothe, Lu Odom, and Jay Jay Martin.

Compulsively, Gary Lee glanced over at Shane Sullivan. There, just a few feet away, sat the smug lawyer who'd filed an involuntary bankruptcy filing against the Broward firm two months ago. A bankruptcy filing no one in the firm ever wanted, and one that had brought a crowd of over three hundred people to the US Trustee's office that morning, many howling for blood.

Shane was himself a long-ago Broward alum, not to mention a Boalt classmate of the infamous TS himself. How perfect, Gary

Lee thought grimly. He remembered his own first year at Broward. How miserable he'd been, working in the trial department for a Marine vet with no tolerance for civilians, let alone intellectuals. How he'd escaped his nemesis by switching from general litigation to bankruptcy law. And how Shane was then hired as his replacement.

The first part of the bankruptcy proceeding went alright. The first few questions came from lawyers representing the firm's many unpaid landlords. Muted questions, as Broward still inspired fear among its peer firms, if only from the grave. Questions Lu deflected with his usual boyish charm and skill.

But then came the copy guy. The dead-broke copy guy.

It turned out that the dead-broke copy guy had come to this country from Vietnam as a young child, a boat person whose parents had died before his eyes from dehydration, using what little water there was in their one canteen to save him and his older sister.

Growing up in foster homes, Ben Vinh had dropped out of high school and started working when he hit his mid-teens. Gary knew from his own experience using the guy how Ben had eventually built a successful small business doing extra-reliable copying projects for large firms; his slavish attention to detail was legendary.

After having mercifully stopped crying once he got past the part about how long he and his sister had been trapped with his parents' bodies on the way to Hong Kong, it was back to tears again when Ben described his happiness in getting the Broward contract in August 2000—more than a year before TS had fled, and while the other Broward partners were still operating under the delusion they had a functioning business.

The contract Ben Vinh was talking about gave Vinh Copy Services all of the Broward copy work in the Bay Area. On credit, needless to say. And, in the seventeen months between Ben Vinh's getting his dream contract and the shut-down of Broward's operations in January 2002, Vinh Copy Services ran up an unpaid bill of over a million and a half bucks. Of which Broward had, thus far, paid about $100,000.

None of this was complicated or surprising. As Gary well knew, back during 2001, while old Ben was being screwed day by day, there was just too much pressure on Broward to keep paying its partners their full draws to allow for paying people like the overly trusting Mr. Vinh. Because not paying partners all their money, why, that would cause defections and defections would hit the press and bad publicity would then panic the bank. Catastrophe would surely follow. And catastrophe had to be avoided, so Vinh Copy Services would just have to wait for its money. And hope for no catastrophe.

Ben Vinh said he'd already lost his business and his home, forty other immigrants now had no jobs, and if it weren't for his wife and kids, he'd kill himself right there and now. It wasn't until Ben Vinh actually used the word "kill" that Gary suddenly realized the examination room at the US Trustee's office didn't even have a metal detector. But Ben Vinh wasn't really going to hurt anyone. He was just a nice man who'd always worked hard, and now he had been screwed out of all his money. Ben Vinh said he had no illusions about that last fact.

No, all Ben now said he wanted was for Lu, who was sitting right there in a US government office, a place where they were supposed to answer his questions, to tell him how he and his two friends, Steve and Jay, could have taken hundreds of thousands of dollars in paychecks when their firm wasn't paying him, the poor man next to them, for honest work. Work they and the other partners had ordered done and then collected money for from their own clients every month.

Ben Vinh was weeping and yelling at the end. "How could you?" he kept saying, in his heavily accented English. "How could you? You, you who are the law, how could you?" And all Lu, Steve, and Jay could do was look horrified and scared at the same time. And say they hadn't done anything, because they weren't in charge of anything, at least not until after the firm shut down at the beginning of 2002. They couldn't help Ben, even by answering his few questions.

His pals were telling the truth, Gary Lee knew, but so what? The whole process was just a forum for allowing people like Ben Vinh to hurl on somebody. In fact, Gary Lee realized, facing Ben Vinh was probably worse for Lu and Steve and Jay than just wiping some anonymous vomit off your face. Here they all knew

188

Ben Vinh from better days. How he'd personally saved each of them on multiple desperate projects. And they had all thanked him personally for it, too. Because Ben was just a peach, a real peach. Always had been. Poor sap.

Chapter Twenty Six
Chambers of the Honorable Charles Rogers
US Bankruptcy Judge
US Bankruptcy Court for the Northern District of California
(San Francisco Division)
{Evening, Thursday, December 2, 2004}

Charlie Rogers liked lawyers. A long time PW&S partner
before he had been appointed to the bankruptcy bench in 1995, he
had nothing but good feelings and the highest regard for the people
he had worked with in his old firm. And when he had accepted his
bankruptcy judgeship from the 9th Circuit, he had never dreamed
he would ever preside over a bankruptcy involving a firm like
Broward. Such a notion was unthinkable.

Not that the main bankruptcy case in Broward had wound up in
his court. That nightmare of non-paying Broward clients and
disappointed Broward creditors belonged to his colleague and good
friend Bankruptcy Judge Tom Burton, whose chambers were
located up one floor in the nondescript downtown San Francisco
commercial office building which housed the San Francisco
Division of the Northern District of California's bankruptcy court.

The piece of the Broward bankruptcy case Charlie had caught
some months before was a mediation between the Broward
Chapter 7 trustee, Irving J. Cornelius, and several hundred
Broward partners. Shane Sullivan was representing Irv Cornelius,
and he had all of these very angry former Broward partners in his
crosshairs based on a novel, but nonetheless somewhat persuasive,

190

legal theory. Sullivan claimed that most, if not all, the payments made to its partners by Broward in the two years leading up to Broward's dissolution vote had to be repaid to Broward's estate—and ultimately made available to Broward's creditors. But only after, of course, a healthy slice of any amounts recovered were first paid over to Shane Sullivan for his contingent fee.

Charlie had already been somewhat aware of the back story of Shane Sullivan's relationship to the people he was suing. What he hadn't known, however, was certainly augmented by the multiple accusations of inappropriate bias coming from all the separate armed camps into which the various defendants had withdrawn once *Cornelius v. Boothe* had first been filed by Sullivan LLP.

One group said that Shane Sullivan had been fired from his employment at Broward due to insubordination. Another group's brief claimed Shane Sullivan had once formally accused Broward of judge tampering. Turner Smiley, who was separately represented by the famous—and famously arrogant—Steve Neilson at Cole Good LLP, filed a mediation brief which began by noting that Sullivan LLP employed Helen Wilson, Esq., who, like Shane Sullivan himself, was a former Broward attorney. Ms. Wilson, Mr. Neilson begged to inform His Honor, had been hospitalized at Napa State for more than a year due to continuing suicidal tendencies after she had made a failed attempt at killing herself the evening she had threatened Mr. Smiley's life and then been sued by Broward for a stay away order. How could Mr.

Smiley be expected to negotiate with a firm populated by persons so clearly on a vendetta against him?

Nothing anyone had said about his old friend Shane came as a surprise to Charlie Rogers; Charlie knew as well as anyone how insubordinate Shane could be. Why, the man had frequently lashed out at the judge himself, and in open court no less. Never meant any harm by it, just had no sense of limits when it came to making a point. Wasn't all torn up if you bit back, either. So, Charlie always looked forward to having Shane start a brawl, even if Charlie himself might wind up getting his own hair mussed a bit in the process. More fun than most of what went on before him.

As for Shane's having once charged Broward with judge tampering, who knew? For one thing, the record of proceedings before the Commission on Judicial Performance were entirely sealed, and Charlie considered it a breach of legal ethics for Sara MacCarty to have provided him with a declaration summarizing the information she had presented to that body when Shane Sullivan's complaint against Joan Marie and Fran Meyer had been received. For another thing, Charlie Rogers knew whose niece Sara MacCarty was, and he also knew exactly what the now long-deceased Hermann Philips had been capable of, even in his dotage. PW&S had always kept well abreast of what their Broward competition was like, even if Shane Sullivan had been a naïf when he was a youngster.

As for Ms. Wilson's nervous breakdown, all Steve Neilson's callous reference to that fact had done was inflame Charlie against both the lawyer and his client. People from all walks of life came into his courtroom every day, many of them driven out of their wits by financial problems. Charlie couldn't counsel them, either psychologically or legally. But he could, and did, very much, try to leave them their dignity. And Helen Wilson's dignity was something Mr. Neilson apparently thought should be the first thing to go. Well, the hell with that, Charlie had thought when he'd finished reading TS's mediation brief.

There had been 318 equity partners when Broward had come crashing to the ground at the end of 2001. In the two years prior—during which Shane Sullivan claimed Broward had been insolvent—these partners had collectively received approximately $350,000,000 in draws, equaling about one-half of Broward's $700,000,000 gross income during that period.

If that money all came back into the Broward bankruptcy estate, three things would follow: Sullivan would become rich; Broward's creditors would be paid in full; and many of Broward's former partners would lose their homes and whatever savings and investments they had, at least other than what they had tucked away in their 401(k) plans. Like O.J.'s fortune, those were exempt from execution by creditors. For doing nothing but going to work and doing their jobs, Charlie shuddered, imagining how he would have liked being put in such a situation if PW&S had collapsed while he had been there.

But there it was. It wasn't him. And it wasn't his decision anyway. Just another case to dump short of trial, really, no matter how close to the bone its allegations cut or how unfair the result urged by Shane's allegations seemed to the judge.

Sullivan's brief was short and to the point. It focused on California Corporations Code section 16957, a statute everyone agreed would ultimately determine whether and to what extent the Broward partners had to give back what they had gotten from Broward in 2000 and 2001. Section 16957 had, in fact, been ghostwritten for the California legislature—and this was ironic, even by Charlie's ghoulish standards—by a Broward partner who was now himself a defendant in *Cornelius v. Boothe*. It had first been enacted in the 1980s as part of California's then-new Limited Liability Partnership law, a raid on the federal and state treasuries designed to allow professionals to manage their businesses like corporations without having to pay corporate income tax.

Nearly every sizable California law firm had adopted the LLP form. But, while some LLPs had failed, no LLP of Broward's size had ever gone bankrupt, thereby putting a pit-bull trustee like Irv Cornelius in place to hire a pit-bull litigator like Shane Sullivan to test the outer limits of how far 16957 could be pushed in order to beggar the Broward partners.

A perfect shitstorm, Charlie concluded, when—after reading and re-reading all the hundreds of pages of submittals from the warring parties—he finally sat down alone in his large private office a week or so before the long-scheduled mediation of *Cornelius v. Boothe* and tried to think through how best to prod the parties to a resolution that would not be unfair to anyone.

194

Wouldn't be at all difficult if he was also the trial judge. Then he'd just call Shane in first, tell him that he, Charlie, hated his case. Too unfair, he'd have said to Shane. You can't just chomp down on all these working-stiff partners. Not just based on the fact this Smiley guy went crazy with Bank of America's money. 16957 can't allow that. Not in my court. Take two cents on the dollar or go home with nothing. Shane would then negotiate for five cents and Charlie would get him four cents.

But Charlie didn't have the horses to bully Shane that way. He wasn't the trial judge. So, all Charlie had to work with was his supposed opinion of how Tom Burton would rule if the case were tried in front of him. Which was not at all how Charlie would himself likely rule in that role. And that important fact Charlie knew Shane would have already surmised. Tom had been a government lawyer before taking the bankruptcy bench. He had never earned the kind of money Charlie had made as a high-powered PW&S lawyer, and so Tom would not likely share Charlie's empathy for the mess a large judgment would make of the former Broward partners' upper-middle-class lives.

Tom was more likely to focus on the mess the Broward bankruptcy had made of the dead-broke copy guy's life. Whom Shane would probably have sit through the trial, if Charlie knew Shane. Which he did.

Wonderful thing, mediation, Charlie thought. In many ways even more fun than judging. Went faster, gave the judge a more active role. But, ultimately, mediation put you at the mercy of the fucking litigators. That was the downside. Take a guy like Sullivan. Mildly uncontrollable in the courtroom. Nothing a strong judge, gavel in hand, couldn't deal with. But, in a mediation, Shane would pants anyone, especially a mediator—assuming the mediator wasn't also the trial judge—who missed a point or tried to bully him. Just as fast as he'd insult his opponents to the point of precipitating a walkout.

Shane would deal, of course. In fact he'd deal on the most rational basis imaginable. But the process, my goodness, it was not what Charlie felt he'd signed up for when he'd taken the bankruptcy bench as an alternative to early retirement at PW&S, where you were out the door at sixty-two.

If *Cornelius v. Broward* weren't so fascinating, and Tom Burton hadn't been so insistent, Charlie would have turned the case down. He'd have told Tom to send the mediation to Oakland, where the Chief Bankruptcy Judge—who didn't care for Sullivan's style—would probably facilitate settlement by throwing Shane out a window the first time Shane uttered a peep.

Now it was 10:30 PMon the last day set aside for mediation. The parties had ordered up a private court reporter, and Charlie had gone downstairs in his private elevator to let the woman into the building so she could make a formal record of the settlement he'd achieved after a marathon three-day session.

What a cyclone the process had been. Even with most clients relegated to telephone standby, there were still some thirty defense counsel and Shane to deal with. It had been clear right from the start that Shane and Steve Neilson were unable to speak civilly to each other. Charlie found it hilarious that Shane let Helen Wilson do his talking when it came to dealing with that luminary. If Shane knew what Neilson had put in his "court's eyes only" mediation brief about Shane's female partner—whose good looks had been largely restored by plastic surgery and good dentistry—why, I'd have to bring in the Marshall, Charlie thought. But what Shane and Helen didn't know didn't hurt them, and Helen kept an open line of communication between the plaintiff and TS.

There were a lot of other angry, even irrational, people who made their way into the judge's waiting room. Sara MacCarty, for example, was part of the process because she was *in pro per*. Charlie quickly realized there was no talking to her, so he told her to go back to her office and wait for his summons.

Gary Lee was there. He was attending in person only because the Broward Liquidation Committee—which had separately hired Charlie's great friend and mentee, John Chandler, as the Old Broward partners' main defense counsel—had asked him to.

Gary Lee acted dispassionate, but one glance told Charlie how much Lee hated Shane Sullivan. No doubt about that. Took his former colleague's greed very personally indeed. In fact, Gary Lee only had one house, not much money in his 401(k), and a wife who had never been well. And yet here was Sullivan, who knew all that, and still wanted to make a buck at Gary Lee's expense. Welcome to a life in the law, Gary reflected bitterly. Where the friends you make in youth eat you in old age.

The offer was out for fifty cents on the dollar for anybody who would take it. Once Charlie convinced Shane to lower the offer to fifty cents on the dollar for any compensation above $300,000 a year or $25,000 minimum, about a hundred of the younger partners, including all those who had just made partner in either 2000 or 2001, had peeled off. Shane had $5 million in his pocket with that first wave of settlements done. Enough to keep his office going if he had to try his case. A point lost on no one. More importantly, an object lesson to everyone left in the room that a settlement was achievable, no matter who hated whom more.

The next layer of partners had been much tougher. Mainly laterals there, some making nearly a million a year each. With them, as with the youngsters, it wasn't personal with Shane. Nobody knew Shane from Adam. He was just some vulture trying to pick at remains, and these guys didn't consider themselves dead meat. In the end Charlie had worn everybody down, finally just going around Shane and giving Irv Cornelius a little private talk on how crazy Shane could be sometimes, and how listening to Charlie was always the safe thing to do.

That lecture had predictably intimidated Irv, who hated being criticized by any judge, and who didn't like Shane much more than the Chief Bankruptcy Judge did. Shane was not on board the *Cornelius v. Boothe* train for his winning personality. Irv just flat-out respected how aggressive he was.

In the end, Charlie's tactics brought Irv's price for the mid-level Broward partners down to twenty-two cents, with a rise in their deductible to $500,000. Shane was utterly pissed when Irv came out and confessed how Charlie had gotten him alone in a room to accomplish this. Before Charlie could even communicate Irv's new position to the other side, Shane had stormed into Charlie's office and begun berating him.

That was when Charlie put his foot down. "Stop. I mean stop right now, Sullivan. I may not be your trial judge. But I am a sitting judge of this court, and if you say another goddamn word to me in that tone, you will find yourself in the middle of a disciplinary proceeding."

Shane stopped. His mind raced. What kind of disciplinary proceeding could this guy really threaten him with? Everything, short of coming to actual blows, is sealed in a mediation. But still he stopped talking. Waited to hear what was coming next.

Shane's tenuous struggle to control himself was something entirely rare in Charlie's observation of the younger man. Made Charlie feel guilty for the shameless dirty trick he'd just played on Shane. Made him want to laugh out loud at the same time.

So, he laughed. And then so did Shane.

"OK. OK. I give up," Charlie said. "It was a rotten thing to do." Charlie was still laughing, even harder now.

"So, you report me for judicial misconduct. And then I'll sure as shit hold you in contempt for being so disrespectful to me that you hurt my feelings a moment ago. And, after we both get ourselves disciplined, then we can go off and be partners somewhere in the Rust Belt. Get John Chandler to join us, and I'll keep you from eating him up and spitting him out once a week. But look, Shane, you were never going to give me what I needed. And it's the correct approach. You know it is. And look, I know your real number. Irv told me. Said you wouldn't like it, but he told me anyway."

Here Shane understood what the judge was talking about: the real, live who-cares-where-it comes-from overall settlement number. $50 million. Which number he had told Mr. Irving J. Cornelius that he, Shane Sullivan, would kill him if he squealed to anyone.

Shane had stopped laughing and was already thinking what he would do, physically, to the much smaller Mr. Cornelius, once he got him alone, when the judge went on.

"And I don't think $75 million is that crazy. I don't know how close I can get, but this next deal will get you to $15 million total, and I swear to God I'll squeeze the big guys who are waiting to play as hard as you want me to for that next $60 million, if you'll just allow me to do this mediation my way and let me keep chipping away at the problem."

This last statement was a non-sequitur, not an outright lie. Irv had given Charlie the $50 million number. Even said he'd take less. But warned Charlie not to tell Shane he'd told. Said Shane might quit on him if Shane found out. So, Charlie had given Shane a little misdirection, and probably saved Irv from a real headache.

Shane, for his part, believed nothing and nobody about anything. But he knew the drill. Mediation was a process, and, unlike many of the more timid souls in his profession, he really did know how to say no and mean it. So, he went along. $15 million was a fair piece of change, and the last layer of partners, the one that TS, Lu Odom, and Sara MacCarty were in, that was where the real munchies were anyway. Personally as well as money-wise.

The last day and a half of the mediation had been devoted to the hundred or so Broward partners who had earned at least $1 million per annum during the firm's heyday. There were even quite a few who had been making $5 million—even, in TS's case, $10 million—a year during those last two glorious years.

By then Charlie had decided Shane's number was not $75 million, or $50 million, but $40 million, which was four times what Shane would ever have gotten if Charlie was both mediator and trial judge—and infinitely more than the big goose egg Shane would have gotten if he'd tried this dog in front of Charlie.

But, boy, getting those last millions had been agonizing. The problem had not been TS. Neilson was highly analytical, and he was happy to have TS contribute a large sum of money to any settlement. All he wanted in exchange was for any settlement to make it clear that TS would only have to pay once, and that the state court lawsuit Joe Wood had brought against both TS and Sklar—suing TS for mismanagement and fraud and Sklar for fraud and interference with contract—would be dismissed based on TS's contribution to settlement.

But Neilson had a problem. John Chandler had highlighted it best. No one he represented, he told Charlie, was going to pay anything if all TS had to pay was some fractional share of the proposed settlement. While his clients looked at Sklar, not TS, as the deep-pocket defendant in their state court lawsuit—and part of any deal they made with Irv was going to have to involve the Broward bankruptcy estate's agreeing that the state court case belonged to the Broward partners and not to the Broward bankruptcy estate—no one was ever going to agree to let TS go that lightly. Never.

In poetry and drama, love conquers all. But in mediation—which, like family law, is an exquisitely painful misnomer for what the process in truth consists of—hate is the best leverage. When he had confirmed Chandler's insight with the other ten or so defense counsel and the various *pro pers* on the Broward side, Charlie put it to all of them as a group.

"Well, people," he began, "outside the door of this office there are Shane Sullivan and Steve Neilson. And Neilson is smart enough to pay Sullivan $5 million to have TS walk, once and for all. And Sullivan is smart enough to take it. Leaving you with no case against TS. And, when Sullivan thinks about it some more, leaving you with the additional risk that Shane will tell Irv Cornelius to go poach your case against Sklar. Which, Mr. Chandler here will tell the less thoughtful of you, is no joke. So, end game, Sklar then settles with Irv Cornelius for whatever Irv can negotiate—and you all are left with no possible upside. Plus, you're still facing Shane Sullivan two months from now in a very dangerous trial in front of Tom Burton. A Tom Burton who probably does not think your clients have some inalienable right to keep their multi-million dollar salaries when Broward didn't pay the guy who did its photocopying. And a lot of peons just like him. Tom and I may even agree on that point."

Charlie was swinging for the stands here. He had a growing dislike for the various individuals he had been exposed to at the top tier of Broward's partnership. Didn't change his view of the proper legal limits of 16957, but letting this crowd of misanthropes and their lawyers see his honest anger toward them was a nice touch, he thought, especially since he was now convinced they all would, indeed, be in a great deal of difficulty should they choose to go to trial in front of Tom Burton.

It was 4:00 PMon the last day of mediation when he gave that very nasty speech. Nothing happened for five hours after that. During all those five long hours the judge sat alone with Shane Sullivan and Steve Neilson. Those two, sensing a possible deal between them, had both acted like gentlemen, with everyone passing the time by telling war stories and dirty jokes.

And then, at 9:00 PM, the case broke wide open,   So
intimidated were they by the prospect of losing their case against
TS and Sklar before it could even be brought to trial that the
remaining Broward partners—including Sara
MacCarty—collectively offered $30 million. The only conditions
were that the Broward bankruptcy estate's claims against TS and
Sklar be assigned to the Broward Liquidation Committee, for the
benefit of everyone participating in this last $30 million payment.
$30 million brought the overall settlement number to $45 million.
Irv Cornelius said yes before Shane could stop him, and
then—ruefully looking up at Judge Rogers, who had taken the
bench to receive the offer—Shane nodded his acquiescence as
well.

Steve Neilson choked out an angry protest. "Outrageous! It's
just outrageous that Your Honor would sit with me and Mr.
Sullivan and give no hint of what Your Honor and Mr. Chandler
were obviously plotting behind Mr. Smiley's back the whole
time."

"Is that a legal objection, Mr. Neilson?" Charlie Rogers
blandly replied, feeling sorry for Neilson, if not for TS. Neilson, he
had decided, was not a bad egg. Too successful for his own good.
And way too thin-skinned. But that was what came from having a
father who had been Dean of Yale Law School.

John Chandler sprang to his feet. "Mr. Neilson's remarks are
unfair, as Your Honor well knows. Your Honor never suggested
this method of settlement to our side. All you did was help us

understand our position, for which I, in particular, am most grateful."

Shane laughed, though only to himself. Both he and John Chandler thought the world of Charlie Rogers. And Shane thought the world of John Chandler, a lawyer who had once saved him from personal financial disaster right before this very judge. But the sycophancy of twenty-first-century courtroom practice in the federal courts was something Gilbert and Sullivan would have enjoyed choreographing had they lived to see it. Shane hated authority in general, and so he much preferred Steve Neilson's in your face style to John Chandler's polished-apple-for-the-teacher-approach to advocacy. None of it mattered. By 11:00 PMthe settlement had been formally put on the record. TS was left in the gutter, fully exposed to his ex-partners' state court lawsuit.

Shane hadn't gotten rich, at least not personally. By 2004, he had acquired a total of eleven partners to share his good fortune with. But, with a third of an overall $45 million settlement coming in, Sullivan LLP would soon be having its best year ever. Shane noticed that Helen Wilson had acquired a glow that he hadn't seen since law school. The former Broward partners certainly weren't TS's only enemies. There was no shortage of such folks, that was for sure.

Chapter Twenty Seven
Superior Court in and for the
City and County of San Francisco
{Afternoon, Sunday, April 2, 2006}

The jury in *Martin v. Smiley* delayed reporting that they had a verdict to Judge Alarcon until they had one last long lunch together. Knowing they would soon be separated, the group had splurged and reserved a table at Citizen Cake, which one of the jurors, a city employee, said was the best place within walking distance of the courthouse. Another of the jurors, one of the better-off ones, had quietly made up the difference between the $20 a meal the lunch really cost and the $7.50 per plate everyone agreed to pay.

It was odd, that better-off juror thought, how—even with all the discord, all the oddball attitudes of his fellow jurors—he actually found he had wound up liking everyone at the table. Yet what a dog's breakfast the case had been. Starting with the trial lawyers. Where had those Broward partners ever found this Joe Wood fellow? And how in the hell had such a charlatan reached so many of his new friends and fellow jurors on such an illogical level?

The man who had bought everyone's lunch, Juror Number 7, was a thirty-nine-year-old Indian émigré and former internet executive. He held a BSEE from San Jose State and an MBA from UC Berkeley's Haas business school. He'd acted as foreman of the

Martin jury, taking advantage of the usual confusion at the beginning of any jury deliberation to appoint himself to that position with no very vocal opposition from anyone.

He had also been the last juror seated, after both sides had exhausted all their peremptory challenges, and he was quite sure Mr. Wood had tried quite hard to throw him off the jury for cause. Which had gotten nowhere with Judge Alarcon, whom Juror Number 7 had come to very greatly admire.

Joe Wood picked his own juries. No fancy consultants for him. And until he'd run out of bullets, and this Juror Number 7 was put in the box, he'd been satisfied he could do what he needed to do with what was a pretty average bunch of people—women mainly. When he'd questioned Juror Number 7, he'd assumed the fellow would play along with Joe's aren't-you-too-important, don't-too-many-people-depend-on-you routine to maybe get Judge Alarcon, who was at least pretending neutrality at that point, to bump 7 for cause.

Snakebite was the result. Not too busy, the guy said. Made his pile in the dot boom and got out early. Working on a few new things but nothing that would keep him from doing his civic duty. Sounded like an interesting case. Had a few brushes with various corporate lawyers when his company went public and had always wondered about how American lawyers did business among themselves.

The actual jury trial had lasted nearly two months. In addition to Joe Wood, Steve Neilson acted for TS and Cotta & Van Atta's John Cotta was there defending Sklar.

Cotta was a Vietnam vet who had lost both legs after stepping on a South Vietnamese Army-laid landmine during Tet. The man's face was so scarred from his battle wounds that plastic surgery had only made him look more fearsome. Much more the kind of defense lawyer you would find in rough and tumble East Texas than in effete San Francisco.

It was a straight swearing contest, really. Gary Lee and Leticia Jones were up first. They told the truth, straight up. About how ninety-one-year-old Lew Flood had misused his control over Bank of America to force a combination on Broward and how the only thing which had stopped him was his having the life crushed out of him and his partner Ken Smythe by the collapse of the South Tower at about 10:00 AMon 9/11. Right while TS, Gary Lee, and Leticia Jones were all in Sklar's offices, waiting to hear from Sklar's Executive Committee what Broward's fate would be. A Sklar Executive Committee which had come from far and wide to vote on the matter.

Other than making the point that there was no paper trail supporting this story, John Cotta had not cross-examined either of these first two witnesses. Steve Neilson had asked nothing at all. Just glowered to show his personal disbelief.

Next came TS. He told some of the truth. No, he said, no one had threatened Broward in his presence. He would have reported that to Bank of America, even gone to the US Attorney if such an outrageous thing had even been suggested. But it was true he had been at Sklar's offices when the 9/11 attack occurred. And it was also true that the reason he was there, along with his two colleagues, Gary Lee and Leticia Jones, was to talk merger.

A merger that would have saved Broward and recognized all the good things he had done for the firm, if it hadn't been wrecked by the 9/11 attack and the death of his two close friends, Lew Flood and Ken Smythe. Both of whom had been truly honorable members of the legal profession. Here TS had become tearful.

Joe Wood tried to penetrate TS's contrived story, but his strength lay in argument, not cross-examination. And TS was a formidable witness, radiating sincerity, cloaking himself in the terror he had felt when the Twin Towers had gone down, making Joe look slow and unsure of himself. Though Joe did not linger long with TS, it was still painful to watch.

John Cotta was a different story. He was no empathetic preacher boy turned lawyer. He was an antagonistic cross-examiner and one who got away with more than most courtroom advocates either would or could. After all, sitting there in a wheelchair projecting only nubbins for legs, who could hold a little mean-spiritedness against him? John Cotta wasn't just mean, though, he was also Princeton '65, Yale Law '72, and even smarter than those elitist credentials meant he should be.

Broward owed Bank of America $100 million, he first got TS to admit.

And Broward hadn't paid that $100 million back, had it, he'd then honed in. TS equivocated on the latter issue, talked about relationships, lots of friendly meetings, but Cotta's point was made.

Next, Cotta focused TS in on how completely inappropriate it would have been for Sklar to be talking merger with the same Broward that owed Sklar's client, Bank of America, all that money, at least without first telling the bank what was going on.

TS agreed with that proposition, not seeing the trap as clearly as he should have. The truth was that Cotta bothered him. Anyone he couldn't charm bothered TS. This was worse. Cotta's attitude went beyond viewing TS as not charming. Cotta saw TS as edible.

"Do you know if Broward ever mentioned a possible merger with Sklar to Hadley Bennett while Sklar was representing Bank of America, Mr. Smiley?" Cotta asked him.

Smiley paused to think that one over. While he paused, Cotta looked toward the back of the courtroom, and in popped Ms. Bennett herself, looking severely at TS. Her angry face made up his mind for him. Better to say nothing, he thought, even if such silence was somewhat inconsistent with all that phony praise for his two dead tormentors at Sklar.

"Don't know what went on between Sklar and the bank, Mr. Cotta," he said blandly enough. "Lew and Ken were fine men, and I'm sure they did the right thing."

"The right thing, Mr. Smiley?"

"The right thing?"

"Are you so lost to all ethics that you don't understand the only right thing was to withdraw from representing Bank of America if you happen to be telling the truth and Sklar was going to do a business deal with Broward? Are you seriously suggesting anything else? Are you?"

TS could only make a weak, unrehearsed reply to the effect that he was no expert on legal ethics, and that it was really all Sklar's problem, not his.

This brought Cotta down on him like a wolf on a laggard sheep.

"You know lying to this jury is an ethical problem, Mr. Smiley, don't you? You know perjury is a bad thing?"

Steve Neilson began shouting some kind of objection. But by then TS was terrified. He just wanted off the stand, and Cotta seemed to be throwing him a bone when he didn't wait for an answer, ignored Neilson's shouts, and instead finished with the rhetorical flourish that if Lew Flood and Ken Smythe were really the fallen American heroes TS said they were, then no way did they try to merge Broward into Sklar while still representing Bank of America. No way at all.

TS said nothing. The judge called a recess. On the break, TS told Neilson not to ask him any more questions.

Joe Wood knew the damage Cotta had done his case, but he also saw what a victim TS would make if TS were subjected to further cross-questioning and, as a result, Cotta got yet another shot at him. So, Joe also passed on asking TS anything more, and TS was off the stand. No one from any of the three sides went near him again.

What the rest of the trial had consisted of was hard to say. Joe Wood called all of the surviving fifty-one members of the Sklar Executive Committee. He asked each of them if it wasn't true a merger with Broward had been on the agenda when the 9/11 attack had interrupted the meeting. Fifty-one times, the answer was more or less the same.

"Not possible." "Nothing on the agenda about that." "Don't know anything about it." "There would be a file, a submittal." "No paper trail." Just plain "No." Even an occasional "How dare you?" —though, since the fact the Broward partners were on site that 9/11 morning made even Cotta suspicious of his entirely untrustworthy clients, Cotta had cautioned the Sklar partners about appearing too self-righteous.

This *auto-da-fé* had been agonizing for 7 to sit through, as he never believed anything that wasn't written down. But Joe Wood's approach did make points elsewhere on the jury. The Sklar senior partners were what they were. Arrogant cut-throats to a man. And the fact there was not a woman among them was not lost on their audience of mostly women jurors either. They did not project at all well when contrasted with Joe Wood's likable nature.

Then Joe had thrown out the few secretaries and paralegals he had in his bag who had overheard rumors of a Broward merger. Those willing to testify had, not coincidentally, lost their jobs after Sklar had cut back sizable numbers of staff in the economic contraction that followed 9/11. None knew much; all they really proved was what a bad place Sklar was to work. Which, again, made a point Joe wanted to make. Needed to make.

The rest was experts proving how much it was all worth. Hundreds of millions, according to Wood's parade of such witnesses. None of whom had much to say back when Cotta cross-examined by noting how broke the firm had been on 9/11. Neilson said nothing at all.

When it came Cotta's turn, he called only one witness: eighty-four year old Rhea Green, the woman who had been Lew Flood's admin for over fifty years. Rhea Green had finally retired from Sklar after her boss had perished in the 9/11 attack, Cotta established. Since then she'd had bladder cancer and begun wearing a wig after her hair had failed to come back after chemo.

The wig was a real fright. But it only served to make Rhea more human, especially to the eight women on the jury. Cotta had picked it out himself, telling Rhea she could have her own much more stylish hairpiece back when a verdict came in. Never take the stand with a good haircut, he'd told the old lady, with a wink. Rhea, who was as good a judge of legal talent as any Sklar hiring partner, did as Cotta requested.

Rhea Green, of course, knew the truth about the Broward deal. But she'd been covering up for Lew Flood for as long as she could remember. She was not going to see Lew's memory sullied by some Texas charm boy who, as far as she was concerned, was just taking advantage of the fact the old man wasn't around anymore to scare up some easy money.

In the event, Rhea's appearance on the stand was eerie in the extreme. It was as if Lew Flood had come back from the grave to defend himself. All the dead man's honors; all his many charitable good deeds; all his personal kindnesses toward employees, most directly as applied to Rhea herself, were laid before the jury.

And then, the fateful day. Lew's heart attack. Ken's brave effort to rescue Lew from an impossible situation. The eight men who had died in the buried copter.

Finally, hearts and flowers exhausted, Cotta put to her the critical question: "Ms. Green, were there three partners from Broward at Sklar the day of the attack?"

"Yes," Rhea had answered.

"Why?"

"I'd need to check my daybook before I answer that, Mr. Cotta," Rhea had replied.

John Cotta handed Rhea a black and white spotted child's notebook. The document had been previously stipulated into evidence. She looked at the jury, and then, in a movement that had been carefully planned beforehand with Cotta, she held up its cover so the jury could see it. After a moment, she explained.

"Used these little beauties all my life, from P.S. 108 to the last day I ever worked in an office. Says here, at page 48, Lew Flood, Ken Smythe, Turner Smiley, Leticia Jones, Gary Lee. Meeting regarding Bank of America. 11:00 AM 9/11/2001. That's what it says."

And it did say that, because Rhea was too smart to ever write anything incriminating down, anywhere, anytime. Lew had known she was a gem, and had refused to let the firm retire her.

Cotta pressed on. "Did you prepare an agenda for the 8:00 AMmeeting of the Sklar Executive Committee the day of the attack?"

"Sure did. Always did. Put down everything there was to discuss, too. Lew would chew me out good if I missed something. Not that he ever had to."

It was Academy Award acting, in many ways a reflection of the fact Jews do not believe in hell.

"Anything there about a Broward merger?"

"Goodness no," the withered, leather-skinned old lady said, trying her hardest to administer the coup de grace to Joe Wood and his clients. "Why, Mr. Cotta, a lawyer can't be after suing someone for money on behalf of a client and then be buying the defendant out at the same time. Even I know that, and I just went two years to high school."

Neither Joe Wood nor Steve Neilson cross-examined. The really good lawyers—the ones you want on your side in a pinch—such lawyers do not ask questions of dangerous witnesses just to hear themselves talk. They bury their dead and move on. Hope a jury's natural forgetfulness in a long trial will dull the pain. Throw their own blows in their own good time.

Which is where Steve Neilson went next. He tried to dull TS's pain through several weeks of expert testimony disputing the former Broward partners' mismanagement claims against TS. This was followed by rebuttal experts from Broward, whose job was to refocus the jury on how big a financial disaster TS had made of a healthy business.

At which point the trial evidence closed, and it was showtime. Mainly for Joe Wood.

Joe's opening speech started out simply enough. Gary Lee and Leticia Jones were telling the truth. It wasn't some unrelated meeting about the money Broward owed Bank of America that had nearly gotten the three Broward partners killed on 9/11. They were there to sign off on whatever Lew Flood told them they had to agree to.

No paper trail. Lying Sklar partners. A lying Sklar legal secretary. What else could you expect? And, as for the defendants both playing on the deaths of Lew Flood and Ken Smythe, well, no one deserved to die that way, but that didn't justify what those two men had done to Broward.

If you just wrote down what Joe Wood had said, it didn't seem like much at all. But, just like what Steve Boothe had seen on his VHS tape when Joe had the crowd in Corpus going, his hands in those baskets filled with snakes and his eyes rolled toward the heavens, it wasn't what he said, it was how he said it. Wood's uncanny ability to connect with the jury convinced Neilson that TS was doomed. It even left Cotta shaken.

Cotta spoke next. Said everything 7 thought he should say. No paper trail proved there was no proposed Sklar/Broward merger in the works. Using the fact people were dead to make money was a very wrong thing to do. He was brief and to the point. But he just didn't compare to Wood.

Neilson was much the worst of the three speakers. Much longer than either of the two others, and all focused on how TS had not mismanaged anything, as if that was TS's only problem. No one paid much attention to him.

Wood's closing was one of his best. A seal-clubbing, really. It was so good, in fact, that no one could remember what he had said when it was done. But it left nearly everyone who heard it with the clearest possible sense that a great wrong had been done, and that Lew Flood, dead or not, had to be held to account for it. Big time.

The evening after arguments were done,Steve Boothe told Joe that he and his partners felt Joe had done the best job possible under difficult circumstances. Circumstances like Judge Alarcon, who had been pot-shotting Joe from the get-go, and who had rudely interrupted Joe's final closing several times when the judge realized the jury was slipping away from him and into the arms of a man he considered a complete huckster.

The jury's first straw vote had been six plaintiff, two defense, and four on the fence. If 7 and his initial ally, Juror Number 2, had any knowledge of jury statistics, they would have quit right then and let Joe Wood have his verdict. But 7 wasn't in any hurry, and 2 wanted to be a lawyer; he was anxious to see how the process worked no matter how long it took. Even if it cost him his crummy job.

The other thing that killed Joe Wood was how good 7 was with people. In the US since he was six, 7 had been President of every school class he'd ever been a member of—at least after he'd mastered enough English to say more than just hello. In business, 7 had acted as liaison between management of his internet start-up and hundreds of software engineers, keeping those often anti-social prima donnas of high tech all pulling on the same oar. Mainly, 7 was patient. That was how he got things done in life.

You had to get to nine. It took 7 a week to get from six plaintiff, two defendant to six and six, with a good deal of movement in all directions. Another week and it was five plaintiff, seven defendant. By the beginning of the third full week of deliberations, everybody on the outside was going nuts trying to figure out what was going on inside the jury room.

Finally, at the end of that third week, with the jury hopelessly deadlocked at four plaintiff, eight defendant, 7 broke things his way. He took advantage of the fact that, by then, some jurors just wanted to go home, regardless of outcome.

"Look, folks," he said. "We have a very honest disagreement about who Lew Flood was, and what he did. But no matter how persuasive Mr. Wood is, the plain fact is we never got to meet Lew Flood, and he never had any chance to try and explain himself. And that's not anyone's fault, since the poor man was killed in the attack. But this Turner Smiley fellow, him we did meet. And we've been so focused on Lew Flood, who's dead, we haven't really talked about Turner Smiley. So, here's what I say. Smiley ran Broward into the ground, and he didn't keep hardly any of his partners in the loop. While I think the fact that Broward was broke proves Sklar never tried to merge with Broward, that doesn't matter as far as Smiley is concerned. Smiley still has to pay, regardless. So, why don't we all agree to vote the same way? The money, all the money, that the four people in the minority want to award against Sklar and Smiley, why, we'll just all vote to award every dollar of that money against Smiley only. Split the baby and go home. We don't owe it to all these lawyers to keep beating each other up over this."

The way the complicated special verdict form read, you could only do what 7 had suggested if you found both Smiley and Sklar innocent of fraud and Smiley separately guilty of neglect. It wasn't a problem. Just tell me how to vote on each question, was the general sentiment among the exhausted jurors.

When the jury came back after that last lunch together, their damages number against TS was $200 million. Quite a bit more than TS either had or ever would have. And, given that fact, a practical catastrophe for everybody involved in the case except Sklar itself.

After the verdict was read and the jury polled, John Cotta had wheeled himself over to Joe Wood, who had given him a terrible scare. He whispered, sympathetically, "Hard cases, man, it's the hard cases that make bad law." Cotta then put out his hand.

"Win some, lose some," was all he got back from the imperturbable Joe Wood. The Texan then shook Cotta's proffered hand, left the courtroom and returned home to Corpus that evening.

Steve Neilson—who had never suffered a verdict anywhere near the size of this one—shook no one's hand. Nor did he make any cute remarks. He just packed up and left. TS got word of what had happened from a Crowley paralegal later that afternoon. Along with a very sizable bill for services rendered, due when submitted.

Chapter Twenty Eight
Glenbrook, Douglas County, NV
{2007}

There had been the usual post-trial motions after Joe Wood's pyrrhic victory over TS. Neilson had gotten several jury declarations demonstrating that it was a legally improper compromise verdict that had done TS in. But Cotta had gotten an equal number of sworn statements reciting how, in the end, there just wasn't enough evidence of fraud by anyone, and that the only thing more probable than not was that TS had been a poor manager, even a reckless one.

Bill Alarcon had no doubt that what the jury had rendered was a compromise verdict. But he also knew that he, as the trial judge, was entitled to decide which jurors to believe and which jurors not to believe about any possible misconduct during jury deliberations. With no practical fear of reversal no matter whose side he took.

Alarcon's main reaction to the trial he had witnessed was his abhorrence for Joe Wood. He knew TS had nowhere near enough money to pay anybody any $200 million. He also knew that if he touched the verdict, he'd be giving that Wood another shot at Sklar before a different judge and jury. Where the man would probably hit Sklar, which had the money, for hundreds of millions. No way was he going to be part of that. So, the verdict stood.

At that point, since it was only a negligence finding, and thus dischargeable in bankruptcy, TS gave up, filed for personal bankruptcy, and turned over his non-exempt assets, totaling about $12 million, to his ex-partners. TS's personal bankruptcy was the last straw for Herbert Chambers, LLP, which fired him. He had $7 million in his 401(k). His parents' estate plan had made him and his two siblings the beneficiaries of a substantial spendthrift trust. Time he was done working, TS thought, when the enormity of his fall from grace finally hit him. Rather than fight with anybody about anything, TS responded to the loss of his last job by resigning from the Bar and leaving California.

He still loved the outdoors, cross-country skiing in particular. So, he moved to Glenbrook, Nevada, a residential enclave on the shore of Lake Tahoe, between the billionaire-dominated community of Incline Village and the proletarian gambling hell of South Lake Tahoe. No gaming was permitted in Glenbrook. It was just a nice planned community, in a state bordering California, that had no personal income tax. Glenbrook also had enough divorcees hanging around the bar at its golf-course clubhouse to keep anyone with a functioning prostate indefinitely amused.

TS didn't bother anyone and no one bothered him. The only decision he had to make every day, he would often joke to an entirely new circle of friends, was what time to switch from coffee to beer.

Chapter Twenty Nine
New York, NY
{Afternoon, Monday, September 29, 2008}

Heartspring School cost only $30,000 a year when Ellen Smiley had first been institutionalized at age six. Nearly thirty years later, the annual bill was running well over $100,000, and there was no end in sight to the increases. Inflation was only part of the problem. Ellen Smiley's increasingly unmanageable behavior—which required such high levels of staffing that Helen had been told there was simply no predicting where costs would go—was the killer.

The annuity Helen had bought with the Smiley family's trust fund was capped at $50,000 a year. Its virtue was that it would pay as long as Ellen lived, which would very likely be long after Helen Wilson was gone. $50,000 would always buy care better than what Ellen would get if she was placed on the Medicare rolls. Anything was better than that.

But Helen wasn't satisfied with budgeting Ellen's care. Heartspring was posh. Ellen would never be harmed there. No matter how outrageous her behavior, the Heartspring staff would care for her, and warm to her, and calm her. Helen knew a good deal when she saw it, and Heartspring was certainly that. At any price.

It was her need for money, not anything to do with TS, that had given her such a glow when Shane had brought in that $45 million settlement in *Cornelius v. Boothe.* Her personal share, as co-lead on the case, was $4 million. Shane had taken $5 million, with the other $6 million divided among partners who hadn't worked the case but who had shared in the financial risk.

At that point, she had begun to breathe easier. She paid back a $500,000 second mortgage she'd taken out against her modest San Francisco condominium, monies she had previously used to bridge the gap between the $50,000 annuity and what was needed to keep Heartspring current over the past ten years. Paying that loan off was something she had never really thought she'd be able to do. Working for Shane was just not that lucrative. Too much tilting at windmills.

She'd taken the rest of her big payday—which was, after taxes, about $1.5 million—to a stock broker, one she'd been recommended to by Shane. A Shane who didn't invest in anything but Treasuries, and who'd said two things. First, don't invest in the market. Any kind of public security is usually rigged. Second, if you insist, then Kent Birnbaum is probably OK. At least he's somebody my brother-in-law, the internet genius, speaks highly of. And I use him to buy T-Bills.

Now she and Mr. Birnbaum were sitting over coffee at one of the hundreds of Starbucks scattered all over lower Manhattan. The stockbroker was out of a job, caught up in the Lehman Brothers bankruptcy that had been filed the week before. And trying to explain to a very angry Helen Wilson why he had invested all of her small account's funds in Lehman Brothers own, now worthless, paper.

That Birnbaum's strategy was eminently sensible—i.e., a retreat to cash equivalents in a rapidly declining equity market, rather than sticking around like a dope to keep on getting creamed—made no difference to a practically murderous client like this Ms. Wilson. Or to many of his other smallish clients, none of whom got how impossible the notion of a Lehman collapse had been for everyone on Wall Street.

And they all had their squeals. This one had a kid in some fancy hospital. Without the money she'd have to mortgage her house again, only she couldn't get a loan. So what, he found himself thinking. At least she had a job. And a senior partner who'd apparently stuck with her through other troubles.

That guy, Shane somebody, was a client of Kent's as well, but not a very exciting one, as he never bought anything but government securities. This Shane fellow, he'd told Kent a bit about this Helen person when he'd pointed her Kent's way, and he'd even asked Kent to take extra special care, treat her account very conservatively. Which, for Christ's sake, Kent felt he had done. Except that George W. Bush had pulled the plug on his long-term employer and now everyone had egg on their face.

The conversation was going nowhere. Helen had known her money was gone when she got on the plane from SFO. Why she wanted this obviously insensitive jerk to explain it to her in person she herself couldn't imagine. The truth was she was just beside herself. She needed that money, it wasn't supposed to have been gambled away. And the idea it was all some big shock that this big-shot brokerage failed, why, a child could see through that one. What must have been going on inside that firm for a failure like this to have occurred? They all had to have known, including this lying sack of shit.

She hadn't said much. Just let Kent Birnbaum talk, make his excuses, tell her his own troubles. But when she shared a bit of herself and then saw how little impact her concerns over Ellen had, something broke inside. It was as if she was back in her Berkeley apartment, trying to get TS to show an interest in what autism meant.

The cardboard cup before her on the table contained scalding-hot black coffee she was unable even to sip. She threw its contents right in her ex-stockbroker's face, temporarily blinding Birnbaum and leaving him with very painful second-degree burns. While he was still screaming for help, Helen left by the back entrance. Then she grabbed a cab to Newark, not knowing what she'd do next.

Chapter Thirty
Las Vegas and Lake Tahoe, NV
{October 2008}

She hadn't known what the New York police might do, once Birnbaum calmed down enough to tell them what had happened. Given how pissed off everyone was at their stockbrokers that fall, they might just leave her alone. But that coffee had been really, really hot. And she had no idea what kind of damage she'd done, just tossing the whole thing at the guy that way.

So, when she'd gotten to Newark, no luggage, everything still back in her hotel room, except her purse and the clothes on her back, she'd taken a plane to Las Vegas. That seemed like someplace where you could remain anonymous for a while.

Then one day, when she'd come back from the movie theater she'd gone to in order to escape a hot spell her own cheap hotel's air conditioning hadn't dealt with as effectively as the massive Cineplex did, the teenager at reception had eyed her suspiciously.

"Las Vegas Sheriff came looking for you, lady," the pockmarked youth sneered. "You kill somebody, lady, or what?"

Helen knew the kid assumed she was a hooker. Helen was not insulted. There were so many whores in Las Vegas it seemed to Helen that practically every female in town was one. Especially any woman holed up in a rat trap like hers.

But in Las Vegas, hooking was as common and legal as smoking, so when the Sherriff came after a hooker, it usually meant she'd rolled a trick. Sometimes even killed him and left what remained of him out in the desert. For Mr. Bad Skin, that meant Helen was going to equal a little fun in his day. Sort of what passed for a Vegas human-interest story.

When she saw how bemused the little savage was at the prospect of her imminent arrest, she did what she'd done in New York. Overreacted. This time by hauling off and slapping the teenager. Who responded by reaching over the counter which separated them and hitting her right in the mouth, punching out one of her carefully restored front teeth and otherwise knocking her unconscious. She only woke up when he dumped the pail of filthy water he'd been using to mop the ground-floor toilets over her bloody face. Then he told her to get the hell out or he'd call the cops.

Out on the blazing hot street, she checked her purse. Her wallet was there, alright, credit cards, I.D., all still intact. But all her cash was gone. She snuck into an open men's room at a gas station and cleaned herself up as best she could. Then she walked several long blocks to a rundown Western wear and sporting-goods place. There, being careful not to smile and thereby display her ruined mouth, she used her credit card to buy fresh jeans and a clean white shirt.

And, on impulse, a handgun. A shiny nickel-plated one, small enough to put in her purse. This is the last time some punk is just going to beat me up, she thought, as she loaded the five .22 shells the store threw in, one short of a full load to prevent accidents. She even considered going back to her hotel and pointing the gun at the sorry little bastard to make him give her back the $500 he'd stolen and apologize for humiliating her. Until she realized he probably had a gun of his own behind the counter. A bigger one that he knew how to shoot a lot better than she did.

Why she wound up driving to Northern Nevada later that day was never clear. All Helen was ever able to tell Shane and Elias was that she had felt she had to leave Las Vegas. Didn't want to go home. Just thought driving the rental car she'd picked up at the airport the day she'd arrived in Vegas on up to Tahoe seemed like a good idea. Go see a dentist up there, maybe call Shane and see if he could figure out what she should do next about what she'd done to Birnbaum in New York. It was just a little hot coffee. Maybe they could just pay the man off. He looked pretty desperate for cash.

Once in Tahoe she'd checked into a motel on the California side, taken a shower, and changed into the fresh clothes she'd bought earlier in the day. The local all-Tahoe phone directory in her room had a listing for TS, who she knew had moved to the Nevada side. He had a public listing because he'd taken to telling new women acquaintances. "Look under Smiley," he'd say, "it's the only one in the book, either side of the lake."

Late the next morning, she called his place, hanging up when he answered the phone himself. An hour later, just after noon, she'd driven into Glenbrook, passing a lightly manned security booth at the entrance without stopping, and headed to TS's place.

While Glenbrook security was out looking for her car—which she parked several blocks from TS's home, to avoid detection—Helen had walked to his house and rung the bell. When he came to the door, she smiled broadly, displaying her missing front tooth.

TS was scared witless. The woman not only looked a fright, gap-toothed and dressed in oversized men's clothes; what was worse she was holding a small gun of some sort on him.

He tried to calm her. "Look, Helen," he said, "we've had our problems. But never violence. Not that."

She said nothing. Just gestured for him to step inside, out of public view, so security wouldn't find her. As best she could later recollect as to what she was doing there, she wanted him to make some financial provision for their daughter Ellen. Just to help Helen get over the hump of having all her investments go south.

But there was something in his insolent smile, something so clearly out of place with the fact of her actually holding a gun on him, that made her think twice about asking for his help. He had smiled that same smile the day he'd recorded her angry threats against him in his private Broward office.

TS, meanwhile, saw something in Helen's face that made up his mind for him. He launched himself at her. Helen's gun discharged. It made no great noise. TS fell straight back. A large pool of blood formed under his head. Still clutching her .22, Helen sat down on a couch and waited for the local cops. Her only thought was where all this would leave the child she still thought of as Baby Ellen.

Chapter Thirty One
Douglas County District Court
Minden, NV
{March - July, 2009}

Nevada is not a nice place. Mostly ugly scrub, its share of Lake Tahoe is its most scenic spot. Which it has desecrated in the worst way imaginable by putting up one gigantic casino after another on its side of South Lake Tahoe.

As evidenced by this planning nightmare, Nevada's long overt domination by the Mob and its continued reliance on gambling had worked a deep malaise into the state's civic culture. Its courts, legal profession, and lay juries were in no way any better than any other aspect of Nevada's governing apparatus.

Judges ran for election with massive funding from casinos. The gaming industry's primary interest in the Nevada judiciary was how quickly it would act to turn unpaid markers given by gambling addicts fleeing Nevada into legal judgments that were enforceable in the addicts' home states as sister state judgments.

Nevada juries populated by any number of pit bosses, blackjack dealers, bouncers, showgirls, lap dancers, and even an occasional escort, were the norm. Such low-lifes weren't all there was, but they were always there, always a factor. This was especially true in Douglas County, a huge, largely unpopulated swath of Nevada, where—unlike Clarke County, the county in which Las Vegas is located—there were no manufacturing jobs.

232

Douglas County's only real population center was South Lake Tahoe. A place where, critics said, the scum met the lake, at least when the scum—typically California tourists up from Sacramento or Stockton or some other such bumblefuck place—chose to go out of the windowless casino buildings and down to the lakeshore to snort cocaine or have sex.

The county seat of Douglas County was "over the hill" —a reference to the flat, dust-blown Carson Valley—in a town of some two thousand souls named Minden. On the outskirts of which very small town the descendants of pioneer Basque sheep ranchers still ran large flocks.

Helen Wilson's prosecutor, Francis Xavier Ilocano—who went by the nickname Fix when in the company of his many friends—was the eldest son of one such long-resident Basque family. Not many knew it, but Saint Francis Xavier—the Roman Catholic priest who, along with his more famous contemporary, Saint Ignatius Loyola, had cofounded the Society of Jesus during the Counter-Reformation—was an ethnic Basque.

The name had traditionally been given to the firstborn son of any branch of the Ilocano clan, along with a fervent prayer that the child might manifest a vocation to the priesthood. While Fix had never wanted to be a priest, he had a sincere Roman Catholic faith for all that. The disgust he felt for the so-called Nevada gaming industry was reinforced by what he had seen as a teenager, when he and his sixteen- and seventeen-year-old buddies had taken to driving over to the lake for the fun of trying to sneak into the

233

casinos to play at the card tables. There they had wound up routinely witnessing the grossly licentious behavior at Harrah's and Harvey's and their like. Unlike his friends, Fix had not found any of it funny.

Fix had gone to the University of Nevada at Reno at eighteen to study animal husbandry. Then, at twenty-two, quite unexpectedly, he had started McGeorge School of Law in Sacramento, telling his parents he didn't want to run stock for the rest of his life. After graduating from McGeorge in June 2002, he'd spent the next four years in Army JAG. Most of it in Iraq, dealing with all kinds of harsh shit. Fragging. Self-inflicted wounds. Spooked troops knocking off civilians for no good reason.

He'd gotten married to another JAG officer while overseas, a lady who was from someplace even more flea-bitten than he was. When their second tour in Iraq ended, neither of them wanted anything more to do with the military. They'd both resigned their commissions on the same day. And then they'd gone back to the Ilocano ranch to figure out what to do next.

It was then 2006. Hardly anybody in Douglas County voted in elections, especially off-year ones, and—since the last DA had been caught in an FBI sting—the office was up for grabs. While there were several candidates, the Ilocanos delivered a majority of the few votes cast by turning out every farmer, rancher, and regular hand in the Carson Valley to vote for Fix.

The gambling interests in South Lake Tahoe, and even down as far as Las Vegas, took note, and were concerned. It was too late to do much about it by then, though, and besides, they had already bought and paid for Douglas County's only District Court Judge, Frank Jonas. Jonas wouldn't face re-election for another five years, and without a sympathetic ear on the local bench, what harm could some rogue DA do anyway?

By the time Helen's trial for shooting TS began that March 2009, District Court Judge Frank Jonas and District Attorney Francis Xavier Ilocano were bitter enemies. For nearly three years, Jonas had frustrated every effort Fix had made to clean up the Nevada side of the lake, dismissing indictments for drugs and prostitution as fast as the DA could obtain them from the local grand jury. The judge had counted on the indifference of a passive electorate to spare him from any criticism of what was politics-as-usual, Nevada-style. Jonas miscalculated, however. By 2008, the grand jury had become so fed up with his trampling on the county DA that it had issued a report highly critical of the judge himself, using statistics to condemn the man as insufficiently tough on crime. A politically charged accusation if ever there was one in a Red state like Nevada.

In response to the grand jury report, the Nevada Republican Party leadership had told Jonas he would have to step down in January 2011, something the then sixty-one-year-old judge was loathe to do. Especially since he'd only gotten into political trouble by following orders from above to shut down the new DA any way he could. But without Nevada Republican Party TV-advertising dollars, Jonas knew he was licked before he could even begin campaigning. So, by March 2009, Jonas understood that in less than two years somebody else would have his job.

What was much worse than Jonas's being forced to contemplate his own early retirement was the fact that Fix himself was very likely going to be his replacement. Running as a Democrat, the DA had already announced his candidacy. With all the publicity this shooting was getting—network TV trailers parked all around the tiny one-room Minden courthouse, crews filming somebody or something day and night—it seemed all Fix had to do to become the Honorable Francis Xavier Ilocano, Nevada State District Judge for Douglas County, Nevada, was win some lay-down felony case.

In March of 2009, Helen Wilson was then sixty-two. Because TS had survived, she was only being tried for attempted murder and the lesser included offense of assault with a deadly weapon. The primary charge carried a minimum twenty-year sentence, with no possibility of parole. The secondary charge carried a sentence of between ten and twenty years, with no possibility of parole until she had served at least half her term in a Nevada State Prison.

While TS was alive, he'd had to endure a series of very dangerous surgeries to relieve the pressure on his cranium caused by internal bleeding which occurred while he went untreated as well as to remove the slug Helen's gun had left in him.

The last of these surgeries wound up putting him into a coma. When he came out, he'd lost all control of normal motor function on his left side. There was substantial deterioration in both speech and cognition. While he was able to live at home, he'd had to engage a live-in nurse. Overall, he went from a guy in his early sixties who was in sufficiently terrific shape that he could pass for late-forties to a guy who looked geriatric. And he felt that way, too.

As near as the Douglas County Sherriff could reconstruct events, after she'd left TS bleeding out on his living room floor, Helen had walked down from TS's house to Glenbrook's private beach. From there she'd gone north along the East Shore of Lake Tahoe. After she'd hiked all the way up to Sand Harbor, she'd emptied the gun and thrown the unused rounds as far out into the lake as she could. Once she'd disposed of the bullets, she'd kept walking north. She'd arrived in Incline Village and checked into the Hyatt Regency around 7:00 PM. Following check-in, she'd gone to her room, taken a long, hot shower, and wrapped herself in a thick hotel robe. TS, meanwhile had lain unconscious and untreated for seven hours until, finally, one of his lady friends had shown up at 8:00 PM, ready for an evening out.

A massive canvas of Lake Tahoe hotels and motels following discovery of Helen's rental car illegally parked near TS's home had found Helen ensconced in the Hyatt at around 9:30 PMthe evening of the shooting. By that time, Helen had already talked to Shane Sullivan and Elias Borah, and the two of them had quickly

237

hired a Nevada lawyer to act on her behalf. That attorney was waiting in the hallway outside Helen's hotel room when the authorities arrived, and he accompanied Helen from the Hyatt to the Minden, Nevada jail cell which had been her home ever since. Acting on her counsel's advice, Helen had not uttered one word to any Nevada cop or DA, let alone confessed to a thing.

The most thorough Nevada National Guard search imaginable of the East Shore of Lake Tahoe found Helen's discarded bullets, but it failed to turn up any weapon. Which was just dumb luck running in Helen's favor. The gun—which Helen had, in fact, buried at the same spot in the lake where she'd thrown the bullets away—had wound up being taken out of California by a Utah family passing through Northern Nevada the day after the shooting.

The family's kids had been allowed in for a quick swim in the shallow waters of Sand Harbor, while their mother unpacked a picnic lunch. The second child, a boy of seven, had seen something shiny, imperfectly buried on the lake bottom, between two rocks. He smuggled it into the minivan for further examination later on. When, several hundred miles to the East, the boy's two sisters finally tattled on him, his horrified parents had first made sure the gun was unloaded, and then tossed it away at the next rest station on I-80. The firearm then went from the rest station to a Southern Idaho landfill. TS's shooting never made any headlines in Salt Lake, so there was never any connection made by anyone between the mysterious weapon and any unsolved crime.

Nor was Helen's credit card any help in establishing the fact she had a connection to any weapon. Those credit card records, of course, showed her clothing purchase from a Las Vegas western wear store, and the store also sold guns. But her gun, which was sold to her without the required waiting period, and which had never existed as far as any system of registration was concerned, had been charged as "used hiking boots." The store owner would not cop to selling Helen a gun, whoever Helen might have shot. Wasn't his problem.

So, on the first day of Helen's trial, Fix had no confession and no weapon. But what he did have was a still breathing victim, TS. A TS who, once he had recovered to the point of even minimal coherence, was able to give a sworn statement describing how Helen had showed up at his home, pointed a gun of some kind at him, and made him step inside. How, when he'd tried to disarm her, she'd apparently responded by putting a bullet in his skull. TS admitted he hadn't seen her pull the trigger. And he admitted that he might have precipitated the shot by rushing her. But he was quite sure he hadn't shot himself. That latter fact was something paraffin tests, conducted when his inert body was first discovered, fully confirmed. Somewhat circumstantial, all in all, but, with eyewitness testimony like TS's, a powerful case for all that.

And, once you left the crime scene, the case was an embarrassment of riches. A personal history between TS and Helen fraught with marital and professional discord. Tape-recorded death threats from ten years back that were filed in official San Francisco

239

court records. Helen's lengthy stay in a mental hospital, though one had to be careful with that, lest a desperate defense plead insanity. Helen's callous behavior in walking out on TS after she'd shot him. Not to mention her checking herself into the area's best hotel to relax after such a brutal shooting. The only thing missing was a photo of her sipping iced Champagne over TS's prone body.

Shane and Elias had come up to Minden to help their Nevada lawyer try Helen's case. Shane had never seen Elias so glum. For one thing, he told Shane, Elias couldn't figure Helen out. Had no idea if she was a real killer—which type he was only too comfortable defending—or a head case. She'd done the shooting, though; there was no way to throw any doubt on that point in the face of TS's anticipated testimony.

A claim of accidental shooting was difficult—not because it might not be true—but because Helen's failing to call for help became so inexplicable once the defense argued that she hadn't really meant to shoot.

And even with a documented history of mental illness, any formal insanity defense was always tough. What the law considered nuts versus what the psychiatric profession gave a Diagnostic and Statistical Manual of Mental Disorders number to were worlds apart.

But between the assault on her stockbroker in Manhattan and her sudden unhealthy interest in the recently retired TS, some kind of delusional thinking seemed to be the best explanation for

Helen's sudden loss of control over her life. That and Helen's concern for her daughter Ellen—whom Elias had insisted on bringing to Nevada to sit through the trial. That last factor might help with one or more of the jurors.

But there was no overall defense plan. Just a mishmash of ideas, none of which clearly led anywhere. A formula for conviction, in Elias's broad experience.

It was in the pre-trial motions Elias first got a sniff of the discord between Judge Jonas and Fix. Elias had figured Jonas for a corrupt pol, and Helen's Nevada counsel, Frank Farentina—a Mob defense lawyer out of Las Vegas who was closely affiliated with the Nevada Republican Party—had confirmed this in short order. But Fix was another character out of central casting. The not-too-bright-but-incorruptible-small-town-DA. Exactly the wrong guy to have to defend a case like this against.

In the face of a heavy felony like this one, any problems between the judge and the DA usually meant nothing. Someone had shot someone else. That someone was tried, convicted, and went away for a long time. Next case.

But when Fix—after getting wind from the press of Elias's plan to put Ellen Smiley in the courtroom for the duration of the trial—moved to exclude her, Judge Jonas sat stony faced. Very deferentially, the judge had then leaned over the bench and asked Frank Farentina what the defense was thinking.

Frank had been well-rehearsed by Elias.

"Ellen Smiley's mother is in serious trouble. Ellen Smiley has a right to be with her mother in her mother's time of trouble. The fact that she's disabled doesn't mean she isn't a citizen. The policy of Nevada is that the Silver State's courts are open to all."

Transparent nonsense, of course. People were excluded from courtrooms all the time. Ellen had never in her life given a single sign that she knew what a mother was. And, taking no chances that his Pinocchio might spring to life, Elias had ordered Ellen be so tranked on downers that, autism or no autism, she wouldn't know her own mother anyway.

The matter was taken under submission. When Elias looked over at Fix, he could see the DA had no confidence in the ultimate outcome. Nu? Thought the old man. In truth, it wasn't that Judge Jonas had an actual plan to screw Fix out of a verdict. Even he didn't think such a thing was possible. But fucking with his rival's head, never letting him feel like he knew where the judge was going next—well, that was as much fun as the soon-to-be-unemployed jurist could ever remember having, either as a lawyer or a judge.

Fix's real problems started with the preliminary questioning of jurors. Jonas simply wouldn't stop interrupting Fix, barely allowed him to suggest the case involved a shooting. The oleaginous Frank Farentina, on the other hand, was given free reign. If you listened to his lengthy, uninterrupted questions—more speeches than anything else—it seemed the case likely involved some unusual kind of hunting accident, in which an unfortunate woman who couldn't shoot a .22 pistol straight had missed a bear, with unfortunate consequences for her ex-husband. Who was a no-good when it came to child support.

Elias had his doubts about taking such advantage of the judge's hatred for the DA, very much fearing the impact of the actual events on the jury when they finally came into evidence. But, when trying the Simpson case in front of a weak and terrified-by-the-spotlight Lance Ito, Johnnie Cochran had gotten away with a voir dire that made equally spurious promises of what was to come. So, why not try it here? They had nothing else going for them, that was for sure.

Next came the jury-selection process itself. Fix had splurged on an expensive Bay Area jury consultant and several mock trials: farmers, ranchers, their families, in other words all the people who voted for Fix at election time, those people, Fix was told by The National Jury Project, would readily vote to convict Helen. Beyond that, male pit bosses and dealers were ok; their female counterparts somewhat worrisome; but none nearly so worrisome as the female sex workers who made up part of the jury pool. Prostitution bred real hatred for the male sex.

And the sex workers were many. They covered the gamut from the magnificently head-dressed showgirls used by the casinos to service the biggest gamblers, the whales. To lap dancers who readily prostituted themselves for extra tips. Right down to the lowest of the low, the parking lot whores, who turned tricks in campers.

243

Those were just the pros. The amateurs were harder to spot, but they were also a commonplace. And, even among those women who never engaged in selling themselves, grudges against ex-husbands were the norm in a state where it seemed everyone had put one or two bad marriages in their rearview mirror by the time they'd hit thirty.

Each side got twelve peremptory challenges, meaning a juror could be disqualified without reason. Judge Jonas bided his time, played Fix into thinking the trial would be on the square by denying each side's attempts to disqualify one juror or another without using an automatic challenge. After two days, all challenges had been exhausted, and a jury was in place. One in which there were no female sex workers, four male agricultural workers, an accountant from Zephyr Cove, and a variety of people working in menial jobs in the casinos, most of them men. Not a bad jury for the prosecution, especially with such a strong case.

But Elias had a hunch, and he played it. He had Frank Farentina challenge Juror 6, a male pit boss, for cause, with the cause being the supposed stress being away from work for several months would cause the man. Jonas listened to Fix's sputtered objections. That the man himself hadn't asked to be excused. That the trial couldn't possibly last several months. And that it was common knowledge the casinos all paid their employees while they served on local juries. After Fix had finished speaking, and without calling for rebuttal, Jonas quietly granted the defendant's motion.

By the time this second round of entirely biased "for cause" jury selection was over, Elias had put five women on his jury, each of whom earned some portion of her living from prostitution. The rest of the jury was made up of five men and two more women. The men were nothing out of the ordinary, and were all likely prosecution votes.

The two additional women, 1 and 7, were blue-collar types, one a typist, the other a supermarket clerk. They were too homely for any sort of prostitution. Nonetheless, both seemed destined to tilt toward Helen. Fix had established that much when he got each to say she still frequently experienced rage toward an ex-husband.

Which fact was not a problem for either Judge Jonas or Elias. Both of whom enjoyed watching Fix's floundering reaction to the judicial outrages being heaped on him and his case. Jonas out of spite. Elias out of hope. In fifty years of law practice, Elias had never seen the like of what Judge Jonas was doing to knock the legs out from under a prosecutor in front of a trial jury. Any case can be won, he told himself. Any case. Even this one.

Fix's opening statement took all of five minutes, and consisted solely of a promise to the jury that he would prove Helen Wilson had shot Turner Smiley and left him to die, which he nearly had. Elias had Frank Farentina reserve opening until the defense case began.

Badly shaken by the rulings he had been getting from Judge Jonas, Fix delayed calling TS. Instead he decided to build his case from the ground up. First he called various employees of both Alameda and San Francisco Counties to establish Helen and TS's short marriage; who—and what—the now thirty-six-year-old Ellen Smiley was; and the fact of Helen's death threats against TS almost exactly ten years before.

There was no telling whether any of this evidence would have come in over a defense objection, considering Judge Jonas's predilections, but Elias told Frank Farentina to allow it to be admitted. The trial had to consist of something, after all, and the more it dealt with ancient history, the less it dealt with the simple fact that everything the DA had said in his opening was true.

Medical testimony came next. TS had been shot with a .22 caliber bullet fired from very close range. The slug had pierced his skull, knocking him unconscious and causing significant intracranial bleeding. There was no indication he had shot himself, something which a paraffin test would have detected. Unspent rounds found in shallow waters off of Sand Harbor had been handled by someone with Helen Wilson's DNA type, though the match was weak due to the time the bullets had spent in the water and careless handling by Nevada State Troopers. The bullets were of the same type as the slug eventually recovered from the victim's head. But that type was a common one, and these bullets might or might not have ever been loaded into whatever type of weapon had been used to shoot the victim. No such weapon had been found.

If she'd just finished the job, Elias reflected, the prosecution would be going nowhere with this case. The evidence so far was quite circumstantial. Because the crime scene had been trampled on by ER personnel who were more concerned with saving TS's life than capturing his potential killer, Helen's illegally parked car was the only solid thing they had to even put her on the scene. And Fix hadn't brought up that evidence, because the search which had led to Helen's arrest at Incline Village had been botched by an overeager Douglass County Sheriff. That inexperienced young guy, after being taken to Helen's rental car by Glenbrook's private security, had immediately smashed out a window and then broken into the locked glove compartment. Where he'd found Helen's rental information. Fruit of the poisoned tree if there ever was such.

Fix's last witness was TS. The man limped to the stand, badly dragging his left leg. The left side of his face was immobile. His speech was halting, and his mental process seemed equally slow. But, in the end, TS's story came out. His former wife had appeared at his door. Yes, that was her at the defense table. His former wife had a small gun in her hand. She had pointed it at him and insisted he allow her into his house. He had become frightened and tried to take the gun from her. That was all he knew.

Elias rose. So, far he had allowed Helen's Nevada lawyer to do everything, but Judge Jonas had granted him permission to actively participate in the trial, and this was a make-or-break moment for the case.

"Mr. Smiley," he began, "I am Elias Borah, one of the defense counsel for Helen Wilson. Are you able to understand me?"

Elias was trying to create some doubt in the jury's mind as to whether TS's testimony was merely a canned version of events, courtesy of someone who had actually lost the ability to remember much of anything.

TS's mouth worked itself into a crooked smile. "Sure," he said. "Ask away."

Elias resumed his questioning, though more warily now. He could see TS was far from a basket case, however badly his speech patterns had been impaired.

"Was there anything that happened before you became unconscious that made you think Helen Wilson actually intended to shoot you?"

TS hesitated. He'd been looking intently at both his ex-wife and Ellen (whom Jonas had eventually allowed to sit in on the trial) since he'd mounted the witness stand. Helen had a look of sheer, furious hatred on her face. Ellen's face, while quite beautiful, was entirely vacant. He couldn't help notice that Ellen's looks favored him, not Helen.

"There was some, something in Ms. Wilson's face, is all. Something like the way she, she's looking at me, right, right now."

The jury immediately focused on Helen, who made no attempt to conceal her murderous feelings for TS.

Elias cursed himself. This was the most disastrous cross-examination he'd ever conducted. Before he could say "no further questions," however, TS drew the jury's attention back to himself.

"But look," he said, looking past Helen's glower and straight at Ellen's unresponsive face. "I think Helen has every right to hate me."

Fix was on his feet, trying to cut TS off.

Judge Jonas curtly commanded him to "Sit down, Mr. Ilocano." Fix sat. What the hell is this, Fix thought. But before Fix could rally himself any further, Jonas spoke.

"This is a case involving a serious felony. The victim must be fully heard from in such a case. And, if I hear another interruption from you, Mr. Ilocano," Jonas bit off the words, his hatred for the DA really showing, "an objection, a sneeze, anything at all, then I'll have my bailiff physically eject you from my courtroom. And he won't be gentle about it, either."

By this time Elias had retreated to his seat at the defense table. He concentrated on praying his thanks to the God of Israel rather than worrying points of law.

TS resumed speaking, faster now, and without apparent impairment. "I mean, I wish Helen hadn't shot me. And I wish she'd called for help after she did shoot me. Though I assume she just thought I was dead. Of course I'm very angry it happened, but

Helen isn't a violent person. I've looked into what was going on with her at the time I got shot, and I'm sure she just wanted me to help with keeping our child Ellen, who's got a bad disability, safe and well-treated. She didn't think I'd listen to what was needed to protect Ellen unless she pointed a gun at me. And she was right. Without a gun in my face, I'm sure I would have shut the door on her. If I hadn't wanted to get shot, all I had to do was listen to Ellen's problems. Instead, I rushed that poor worried woman and I wound up taking a bullet for my trouble. Well, so what? As far as I'm concerned, I really shot myself. By acting selfishly. Not just last year, but for a long time before that. And now it's me who wants to say sorry. Sorry for it all."

TS finally turned to the jury. He was really crying this time, and so were many of the jurors, even including some of the men. "Don't feel you have to convict anybody of anything on my account," he said. "I'm way past wanting any more bad to come from this."

Chapter Thirty Two
Office of the Douglas County District Attorney
Minden, NV
{Morning, Tuesday, July 7, 2009}

The Wilson jury had hung 11-1 for acquittal. The only thing that had saved Fix from ultimate catastrophe was Juror Number 4, a ranch hand who'd snuck on the jury by concealing the fact that his ex-wife had once taken a potshot at him with a .38. Missed his privates by inches, wounding him up high on his inner thigh.

That incident had made him uninterested in who was busy forgiving whom in *People v. Wilson*. Women couldn't just go around shooting their men, he kept saying, during what was nearly a month-long deliberation. No, sir. Not in any situation where he had a vote.

There had been two other votes for that same position, both male, at the beginning of the deliberations. But Juror Number 3, a 6'2" showgirl who danced on the big stage at Harvey's, had been elected foreperson. She'd worn down the two men by arguing with them a bit, but mainly they realized they were not going home without changing their votes. The seven women jurors were never going to vote guilty, that much was clear.

But no one could do anything with 4. He just sat in the jury room whittling while one frustrated juror after another tried to get him to end the agony. No one had anything to say that matched his experience with an angry woman popping off rounds in his direction, and, while he was smart enough not to explain his real reasons for staying with a guilty vote, that experience made him unmovable.

Even Judge Jonas—despite his being loathe to miss the opportunity to humiliate Fix with an acquittal—eventually took pity on the jury and mistried the case, setting it back on the trial calendar for August 3. That was intended to ruin Fix's annual summer vacation.

Fix had responded by filing papers with the Nevada Supreme Court to disqualify Jonas from handling the next trial, doing a fair job of documenting the judge's entirely improper behavior during the first one. But, whether Fix's petition to disqualify Jonas was right or wrong, the Nevada Supreme Court was just as in thrall to the gaming industry as any other organ of Nevada government. And the gaming industry was no friend of Fix's.

If the Nevada Supremes left Jonas in charge, Helen Wilson might very well get off. And then Fix could forget about being elected dogcatcher. Which meant a plea bargain was the only way out. One that would appeal to the sympathy for Helen Wilson that TS's speech had created, but which would not make Fix look weak.

Elias had suggested an insanity plea to Helen a week after the trial. She was not herself, he told her. No one who knew her understood the violence of her reaction to losing her nest egg. She needed help. So, if Elias could get her into treatment, and, most importantly, help her avoid another dangerous trial, well, you had to think about it. At least think about it.

None of Elias's pabulum about Helen needing help fooled Shane, who knew being involuntarily committed to yet another state mental hospital would be a disaster for Helen. But, as always, the real issue was compared to what. And as bad a reputation as the Nevada State Mental Treatment Facility had, that reputation was nothing compared to Nevada State Prison. Plus, maybe, and with the right breaks, Helen could be out of the Nevada State Mental Treatment Facility in a few years, while losing a second trial could easily mean she would die incarcerated.

Helen didn't appear to care what happened next. Her passivity put both Elias and Shane in a tough spot, as neither wanted to make far-reaching decisions for her. But, with a second trial on the horizon and a ruling from the Nevada Supreme Court on Judge Jonas's disqualification possible any day, there seemed little alternative.

With Helen's lukewarm agreement, Elias had gone to Fix and proposed a deal. Helen would plead not guilty by virtue of insanity, and accept involuntary commitment to the Nevada State Mental Treatment Facility in Sparks, Nevada—for an indefinite period—in lieu of risking a long stay in Nevada State Prison. Frank Farentina assured Fix that Judge Jonas would accept the plea.

Fix knew who Farentina was. More to the point, Fix knew who Farentina's friends in Las Vegas were. So, he accepted Farentina's prediction about what Jonas would do in the face of such a plea bargain without much question. The 11-1 vote for acquittal had shocked Fix, and—though he was sure he could convict Helen in front of any normal judge—he also knew Farentina might succeed in blocking Jonas's disqualification if Fix refused to play ball.

Mainly, Fix was persuaded that, if he pled *People v. Wilson* out, the voters might forget this mess by the November 2010 judicial election. A plea bargain was struck, and, for the second time in her life, Helen found herself institutionalized.

Chapter Thirty Three
Administrative Hearing Room
Nevada State Mental Treatment Facility
Sparks, NV
{Afternoon, Wednesday, December 22, 2010}

Helen Wilson's petition for a transfer out of Mental—as the Nevada State Mental Treatment Facility was known to its staff and patients alike—was heard in a large, dingy, stone-walled room. That room lurked unobtrusively behind an unmarked and securely locked door off an otherwise standard psych ward.

The high-ceilinged space had a wooden stage at the front, and was usually employed for all-hands meetings between staff and the few visiting psychiatrists who occasionally ventured into Mental to check up on patient care. Meetings where shift after shift of Mental's hundreds of nurses, social workers, and guards were subjected to the visiting MDs' entirely unrealistic ideas on how things needed to be done to properly care for the inmate population. Most staff participants either did their nails or balanced their checkbooks. Others plugged into their Ipods.

Visiting MDs were exceedingly scarce on the ground at Mental anyway. In practice, there was no treatment for any sort of psychiatric problem at the institution. Instead, Mental was almost always a life sentence for anyone whom the State of Nevada was paying to keep there. And, given the prevalence of simultaneous prescription-drug and home-made alcohol abuse at the place, this so-called hospital's only really redeeming quality was that its life sentences tended to be mercifully short.

TS had tracked Helen's rapid disintegration at Mental by paying one of the more kindly social-worker types to keep an eye out. The woman had told TS that Helen was worse off than most. Literally drinking herself to death on what Mental's population called pruno. Trading sex for the home-brewed prison hooch when she couldn't make enough of the foul stuff on her own. Paying no attention at all to what pruno and psychotropic medications do to one's liver when taken in mass quantities at the same time.

And so TS went to Shane. Shane went to Elias. And Elias went to Frank Farentina. Frank had friends, and Frank's friends had friends. Money, quite a lot of it, and all of it TS's, changed hands. And a very unusual hearing was ordered to see if Mental's medical staff could be persuaded that Helen Wilson would be better cared for at a private hospital in California.

There had been an undercurrent of resistance right from the beginning. Mental hardly ever let any sort of inmate go. Nevada's obligation to pay for their presence was what paid the bulk of Mental's overhead. While Mental had some civil check-ins, it didn't take long for even the most heartless relations to see what a low rung of Dante's inferno their loved ones had stumbled onto. Those who could possibly flee Mental almost always did, and quickly.

To spring Helen, Frank Farentina argued that her marked in-custody physical deterioration was due to a medically provable ingestion of both authorized and unauthorized substances, particularly alcohol distilled on site from canned fruits served to Mental's inmates at mealtimes. Meaning pruno.

Frank Farentina's briefing claimed that his medical evidence proved Mental was neglecting Helen's care, and that it required her release to another institution on the legal theory that Mental had no right to expose the Nevada State Treasury to a negligence claim by Baby Ellen should her mother die in Mental's custody. It was true enough that the blanket waiver of sovereign immunity contained in section 41.031 of Nevada Revised Statutes gave the State of Nevada an interest in seeing that any fully or even partially state-funded private agencies avoided any first-party negligence which might result in claims being made against the State of Nevada on a vicarious liability basis.

No matter how high minded a way in which it was dressed up, however, Frank Farentina's so-called case was, of course, a frontal assault on how Mental ran and had always been run: as a human zoo, with cages cleaned only occasionally. So, Farentina shouldn't have had a prayer in any administrative hearing before Mental's own MDs.

But TS's remaining millions had bought two MDs, out of the five sitting on stage, well before Frank had walked in. Better yet, a third MD had a gambling problem. Frank's friends in the gaming industry had told that doc that certain large and very overdue markers might be forgotten if the hearing went the right way.

This was a surer guaranty of that last, and most necessary vote, than TS's bought-and-paid-for lock on the first two. If Doc 3 didn't deliver, then he sure as shit knew he was in for a serious and quite dangerous physical beating. After all, as a degenerate gambler—the sobriquet by which all gambling addicts were lovingly known to gaming-industry insiders—Doc 3 knew the harsh consequences which flowed from not paying large markers.

Doc 3's problem was that he just couldn't stay away from betting college football and basketball. He'd played both at Yale, and just thinking about the games took him back to his glory days. Days long past, before he'd wound up in this sorry state in this sorry hospital, two failed marriages having broken him down financially and emotionally. Now, besides never winning a bet, all he did with his off time was bang teenage cocktail waitresses. And lately he'd had to pay through the nose for even that small comfort.

So, as Frank had carefully reassured TS, the hearing was merely an exercise. The real problem, and one he'd kept from TS lest he scare the man off, was that Farentina had struck out trying to buy peace at the Nevada Attorney General's office. There the usually very malleable AG would not listen to either money or reason.

The offer to pay had been made quietly and in a time-honored Nevada way. First there was the large up-front campaign contribution, which was made, out of the blue, with no strings attached. This was followed by a very sotto voce explanation from Frank to an assistant AG, explaining just what it would take to triple the already very large contribution, and in short order.

Here, however, all Frank got back were the AG's weak personal thanks for the upfront money. Along with a sincere wish—again right from the AG, a guy named Harry Napolitano—that no hard feelings would result from Mr. Napolitano's necessary refusal of more campaign largess under the circumstances.

Nobody who landed in Mental after pleading not guilty to attempted murder by reason of insanity could be released in only a few years, at least not without a sincere fight being put up by the AG's office, Napolitano told Frank. After all, Nevada was a proud Red State, and the Nevada Attorney General could not be perceived as soft on crime. Things would just have to go how they went.

What this all meant was simple. Frank would have a good afternoon at his hearing at Mental. After some foreplay with experts, he would then put Helen the basket case on the stand for several hours. With any luck, that would allow him to create a clear record of just how utterly fucked-up and dangerous a hellhole Mental was. The Mental review board would then, on a 3-2 split vote, most humbly and surprisingly accept Frank's version of events; issue a highly self-critical report; and thereby earn the utter and sincere enmity of everyone who depended on Mental for their livelihood. And Doc 3 would avoid yet another life-threatening beating, at least for a few more months.

After that had gone down, though, things would not go smoothly. The Nevada AG would next take a writ of review to the Douglas County District Court. A place where Fix now sat, after all his travails, as the duly elected District Court judge. And, boy, Frank mused to himself, was Fix unlikely to let Helen do anything but rot. Either in Mental, or even in Hell, if it came to that.

Ultimately it would come down to the Nevada Supreme Court, which, while very buyable in matters of general divorce and gaming policy, was unpredictably sanctimonious otherwise. And being in places where results had not previously been bought was not what Frank was either used to or fond of.

However, and for now anyway, TS's money was plentiful, and every long march begins with a single step. So, there was Frank—with an apparently catatonic Helen Wilson by his side on stage, and anxious TS left to fret in the audience—putting his own first foot forward.

The preliminary evidence consisted of Frank's expert internist giving the panel of shrinks—who had all more or less forgotten what real medicine they had learned on the way to their psychiatric specialty—the detail of just how Helen's physiology had worsened during the eighteen months she had been held at Mental. The man—a standout physician who took no insurance patients and who was on private retainer for several Las Vegas casino owners—was clearly outraged that Mental exercised no control over its inmates brewing and consumption of pruno.

He characterized drinking such stuff as little short of self-murder; especially given that, in Helen's case, it took place in combination with high dosages of Lithium and Zoloft that she was force-fed daily by staff nurses backed up by Mental's fearsome security guards.

This was followed by a rebuttal expert from Mental, a senior nurse named Mag Smith. Nurse Smith testified that she had personal responsibility for Helen's care. The woman—who mainly spent her days watching soap operas on a small portable TV smuggled into the very hearing room in which she was now testifying—flatly denied the existence of pruno on any of Mental's wards.

She also denied any possibility that Helen could have ingested such a substance, given Nurse Smith's constant watchfulness. Whatever physical problems Helen had, the nurse concluded, she'd obviously had them before she got to Mental, poor thing. When Frank didn't bother to cross-examine the woman's contrived story, Nurse Smith left the hearing, eying Frank, Helen, TS and finally the MDs themselves with great wariness on her way out the door. Not caring if she was believed, just wanting to avoid any personal trouble.

Finally, two hours into the hearing, it was time for the main attraction: Helen Wilson herself. Frank had no idea what she would say. The woman had refused contact with either TS or him. She had shown no interest in leaving Mental. But he already had the votes to win this hearing no matter what the bitch said, Frank thought to himself, and he knew he couldn't hope to win down the road without putting this crazy lady on. Full steam ahead.

"Ms. Wilson," he opened, "do you know who I am and why I'm here today?"

Helen said nothing. Just looked blankly at Frank. Then—in the familiar way late-stage dipsomaniacs experiencing withdrawal often do—she very audibly smacked her lips. In order to insure her sobriety at this hearing, Mental's nursing staff had put her in the seclusion room on her ward for the previous three days. Now what she wanted was a drink, not some tête-à-tête with TS's fancy lawyer.

Frank tried a different approach. "Do you drink in here, Ms. Wilson?" The question appeared to interest her, and Helen, looking defiantly at the MDs on the hearing panel, gained focus. "Sure," she said. "I drink when I can, as much as I can. There's not much else to get you through the day, let alone the night, in this shithole, you know. The whole thing is a nightmare, and the drugs they give you don't help much. But the juice, that always conks me out, makes me feel good for a while. Makes me feel real bad, too, most times, but then you just start drinking it again, and sooner or later it's all one thing, feeling good, feeling bad, all one thing."

The answer was so lucid, no matter that it was despairing, that Frank decided to probe Helen's ability to think rationally, maybe establish she wasn't a threat, something like that. This hearing was just an exercise, after all, and he had no idea what the Nevada Supreme Court would eventually find moving or not moving about this entirely strange case. Probably, and as usual, just who paid what to whom. Nothing more than that.

"You have a child, right, Ms. Wilson? A child who has problems? A child who needs you?" That question got Helen's attention big time. Not to mention considerably agitating TS out in the audience. He barely avoided shouting out to Frank that he'd better leave Baby Ellen out of this.

"I have a little girl who might as well be dead, Mr. Whoever you are," Helen rasped back. "Just like me, she'd be better off dead.

"You people," she went on, looking now at everyone in the room, and finally seeming to recognize TS, "you walk around, you're alive, and you have a future. Someday, you'll feel different. In the end, we're all on the same conveyor belt to nowhere. But my conveyor belt has suddenly become real short. And my kid, well, there was never any conveyor belt she ever even got to go on. Not even a short one. Eat and drink. Piss and shit. Sleep, if you're lucky. That's all she and I do, and she's a hell of a lot better off than me, because I don't think she knows she's alive. At least I hope she doesn't, because if she did, she'd be like me, and I don't like being me."

Frank had no idea what to do. He couldn't imagine anything this unhappy woman was saying was going to do him any good, either in front of Fix or any other unbought judges. Her angst was so strong, she might well be a danger to anyone who spit on the sidewalk while she was walking along next to them. Her very lucidity made the threat worse, since that lucidity meant she could pass for rational, as fucked up as she was inside. Incongruously, Frank realized—looking at her from very close up, absorbing the wildness of her features—he personally would feel better if this deranged soul was locked up in a high-security institution like Mental. No way did Helen Wilson belong in any low-security private hospital. Not if society cared about innocent bystanders.

It was easier, not giving a shit if he got Helen out. Made Frank more relaxed. But things were going so badly, he knew he had to go through the motions. Keep plunging along. Otherwise, there was at least some risk TS might not pay his next bill.

And Frank was personally curious about one thing, at least. How had Helen, after getting out of Napa State and spending almost a decade working for Shane, gone so far off the rails in 2008? It couldn't have been just her losses in the stockmarket. Didn't make any sense. So, what in Christ Sweet Jesus's name had it been? Frank wanted to know. He'd always wondered about it. So, why not ask her, he thought. Maybe she knew. Maybe she'd even tell him.

"Why throw coffee at that stockbroker, Ms. Wilson? Why shoot Mr. Smiley? Can you remember what you were thinking? Were you thinking anything at all?"

Helen appeared confused by the questions. No one had ever gotten around to asking them of her before. Her plea bargain had been a fraud, even she knew that. Or was it? For the first time, it seemed, she was turning over what she had done in a self-reflective way. Not because she suddenly cared what happened to her. But because she found she was as curious about the answers to Frank's questions as both Frank and TS no doubt were. Not to mention Shane and Elias.

Minutes passed. She asked to go to the toilet. When she came back, it was obvious she had been crying. And retching.

"It was just like I got on this train. And it started going faster and faster. When the money was lost, I stopped sleeping. By the time I got to New York and talked with that Birnbaum guy, I hadn't slept for a week, maybe more. That just hadn't happened to me when I worked for Shane, as nuts as Shane is, and as hard as he drives everybody. That was just work. But that money I'd lost with Lehman Brothers—I felt I needed that money for my kid, and I never thought I'd get another shot at making money like that. So, I just kept thinking about that money, like counting sheep, only I never slept, counting what I'd lost, dollar for dollar, going crazy over it."

She paused. Frank thought he might cut her off, since this wasn't going anywhere good. He looked back at TS, who quietly signaled for him not to interfere. This was something TS wanted to hear, whatever happened to Helen as a result.

"So, you know, the Lehman guy just wasn't listening to my problems. I was just another body down the Ganges to him. And I didn't have a lot of inhibitions left, so I tossed my coffee at him. Didn't even think how hot that goddamn Starbucks is, how they heat it up in microwaves in some of those places. Then I panicked. Went to Las Vegas. Sin city. And I was beginning to get control. Too hot to sleep at my motel. But I'd go to the movies and sleep there, where the air conditioning was good. Then that sadistic teenager was so delighted the Sheriff had come looking for me, I lost it again. Slapped his face. Got beat up and lost one of my front teeth for my trouble. That really got to me. All those bad memories from Napa State. How bad I looked the first time I had no front teeth. How helpless I was after I just lost it that first time. The rest of it, I don't know. TS was such a shit. Baby Ellen needed his money. A gun was easy to buy. And the train I was on, that train wasn't going anywhere good, and I wasn't getting off, even if I could. I mean, here's the truth, I don't know what I have wrong with my head. But there's something. Maybe I feel things too deeply. I know I have too much energy. And when I don't sleep, I lose control. And that's all there was to it. I'm still not sorry I shot TS. The world would be a better place without him. But I didn't even have enough presence of mind to kill the SOB. I was just up there at his house with a gun because it seemed like a logical thing to do. Like getting drunk every day seems like such a logical thing now. People like me, no matter what good things we have, we're not like regular folks. Bad stuff follows us around. I really believe that. Bad stuff follows us around."

Chapter Thirty Four
Douglas County District Court
Minden, NV
{Late Evening, Thursday, March 3, 2011}

The lights were on late in Fix's chambers. He'd called his wife around 5:00 PMand told her he'd eat in town. Then he'd gotten so wrapped up in the opinion he was writing in *In re Transfer of Helen Wilson*, that he'd worked right through dinner. Now it was nearly eleven at night.

Frank Farentina had been wrong about Fix. Fix was not interested in letting Helen rot anywhere. And Fix had been truly appalled by both the administrative trial record and the accompanying report the hearing panel of MDs had issued.

Fix was too wise in the ways of Nevada politics not to understand that Frank had bought the report and the votes that stood behind it. But Fix knew the medical evidence from Frank's internist was real. And all the rest of it logically followed from there.

The whole thing was so outrageous that Fix had decided not only to grant Helen's immediate release to the Betty Ford Clinic, but also to order Mental to show cause why its license to treat persons referred to it by various Douglas County social services agencies, and Fix's own court, should not be revoked.

Fix had seen too many shell-shocked troops in Iraq to think it was ok for mental-health professionals to shit on their charges. Troops with mental problems were often ground up by the military justice system he had served. But sometimes, he knew, such troops were salvageable. In or out of a military context, Fix considered it entirely immoral to leave such vital salvage operations to the not so tender mercy of sorry assholes like the staff at Mental.

Chapter Thirty Five
State Bar Court
San Francisco, CA
{All Day, Monday, September 5, 2011}

The intense publicity which resulted from TS's shooting and Helen's trial had attracted the attention of Sam Moody, Chief Trial Counsel of the State Bar of California. While no one had filed any complaints with that body, Moody took the unusual step of assigning a State Bar Investigator on his own initiative. Fix had been cooperative, and all the DA's medical records associated with Helen's prior institutionalization at Napa State Hospital quickly fell into Moody's hands.

There was no statute which had required Helen to report that hospitalization. But the tape-recorded death threat Helen had made against TS and her subsequent suicide attempt, which were referenced in the Napa State records—those things were both chargeable as crimes.

California Business & Professions Code section 6106 subjected any attorney guilty of moral turpitude—an arcane notion of moral evil which overlapped with the intent elements of many crimes—to disbarment. And 6106 didn't require that the attorney facing disciplinary charges first be convicted of anything.

"This thing has sure gotten a lot of publicity," Moody told his Special Assistant, Jon Gold, once they'd both finished reading the file on Helen Wilson. "And here's the thing. How do we let this lady run around with a law license? I mean, not only does she threaten a leading member of the Bar; ten years later, for no good reason, she just shows up and plugs him. And then she gets herself sent off to a state hospital on an insanity plea. This is not your average practicing California lawyer."

Jon Gold looked at his boss. He understood perfectly. Sam had recently taken this obscure job as the State Bar's Chief Trial Counsel as a springboard to elected office, hoping a record as an aggressive prosecutor of miscreant lawyers would be worth votes in the next San Francisco DA's race. Sam already had plenty of family money to finance a campaign. What he needed was a track record.

Jon himself was no ordinary state bar employee. He'd come over to the Office of the Chief Trial Counsel from the US Attorney's office, lured by Sam's promises that, if Jon helped Sam make something of this new job, Jon would be along for the ride when Sam went on to something bigger. Jon was an experienced prosecutor with a great trial record. Stripping someone as famous as Helen Wilson of her law license was exactly what he was there to do.

Now here they all were—Jon Gold, Elias Borah, and, on the witness stand, Shane Sullivan—sitting in trial before a State Bar Judge. Helen Wilson was not present. Her videotaped deposition at the Nevada State Mental Treatment Facility had been just been played.

Since Helen denied any recollection of events, the main point of that broadcast seemed to be Helen's gap-toothed, heavily tranquilized appearance. "How can the system allow such a clearly dysfunctional type to practice," was Jon Gold's not-so-subtle-message. And that insensitive message irritated Helen's old friend Shane very much indeed.

Shane was there principally on account of his having acted as Helen's supervising attorney during the slightly less than ten years she'd spent practicing between her two institutionalizations. All of which had gone fine, with Shane giving his opinion of the high quality of Helen's legal abilities plus his own observation as to how quickly she'd recovered her mental balance once she'd succeeded in getting out of Napa State and into out-patient therapy in 2000.

"Are you an expert on mental illness, Mr. Sullivan?" had been the first question on cross.

Elias had told him not to take this Gold fellow for granted. Still, nothing to worry about there, Shane thought, biting off an answer.

"Of course not. All I have is a law degree."

"Ever learn anything about the subject as a psychiatric patient, Mr. Sullivan?"

Elias objected, but was overruled. Objections were rarely sustained in State Bar Court.

Shane looked at his questioner. The man appeared to be fishing. Just trying to get under his skin. Shane made a decision.

"It's really none of your business, but no, the answer is no."

"So, I take it from that last answer, you are not under psychiatric care yourself?"

"No." That much was at least true. Shane was between psychiatrists.

"And certainly you've never been institutionalized?" Jon Gold asked him sardonically.

This question was a problem, and Shane knew it. You could argue about the truthfulness of his last two answers. Not learning anything from treatment didn't mean you'd never been treated. Being between shrinks didn't mean you'd never had one.

But saying he'd never "been institutionalized" was going to be hard to explain away, since, of course, he had been. That was no crime. But thirty-five years before, when he'd first applied to become a California lawyer, he'd concealed his stay at McLean. Just didn't want to deal with it or any resulting questions about his mental health. So, he'd held his nose and outright lied on the form. Never looked back.

In for a nickel, in for a dollar, he thought.

"No, have you?" he'd quipped.

No one thought anything of it. Jon Gold used Shane's supposed lack of psychiatric expertise and inexperience with institutionalization as grounds to strike portions of his testimony. And the trial moved on to its inevitable result of recommended disbarment.

TS was particularly critical of the Office of Chief Trial Counsel for raking over old coals. He'd attended every day of Helen's state bar trial, and testified on her behalf in much the same way he'd testified in her criminal trial. When the judgment disbarring Helen had finally come in, he'd gone to the papers and denounced both Sam Moody and Jon Gold for "going on a witch hunt aimed at destroying an already deeply wronged woman." The newspapers, loving the soap opera aspect of the case, had splattered the headline "State Bar Ruling Destroys Career of First SF Woman Bar President" on front pages all over the Bay Area. In response to that blast, Sam Moody had given up any hope of ever being elected San Francisco DA. He'd also quit his state bar job, leaving Jon Gold as Interim Chief Trial Counsel.

This was not some act of patronage. Rationally or not, Sam blamed Jon for the debacle *State Bar v. Wilson* had become. He had abandoned Jon as an act of retaliation.

Chapter Thirty Six
Nevada Supreme Court
Carson City, NV
{Morning, Thursday, February 2, 2012}

No one had been more surprised than Frank when Fix denied the Nevada AG's writ petition seeking to overturn Helen Wilson's administrative release order. Helen had been packed and ready to board a secure bus headed out of Nevada and destined for the psych wing at the Betty Ford Clinic when the Nevada Supreme Court intervened and stayed her release. Here it was, nearly a year later, with Helen in much worse shape even than when she'd been up before Frank's well-greased panel of MDs, and the Supremes were just getting around to hearing the case.

None of it was good. The AG had taken that goddamn Fix's frontal assault on how Mental ran and whether it deserved licensure and turned the case into a referendum on how Nevada treated the mentally ill generally. There were amicus briefs from do-gooders throughout Nevada, as well as the rest of the US. None of whom appeared to understand that, in the Silver State, avoiding imposition of a state personal income tax, and ensuring the availability of cheap blow jobs for locals and tourists alike, were the two paramount social values. Always had been, always would be.

Arguments were limited to ten minutes per side. No one said anything surprising. Frank said Helen was not going to last in

Mental, the State of Nevada would be sued by Baby Ellen, and the only reasonable thing to do was let her go in exchange for a release of the harm she'd suffered in custody due to poor administration of the hospital. Not about large issues. Just about money and keeping the State of Nevada out of federal court, where things didn't always go so well.

Then the AG played let's pretend, saying the panel of MDs had done no independent investigation of operations at Mental and had no choice but to accept Mag Smith's no-pruno-in-the-hospital testimony, especially since Frank had not bothered to cross-examine her.

A month later, the Nevada Supreme Court denied Helen's exit visa, holding no adequate evidentiary record supported a conclusion she had ever ingested pruno at Mental, given that there was no competent evidence the substance existed within Mental's facility.

A month after that, Helen was dead. On autopsy, a high concentration of both alcohol and psychotropic medicines was found in her liver. If not suicide, it was close enough for government work. At least that was how TS, Shane, Elias, and even hard-hearted Frank all saw it.

Chapter Thirty Seven
State Bar Court
San Francisco, CA
{All Day, Friday, October 5, 2012}

Helen's death hit TS hard. Despite her unwillingness to accept visitors at the hospital, he'd been hoping his help with Ellen and his attempt to spring her from Mental might bring Helen around to something resembling forgiveness. With Helen dead, that possibility was gone.

Within just a few months of Helen's April 2012 demise, TS had transitioned from grief to anger. Anger at Elias and Shane for persuading him to give a victim statement supporting Helen's temporary insanity plea, and for otherwise encouraging her to accept incarceration at Mental. In the end, TS just couldn't understand why a case where the jury had very nearly acquitted Helen the first time; a case where there was no weapon; a case where—because of an illegal search, there was no car—and therefore no case without him; why that case hadn't just been retried to an acquittal.

TS's anger obsessed him. Somewhat muted when it came to Elias, since Elias had no long-term relationship with Helen—and thus no insight into her character—it bordered on the irrational when it came to Shane. A Shane whom TS knew Helen would have mainly relied upon in deciding whether to plead out or go back to trial. And a Shane who, as far as TS was concerned, should have known Helen for the menace she'd be to herself once she was institutionalized for a second, indefinite term.

By the summer of 2012, TS was sufficiently recovered from the ill effects of his wounds to have taken up golf, a game he had never played while practicing law. Glenbrook was experiencing an influx of recently retired baby-boom professionals, mainly from Los Angeles and the Bay Area. Lots of them played golf, so there was always a pick-up foursome to be had.

TS tried to avoid playing with retired lawyers. He felt like too much of a curiosity, both because of how big a bang Broward had made when it went down, as well as for all the drama connected to his shooting and Helen's trial and eventual suicide. He felt more comfortable with docs, or if he couldn't get docs, he'd take a successful small-business owner. The investment bankers were mainly all up in Incline Village, so they weren't on the menu.

It was on the back nine in late August 2012 that he first heard about Shane's college breakdown. The guy who told him was a retired food distribution executive from Palos Verdes. He had been in Harvard's Army ROTC unit with Shane back in early 1969.

The man hadn't known Shane well, he'd said, but well enough. There were only thirty-five seniors in the whole program. So, everybody knew everybody.

Everybody who lived at Glenbrook knew TS had been shot in his home by an ex-wife. So, it wasn't possible for TS to avoid talking about that bête noir, he just preferred not talking about it with lawyers, who tended to cross-examine rather than listen sympathetically.

TS had been talking about what a raw deal Helen had gotten, mainly from her own lawyers and her trusted boss, all of whom had shunted her off to a mental hospital rather than try and get her off charges she'd nearly beat once. Shane's name had come up as one of those TS held most to blame for making the decision to put Helen away.

"Well, that's certainly ironic," the man, Blaine Lawrence, had said, "considering what happened to Sullivan in college."

Blaine had then proceeded to tell TS about how Shane Sullivan had arrived in his Harvard ROTC Colonel's office high on LSD. How the cops had been called, and how Shane's name had been stricken from the rolls of those commissioned in June.

"Never saw Shane after the day the story started circulating and never really knew what happened to him after that. Everyone said they'd taken him to a mental hospital. Didn't graduate with the Class of 1969. That much I know. A few years ago they published an alumni list that listed everybody who graduated that year, including people who'd lost touch with the University. Shane may have graduated in another class, that I don't know."

The man rambled on. But he'd planted a seed. TS had a clear memory of Shane's sworn statements about Shane's own mental health history, and he was determined to see what lay behind Blaine Lawrence's story.

He called Steve Neilson for help. While no particular friend of TS's, Neilson was still smarting from the disaster the bankruptcy mediation had wound up spelling for his trial reputation when Joe Wood had taken his and TS's pants down. Sullivan's participation in that mediation had been enough to make an enemy of Neilson. Plus, whatever his faults, TS had always paid his bills, and never complained about the $200 million verdict Joe Wood had achieved. Even thanked Neilson for avoiding a fraud judgment.

Neilson was sufficiently prominent that he had access to David Israel, the gumshoe of choice for the cognoscenti of such things. He was able to turn the private eye loose on Shane within only a few weeks of TS's first call. The instructions were simple. We want to go to the State Bar and complain that Shane Sullivan perjured himself. But we don't want to take them the evidence of perjury, because, if we do that, it will taint their investigation. All we want now are ultimate answers.

Did Shane get locked up? For what and how long? Did he disclose his problems to the State Bar at the beginning? You tell us, we'll go to the State Bar and voice suspicion only. Let them use subpoenas to get at the story the right way.

It only took a week. There definitely had been a breakdown. Some drug involvement. An eventual diagnosis of schizophrenia. Seven months in hospital. No disclosure ever made to State Bar.

No secrets were safe from David Israel, Neilson thought, smiling at the thought of how much trouble this was going to cause

Shane Sullivan as he telephoned TS about the happy results of Israel's investigation. TS had responded to Israel's report by having Neilson write Jon Gold, making a request for an appointment, purpose unspecified.

When Neilson's late August 2012 letter was received, it found Gold in the process of looking for new employment. His short tenure as Interim Chief Trial Counsel had not met with any particular success. The Office of the Chief Trial Counsel was populated with mediocrities with no desire to tackle difficult or unusual cases. Quite the opposite of the US Attorney's Office for the Northern District of California, which was showing no interest in re-hiring Jon. As Steve Neilson was a senior partner at one of several prestigious Northern California law firms Jon Gold had sent his resume to, having the man over for an interview on any subject was certainly OK with Gold.

The interview between Neilson and Jon Gold had resulted in TS's filing a Complaint, mentioning Blaine Lawrence as the source of his concern about the truthfulness of Shane Sullivan's trial testimony. But, Neilson had previously assured Gold, there was more to TS's story than just a golf-course rumor. And Neilson had not been at all averse to hinting that former Assistant US Attorneys were in high demand at his shop as another way of drawing Jon Gold's special attention to TS's Complaint.

No far-reaching investigation had turned out to be necessary in any case. Once confronted with TS's Complaint, Shane had come clean, telling the State Bar all the details of his stay at McLean and his subsequent cover-up of that fact both in 1973 and once again in 2011, when Helen had been disbarred.

The Office of Chief Trial Counsel then filed a Notice of Disciplinary Charges against Shane under Title IV, Part B, Standard 2.3, citing a violation of Business & Professions Code section 6106, a general statute forbidding dishonesty on the part of Members of the State Bar. The maximum punishment under Section 2.3 was disbarment, and that was the remedy Jon Gold—who chose to handle the case himself—requested.

Gold's theory, while attenuated, stung Shane badly. According to Gold, Shane had given false evidence in a disbarment proceeding where the end result was a likely suicide. While it was impossible to say what might have happened if Shane had been truthful, Gold argued that Helen had paid for his lie with her life.

The State Bar Judge, Michelle Brown, a three-term appointee, had been sitting in that capacity for nearly fifteen years. Herself a former State Bar prosecutor, she was entirely a creature of a very closed world. One that mainly dealt with drug and/or alcohol abuse, as well as embezzlement.

Mental illness as cause for discipline was not unknown to her, of course, but usually it was offered up as an excuse for misconduct. Never, either as prosecutor or judge, had she seen a case like this one. Sure, admitted perjury was a serious thing. Especially repeated instances of it—as was the case here—even though limited to one subject and even though spread out over thirty-five years.

But this ex-AUSA's attempt to blow-up that perjury into a *de facto* homicide—it was about all she could do not to dismiss the case after opening statements. Much better not to do that, she knew. Just let the hot dog prosecutor, Gold was his name—someone she knew was hated by the regular state bar prosecutors—make his pitch, then find minimal impact and sentence Mr. Sullivan to a year's suspension or some such. Nice being a judge, she reminded herself. Never need to be anxious when you have the power of decision firmly in hand.

As he listened to argument from the counsel table, first from Gold and then from his lawyer, John Cooper, the guy he'd been using for most of his career to get him out of the trouble he so often landed himself in, Shane's mind was a million miles away. At a lunch and then a funeral.

The lunch was back in the winter of 2002. He'd taken a young man—a high school friend of one of his own boys—to lunch at one of his regular haunts, Café Coppola, located in the Godfather director's gray-green Flatiron Building on Columbus, just up the hill from Shane's offices at the end of Montgomery Street.

The young man, Tom Smith, was lucky to be alive. Two years before, he'd thrown himself out of a sixth-story window, breaking his neck, back, and numerous bones. Shane's kids knew Shane's mental health issues. These had come out at various flash points in

283

family life. Shocked by Tom's suicide attempt, Shane's son, Bill, had asked Shane to meet with Tom—whom Shane had watched quarterback many Lowell High School football games, usually with Bill doing most of the blocking for him—and just talk through Tom's problems. See if Shane could help.

The lunch had not gone well. While Bill had told Tom why Shane might be able to help him—and Shane had been candid about his own experiences with mental illness—the two men were on opposite poles of the manic depressive spectrum. About the only thing Shane really had to offer Tom was the fact that Shane had himself recovered from a truly devastating breakdown; gotten through law school; and then had a successful career without any recurrence of his former delusions.

Tom listened respectfully to this, but said little. His entry-level job at Price Waterhouse was going poorly. To accommodate increasingly frequent psychiatric appointments, he'd had to ask that giant firm's HR Department for special accommodation. Something that—given corporate America's real attitudes toward mental health issues—both he and Shane figured was a ticket to nowhere.

About a year later Bill came home from graduate school and told Shane that Tom was dead. The boy had been travelling in St. Petersburg, on an indefinite leave from Price Waterhouse and supposedly working to improve the Russian he'd majored in at Berkeley. This time he'd made sure, jumping from a high-rise hotel room thirty floors up.

Shane would never forget the funeral. He and Bill had gone together. Tom's dad, a professor at SF State, had spoken to an overflow crowd. There was no mother. Tom had explained to Shane that his mother had her own psychiatric issues, and that she and her dad had split shortly after Tom was born. The woman had been a handful all of Tom's life, and one didn't have to be a geneticist to assume a connection between her ills and those of this most unfortunate child.

The father was heartbroken. He angrily complained that his son felt outcast by his illness. Looking right at Shane—or, at least, Shane would have sworn he did—he complained there had been no role models for his son. That those few who succeeded despite a severe psychiatric disability kept their problems strictly to themselves. Cowed by a public opinion about the mentally ill that would never change if only the failures of the afflicted were publicized.

He called his son his soul mate and, weeping openly, concluded his short speech by saying "Now my soul mate is gone." It was as hard a thing as Shane had ever seen. He fled the church at the earliest opportunity, leaving Bill to offer the Sullivan family's condolences to Tom's father and friends. He had not wanted to face up to Dr. Smith in person, that was for sure.

Now here he was, a defendant in a state bar proceeding. Charged with doing just what Dr. Smith had once accused him of. Hiding from his past. And hurting other people. People he cared about. People like Tom. And Helen. Jesus. Helen. He thought of

285

the coroner's pictures he'd insisted Elias show him. The pain on her dead, now ugly and misshapen face.

He knew the counterarguments, the ones that had urged concealment. Even now—with outpatient psychiatry a commonplace—involuntary hospitalization was still a true stigma. And, in the rough and tumble world where Shane operated—where lack of judgment was the first accusation hurled at one litigating counsel by any opposing lawyer worth his salt—the merest hint of meaningful psychiatric problems, past or present, would be exploited to the absolute hilt.

But those counterarguments didn't wash with Shane, not in hindsight. It wasn't Tom so much. There he had tried, whatever the boy's dad thought. And beyond a desire to be kind, he had no real stake in Tom.

But Helen was different. He'd been so confident Helen wasn't like him, that she was strong. So, he'd told her nothing about himself. And it had worked, at least the first time around. He'd had her committed—not because he thought she was the least bit crazy—but because he couldn't think of any other way to control her anger. And when she'd finally calmed down, he'd sprung her and then just put her to work. Never dug deeper into how she could have let herself get to the point of making so many determined efforts to kill herself in and out of Napa State.

Treated the obvious psychiatric ramifications of his friend's personality as if he himself didn't believe in psychiatry. And all that despite the fact that there is no experience like a long-term involuntary psychiatric hospitalization to make a believer in psychiatry out of anyone. There are no atheists in foxholes.

And now Helen was dead, and TS was her avenging angel. Shane had no doubt it was TS who owned Gold, one way or another. But Shane's own guilt—equal parts based on his failure to see how Helen was coming apart over money and his failure to realize that she'd never make it through another hospitalization—kept his anger against anyone but himself in check.

After the first day of the hearing, before any witnesses had been called, he told John Cooper he wanted to resign from the California Bar. Cooper reacted furiously. "You want to resign with charges pending? Are you nuts?" Cooper caught himself. "Of course you're nuts. That much even I have finally figured out. But look, Shane, I mean, are you really nuts? This case is B.S.   This Gold guy is doing some kind of a political favor for Steve Neilson. I hear he's trying to get a job at Neilson's law firm. So, he's just cooking up this case for maximum effect to make a big splash. And that lady State Bar Judge doesn't appreciate what she's hearing at all. She doesn't like the lying, of course, and she's going to discipline you. But it's going to be a slap on the wrist. And that's all it should be. You aren't responsible for that poor woman's death. She was just a lot more unbalanced than anyone ever realized. That's all. That's it."

Shane looked at Cooper. He hadn't hired him to be a yes man. And he understood his lawyer's frustration at being forced to throw in the towel on what both he and Shane thought was an easily winnable case. But Shane wanted to do something, really do something, to make his regret for what had happened to Helen clear. And to Shane the only thing that would accomplish that would be to resign.

Nothing was decided. Shane promised to talk it over with Elias over the weekend. Cooper repeated over and over how there would be no going back from a resignation, and how the disgrace of resignation would be indistinguishable from actual disbarment. "And for what? Because you feel bad you didn't stop somebody from doing something they would have done anyway? Face it, Shane. You don't know any more about why people do the things they do than anybody else does. You didn't get any mystic insight into people's heads because somebody talked you into dropping acid when you were twenty-one. You are just some guy who was lucky enough to not let getting locked up ruin the rest of your life. If I could, I'd have you committed before I'd let you do what you are talking about doing. Don't put it past me."

Chapter Thirty Eight
San Francisco, CA
{Afternoon, Saturday, October 6, 2012}

Elias had one of those very special Seacliff houses overlooking the Pacific. A lot of Sicilians had perished in order to generate all the defense fees which had paid for it.

Shane, Elias, and their wives were sitting outside on an unusually warm day in what was usually the chilly Seacliff neighborhood. Shane had just finished trying to put his reasons for resigning from the State Bar into a coherent form. As he could see from looking around at his audience, and particularly from his wife's very worried expression, all he had succeeded in doing was convincing everyone he was not himself.

"If you're tired of being a lawyer, Shane, that's simple enough," Elias said, gently. "Win the case, keep your ticket, then go inactive or even resign. Assuming you want to try and pass the bar again at your age if you change your mind. But, my goodness, don't resign this way, under a cloud of guilt. John Cooper is just doing his job telling you that letting this Gold fellow drive you out of the profession based on this cooked-up mess he's thrown against the wall isn't at all appropriate. All Gold wants is to win at least one difficult case while he's on the state bar payroll. So, he can then brag about what he did there for the rest of his career. And bringing you down fits the bill. Where's the justice in that?"

Shane started at Elias's reference to justice.

"Justice, Elias? Justice, you say? Why, I'm almost sixty-four. And you're well over eighty. Are either of us still so naïve that we pretend to know what justice is? Particularly the kind of justice the so-called justice system dishes out? I'll tell you what's just here. What's just here is that Helen shouldn't be dead. What's just is, knowing what we knew—hell, knowing what I knew about what these fucking mental hospitals are like—we shouldn't have been so quick to play the odds and stick her back in one rather than go to trial. Sure she was good as dead if she went to jail. But look at what happened. And if I live to be a hundred, I'll never convince myself I couldn't have been a better friend to her. Starting with not pretending I was any better than she was."

Elias sat stony faced. It was not the first time he'd had a client so racked with remorse that the client wanted to plead guilty. Best not to contribute to the emotions of the moment in such situations, he'd learned.

Elias's wife Zelda—a woman older than her husband and in even frailer health—looked over at Shane's wife, Nancy. She saw that Nancy was terrified by her husband's despair, with no idea how to control him. She also grasped that, whatever Elias might think, Shane was not going to be talked out of resigning.

Changing the subject, Zelda Borah said to Shane: "So, ok, so you resign. But what do you do after you aren't a lawyer, Mr. Sullivan? From what Elias tells me you are very much like him.

Your work is your fascination. If you do what you say you are going to do, you will no longer have that. Why is this guilt over a dead woman, a dead woman who was never more than a friend to you, I assume, worth that?"

Women, Shane thought sarcastically. It all begins and ends with sex for them. She seemed like a nice old lady, and yet here we are, right in front of Nancy, and she as good as accuses me of sleeping with Helen. Which Nancy probably suspects anyway, since I'm acting so nuts right now.

"Anything that ever happened between me and Helen is between me and my wife, Mrs. Borah. But this is not about some old flame. I did care about Helen. And I also feel I had a responsibility to her. I mean, if people who have the same problems can't help each other, then who can? And suicide, a person who needs help to avoid suicide is entitled to help from anyone who can help. But me, I just let it happen. And I hate to say it, so did your husband. But he at least has some kind of an excuse. He didn't have as much understanding of what was going on as I did, and I didn't help him understand. And for that I have no excuse. None at all."

Elias jumped back in. "But what has any of this to do with your license, Shane? Go ahead, put on sackcloth and ashes. Or start a suicide prevention foundation. But don't just let this Mr. Gold end your career. It's not even rational, forget about just. You are a fighter. So, please, my boy, fight this out."

Shane was unconvinced. "I'm not saying resignation is all I'm going to do, Elias, but it is the first thing I'm going to do. It's my way of saying that whatever the legal profession is, whatever it expects me to do, that I don't want any part of it. Since every lawyer I know says I can keep my license if I just fight, that's the one thing I'm not going to do. Instead, I'm going to flush my goddamn law license down the toilet, which is just where it belongs."

Chapter Thirty Nine
Marin City, CA
{Early Morning, Sunday, October 7, 2012}

The whole thing was meshugana. First Shane Sullivan shows up on his doorstep, wife in tow, and goes on a tear about resigning from the bar with charges pending. Now, here he was, parked in Marin City, waiting for Michelle Brown—Shane's judge and Elias's sometime mistress—to emerge from her home and get her newspaper. Back in the early 1960s, Michelle—the first black woman ever hired as a state bar prosecutor—had not hesitated to prosecute lawyers who openly professed radical beliefs. Elias had been just as stubborn in their defense. Improbably, they had found themselves in bed together within hours of each courtroom confrontation.

Even back then, Elias had long been married to Zelda. His affair with Michelle Brown had been an open secret, to his wife as well as to many others. But it was never discussed. Now, more than forty years after his last sexual encounter with Michelle—and as soon as Shane and Nancy Sullivan had gone home the day before—Zelda had calmly informed him that the only solution she could see to "that poor woman's problem" was for Michelle Brown to stop Shane's hearing before anybody could resign from anything. And that he, Elias, was the only one who had a chance of making such a thing happen.

When Elias asked Zelda the why of things, he was immediately sorry he had. "Because," Zelda said. "Because, Elias, because somebody should get something good out of what happened between you and that woman judge. And all the hurt that business caused me."

Marin City is an incongruous ghetto in the sea of Whites Only prosperity that makes up the rest of Marin County, California. Michelle had never made much money, either as a lawyer or a judge, but she still didn't need to live in a ghetto. Just felt more comfortable having other black people for neighbors, she told her white friends and colleagues. Elias' Prius was entirely out of place on a street dominated by American clunkers in various states of disrepair.

Michelle's front door swung open and the judge, wrapped in a well-worn housecoat, headed for the lawn where her copy of the Chronicle had been tossed an hour before. It was all Elias could do to reach her before she'd made it back into her home, where Christ only knew who else might be in residence. Elias had not kept up with Michelle's personal life since the two of them had parted, amicably enough, when Elias had made it clear he would not leave Zelda under any circumstances.

"Michelle, Michelle, please slow down, I'm an old man and we need to talk," Elias managed to blurt out when he was about ten feet from the judge.

The judge was entirely startled by the sight of Elias, out of breath and clearly disturbed, huffing and puffing on her front lawn. He looked so guilty standing there she wondered that he hadn't worn a false beard.

"Jesus, Elias, calm down. If you drop dead on my lawn, people are going to make a lot of wrong assumptions about us, including my new husband back in the house there. Who, thank God, is still asleep, and doesn't usually get up for a while. Now what's this about?"

He managed to talk her into taking the passenger seat of the Prius. He got in and drove off a few blocks, then parked again.

"It's the Sullivan matter," Elias said.

The judge tried to exit the car, but Elias had taken the precaution of locking the doors and using the child-proofing feature.

"Now, calm down Michelle. This isn't the first time we've bent the rules together. And if you don't think what I'm going to ask you to do needs doing, then you can recuse yourself and report me to the State Bar for making an ex parte contact."

The judge said nothing. Just nodded furiously. Then sat staring straight ahead while Elias went into his pitch. About Shane's overwhelming guilt at Helen's death. His determination to resign with charges pending. His disregard for the advice of everyone around him, family, friends, and counsel.

When he saw his old friend softening, Elias played on what he knew would be a major cord with Michelle. Jon Gold's misuse of his prosecutorial discretion to blow up a harmless set of lies into a disbarment rap. Something only an outsider to the State Bar Court's culture—even as sanctimonious as that culture was—would ever have done.

When he'd finally exhausted his argument, Michelle wordlessly tried her door again. Sighing, Elias unlocked it from the driver's seat. Michelle stepped out. Then, before Elias could close the door and drive off, she'd gotten back in.

"So, other than my not disbarring you, just what is it you want from me?"

"A dismissal," Elias said. "And before this idiot can resign. That's the only thing that will stop this whole thing from becoming a first-class catastrophe."

The judge looked dubious.

"He can always resign, Elias. So, why should I go out on a limb to keep him from doing something he's apparently going to do anyway?"

Elias looked at the judge impatiently. "Come on, Michelle, you know as well as I do there's all the difference in the world between resigning with charges pending and just resigning. The first is tantamount to permanent."

Michelle Brown considered. "But even if I did dismiss the case, there would be an appeal. And any interim resignation would still be with charges pending."

"Sure. But unless there was a reversal, the charges would remain dismissed, and Shane could become a lawyer again. Besides, if he wins, he'll rethink. I know him, he's going to get through this, and be sensible. He just needs help. Our help."

Now the judge got to what was really on her mind. "So, you mean to tell me this man, this Shane Sullivan, means enough to you to come up here and deal with me this way?" she said.

"No, Michelle, he doesn't. He's a friend, all right, and I admire him. But Zelda told me this was something I had to do. And you know what? She said it would make up for what the two of us put her through, way back when. But don't ask me why she said such a thing. She'd just met Sullivan, and I think it was something about the man's wife, who'd insisted on coming along, that hit Zelda. So, here I am. Begging. Please, Michelle. You know the case is crap. Just kill it quick. That's what I'm asking. Kill it first thing tomorrow."

Chapter Forty
State Bar Court
San Francisco, CA
{Morning, Monday, October 8, 2012}

When the parties arrived in the State Bar Court's Courtroom 1 on the sixth floor of 180 Howard Street that Monday morning, with Elias scheduled to take the stand as Jon Gold's first witness, they were greeted by an entirely empty room. No judge, no reporter, no clerk. The security guard outside, a Pinkerton who'd just started the week before, knew nothing.

After waiting an extra half-hour for some signs of life, John Cooper had knocked on the locked door behind the bench, only to be greeted by silence. It wasn't until shortly after 11:00 AMthat Judge Brown's law clerk came in, briefly explaining that Judge Brown was working from home and had just transmitted a draft order, which would likely be available to the parties after 2:00 PM. The parties were then asked to leave, and Courtroom 1 was locked behind them.

As there were no motions pending, the law clerk's announcement that some kind of an order would be forthcoming caused consternation on the part of both Jon Gold and John Cooper. While Elias was enormously cheered by this turn of events, he said nothing. Just took Cooper aside and whispered that Shane's defense counsel should prevent Shane from doing anything rash—lie to him, do whatever—but keep Shane from resigning until the parties could see what the judge had in mind. Then Elias went back to his office and told his secretary to hold his calls. He had Cooper's cell phone number and would get a report shortly after 2:00 PM.

Gold, Cooper, and Sullivan were all standing outside Courtroom 1 by 1:30, waiting to see what happened next. The doors were still locked, so the different camps took up seats on opposite sides of the hallway outside the court. The Pinkerton was their only other companion. At about 2:30 the law clerk finally appeared, holding what appeared to be a multi-page document. Everyone sprang to their feet, even the Pinkerton, who was caught up in the tension of the moment.

There was only one copy of whatever it was Judge Brown had to say. Jon Gold seized it from the law clerk's hands and then stubbornly clung to it, despite John Cooper's protests. Neither the law clerk nor the Pinkerton wanted any part of a fracas over who got to read the paperwork first, so it was nearly twenty minutes until Gold finally gave up what he was holding and then marched himself out of the building, muttering.

Cooper read what Gold had handed him, then reread it, and, finally, he smiled and handed it over to Shane.

"You can resign all you want to now, Shane, but it won't be on account of this case."

The order read:

In re Shane Sullivan, a Member of the State Bar of California.

While this State Bar Court recognizes that Rule 219 of the Rules of Procedure is normally invoked only after close of the Office of the Chief Trial Counsel's evidence, here the facts are undisputed. Therefore, as a matter of judicial efficiency, and subject to such further briefing and argument as may be appropriate, the following shall serve as the State Bar Court's "[Proposed] Findings of Fact and Conclusions of Law" pursuant to Rule 219 of the Rules of Procedure.

The matter before the State Bar Court is the adjudication of a Notice of Disciplinary Charges (NDC) filed by the Office of the Chief Trial Counsel against Respondent Shane Sullivan (Sullivan). In the NDC, Sullivan is charged with violation of Business & Professions Code section 6106 on account of two instances of deliberately making false statements under oath in order to conceal a seven-month hospitalization in 1969 on account of a psychiatric diagnosis of schizophrenia.

As set forth in the NDC, the perjured statements—both of which are now fully admitted by Sullivan—occurred (i) at the time of Sullivan's 1973 application to become a Member of the State Bar and (ii) in connection with Sullivan's testimony as a character witness in another State Bar Court proceeding, <u>In re Helen Wilson, a Member of the State Bar of California</u> (Wilson Case), which earlier proceeding resulted in a recommendation for the disbarment of Helen Wilson (Wilson) in 2011.

In opening statements, the Office of the Chief Trial Counsel relied on Wilson's apparent 2012 suicide in order to argue that "the extent to which the victim [was] harmed" for purposes of judging "the magnitude of the act of misconduct and the degree to which it relates to the member's acts within the practice of law" under Title IV, Part B, Standard 2.3 should include this State Bar Court's consideration of the death of Wilson.

Sullivan has been a Member of the State Bar since December 1973. There is no record of previous discipline. Prior to becoming a Member of the State Bar, and in 1969, Sullivan was hospitalized for seven months in a private psychiatric facility located in Belmont, MA. While committed he was diagnosed as a schizophrenic.

After being released from hospital, Sullivan completed his undergraduate education and then attended law school at the University of California at Berkeley, graduating from the latter institution in the same year he became a Member of the State Bar.

When asked a question on his State Bar membership application form concerning his psychiatric history, if any, he deliberately concealed both his commitment to a mental hospital and the fact he had been diagnosed as a schizophrenic while being treated there. Much later, in 2011, Sullivan again deliberately misrepresented his psychiatric history when asked a related question during the Wilson Case.

This State Bar Court does not condone perjury in any form. A false oath is a fraud on the government and, as our Supreme Court said in In re Vincent W. Hallinan, a Member of the State Bar of California (1957) 48 Cal. 2d 52, "there is no moral distinction between defrauding an individual and defrauding the government, and an attorney, whose standard of conduct should be one of complete honesty ... [and who is guilty] of either offense is not worthy of the trust and confidence of his clients ...."

There is, however, and as this case demonstrates, a reductio ad absurdum to everything. Two instances of perjury on the same subject matter separated by over thirty-seven-years is hardly the basis on which any ordinary disbarment proceedings would be brought. Moreover, Standard 2.3 does not mandate even suspension every time a Member of the State Bar is caught in an act of dishonesty. Rather, under the language of Standard 2.3 itself, the degree of punishment for attorney dishonesty is focused on a combination of the magnitude of the act and the harm it caused.

Here, coming right at the outset of a legal career, the magnitude of Sullivan's initial dishonesty was admittedly grave. (See In re Laura Beth Lamb, a Member of the State Bar of California (1989) 49 Cal. 3d 239 [disbarring a wife who—following her own 1983 admission—impersonated her husband in order to take (and pass) the California bar exam in 1985 on her husband's behalf].) The magnitude of Sullivan's initial act of dishonesty, however, must be judged in light of the thirty-seven years which have now passed without discipline.

Moreover, and to the extent this State Bar Court might otherwise be inclined to publicly discipline Sullivan's initial misconduct—if for no other reason than to discourage others who might be inclined to conceal information relevant to their fitness to practice law from the State Bar at the time their application for admission was being considered and then compound the problem by lying under oath about the same subject matter to cover-up their initial perjury—the conduct of the Office of Chief Trial Counsel in bringing this case presents such an apparent case of prosecutorial misconduct in its own right that this State Bar Court has concluded it would be inequitable to further embarrass Sullivan by public reproval, let alone to order either a suspension or disbarment.

By way of further explanation, the Office of Chief Trial Counsel, acting through its designated prosecuting counsel, Jon Gold, Esq. (Gold) argues that the outcome of the Wilson Case might have been different, and even that Wilson might still be alive, if only Sullivan's testimony had been truthful respecting his own personal experiences with psychiatric hospitalization.

The argument—supposedly made to justify disbarment under Rule 219 of the Rules of Procedure—is presumptuous and absurd. Even assuming Wilson's suicide were somehow the result of her disbarment, this State Bar Court has concluded that Wilson's disbarment was nonetheless required for the protection of the public. While determining the initial fitness to practice law of individuals previously afflicted with mental illness requires the State Bar to balance the rights of such individuals against the need *to protect the public from possible future harm, the existence of mental illness provides no defense to a later disbarment, if such disbarment is otherwise justified. (See <u>Snyder v. State Bar of California</u>(1976) 18 Cal. 3d 286.)*

Wilson shot another person with whom she had a long and acrimonious personal relationship. This lack of self-control made her disbarment necessary. Such disbarment was not a function of anything other than the admitted facts of the Wilson Case. These facts make the claim that Wilson's apparent suicide was caused by Sullivan's 2011 perjury impossible to prove by clear and convincing evidence, as is otherwise required by Rule 213 of the Rules of Procedure.

The appropriate discipline in <u>In re Shane Sullivan, a Member of the State Bar of California</u>, is a private reproval of that individual under Rule 270(c) Rules of Procedure.

The State Bar Court also finds that Gold knew, or should have known, that the Office of Chief Trial Counsel's request for disbarment of Sullivan in <u>In re Shane Sullivan, a Member of the State Bar of California</u>, was without merit and, in addition, that Gold appears to have brought this matter before the State Bar Court for a purpose other than to obtain appropriately limited disciplinary relief against Sullivan.

NOW THEREFORE, IT IS HEREBY ORDERED AND ADJUDGED:

Pursuant to Rule 270(c), Rules of Procedure, Sullivan is privately reproved for his failure to disclose his psychiatric history to the State Bar in 1973 and again in 2011.

Pursuant to Rule 218, Rules of Procedure, Gold is referred to the Office of Chief Trial Counsel for possible institution of disciplinary proceedings for prosecutorial misconduct.

Dated: October 8, 2012

Michelle Brown

Judge

California State Bar Hearing Department

Later that afternoon, John Cooper, Shane Sullivan and Elias Borah gathered in Elias's Union Square law office. Shane was extremely agitated. He had fully expected to resign with charges still pending before Judge Brown, and he was entirely frustrated by the fact that the judge's ruling appeared to deny him even that sorry manner of expiation.

John Cooper, on the other hand, was exultant. As Elias noted with some amusement, Cooper was more than half way to convincing himself that his opening statement had been the thing which had pushed Judge Brown to issue what was, for certain, a most unusual order.

For his own part, Elias was entirely admiring of how thoroughly his old friend had worked her way through the daunting analytical problem of throwing out a case that had never begun without any legal authority permitting her to do such a thing.

Siccing the Office of the Chief Trial Counsel on the very unpopular Chief Trial Counsel himself had been her masterstroke. It was Elias's bet that Jon Gold would now resign rather than face internal charges, and that no challenges to Judge Brown's entirely illegal ruling would be filed by his successor. This, of course, was what Michelle was betting on as well.

Even the judge's opening citation to the Hallinan case was poetic justice. *Hallinan* was, after all, the very first case Michelle and Elias had ever litigated against each other and had marked the beginning of their affair. Given Vincent Hallinan's well-known contempt for rules of any sort, that old Commie must be smiling down from heaven at the utter hypocrisy of it all, thought Elias. A perfect day, the old man thought. Yes, indeed, a perfect day.

Chapter Forty One
Faculty Club
University of California at Berkeley
Berkeley, CA
{Evening, Friday, November 15, 2013}

Getting TS to accept a limousine ride down from Glenbrook and speak at the Boalt Class of '73's fortieth reunion had not been easy. After failing to get even a return call, the Development Office had finally enlisted Professor Vett's help, and that eminence had gently reminded TS of two things. That TS was the Class of '73 president, first of all, and that it was school tradition that still-living class presidents act as masters of ceremony at their fortieth reunion. And that it had been Vett's telephone call to a senior Ludwig Smith partner which had resulted in TS's one and only job offer out of law school.

With TS as the featured speaker, attendance at the reunion dinner was remarkable. There had been just short of three hundred grads. About forty were dead. Fully half of the remainder were in the room, with their significant others in tow; all in all, a crowd of about two hundred people. TS was not the only celebrity the class had produced. One guy was a sports agent who had been the subject of a highly sanitized Hollywood movie. Another member of the class, this one a guy who had never practiced law, was a real-estate billionaire. And then there was the minority admit, a black woman who had sued, and beaten, the Oakland PD in so many wrongful shooting cases that she had not only become wealthy, she had also succeeded in nearly eliminating that most extreme type of police misconduct in what remained an otherwise entirely woebegone and undisciplined city.

Those were the standouts. The rest of the crowd was just what you'd expect at any late-in-life-reunion. Risk-adverse mediocrities, many already retired. Worried about an erratic stock market, falling house prices, and finding doctors who took Medicare. Would have stayed home except for the Lions versus Christians aspect of seeing TS try to explain what he'd been doing the last forty years.

TS had not been back to Boalt since graduation. Once he'd entered the already crowded room where the reunion was being held, one look at his long forgotten classmates and he was sorry he'd come. He now mainly travelled in a wheel chair, however, so there really was no turning around and leaving. Instead, he'd collected a big crowd around him; tried to put faces with names; and finally just decided to get drunk and the hell with it. His large-print speech, written by his old P.R. firm, was neatly folded in his jacket pocket. He didn't figure he had to stay sober to read such tripe out loud to this bunch of losers.

An hour, maybe an hour and a half later, there was TS, standing in front of his classmates, feeling the old vim.

"Ladies, ladies and gentlemen, 'Twenty-one today, thirty tomorrow.' Remember that one? How about, 'Don't trust anybody over thirty?' Well, we were twenty-one once, and we sure didn't trust anyone over thirty at the time. But none of it kept us from growing old. Now I know some of you are aware that Helen Wilson, our classmate and my former wife, is no longer with us. And I assume many of you are familiar with the lurid facts surrounding her passing. Not to mention the failure of Broward LLP, the San Francisco law firm I once led. So, it's fair to say I've had an eventful career. And not all of it an unqualified success. In fact I think I held the Northern District record for largest individual bankruptcy right up until the Panic of 2008. But so what? Like the song goes, 'I'm Still Here.'"

TS had already spotted Shane in the audience. Didn't bother him. The guy had resigned from the State Bar even after beating the rap for causing Helen's death, and TS had stopped thinking about him once that had happened. Probably buy Shane a drink when the evening was over. God knows they'd been through enough together.

But then, just to the left of the Dais, there was Leticia Madison, for Christ's sake. What was she doing there? There was an explanation, of course, but not one that occurred to TS.

Leticia had found herself unemployed once Broward had gone down. And then, after she'd testified against Sklar, the word unemployable better described her situation. But she was no quitter, and she'd used the relationships she'd built up as head of Broward's HR Department with the Boalt Dean to obtain an administrative job at the law school's Admissions Office. A place where her lust for power was somewhat sated by her resulting ability to toss out highly qualified students whose resumes she didn't take a shine to, all without meaningful review by anyone.

Everyone in Boalt administration had to help out on reunion nights, where all classes gathered every five years after the date of their graduation. Leticia was supposed to be taking candid-camera-type pictures, and was using a small digital model that she'd tuck back into her handbag as she went between reunion classes. She'd been as shocked to see TS as he was to see her.

As the UC Berkeley PD later reconstructed events, that was where things began to go seriously wrong. TS had risen from his wheelchair and was standing while he gave his speech. Laid out on the table in front of him was an apparently antique metal cane that he sometimes used to support himself when he chose to walk. A cane the model for which had first been manufactured in England in the late nineteenth-century, a time when London gentlemen feared for their lives while walking the streets of that then largely unpoliced metropolis. As such gentlemen did not want to appear so cowardly as to go armed, they had their innocent-looking canes double as guns, many such cane guns holding two or even three slugs.

TS had bought an antique cane gun at a firearms show in Reno. He was unable to fire it accurately, however, so he'd had a local gunsmith make him a custom version. Violating numerous Nevada and federal laws regulating the manufacture and sale of concealed weapons in the process. So what, TS had thought. He had enemies, he knew that much. And no one was ever going to get the drop on him again. Once burned, your fault. Twice burned, you had no one to blame but yourself.

He was drunk. He was tense. He was greatly disturbed by the hatred he thought he saw harden on Leticia's face. And, to top it all off, when he saw Leticia dive into her purse and then aim something shiny with a rounded barrel at him, TS became truly terrified.

He reacted by reaching down for the cane gun and firing it at his former colleague. Two shots went off in quick succession. As Leticia fell, TS saw that all she had been pointing at him was a digital camera with a moving zoom lens.

At that point, TS threw his wheelchair aside and charged through the antique double glass doors that stood behind him. Doors that led outside to the bucolic, dim-lit Northside of the Berkeley campus.

Most of the audience had at least one cell phone. The emergency numbers of every conceivable police force and Sheriff's office in a twenty-mile radius lit up. Alicia Burden—the black lawyer who'd dealt mainly with shooter cases—knew just who to call at the UC Berkeley PD in the shocked aftermath of such violent behavior.

She had the chief of that organization on a private line within moments. A white man had gone crazy, she told him. He'd shot an innocent black woman with some kind of long-barreled weapon that looked like a cane. "And be careful, Chief," she added, "that crazy white guy still has his weapon with him."

Outside, TS had gotten about a quarter of a mile away. His left leg was dragging. It still suffered from the damage Helen's shot had done to his cranium. He used the cane gun for support. Some hundred or more sworn peace officers from the UC Berkeley PD, the City of Berkeley PD, the Oakland PD, and the Alameda County Sherriff's Office were converging on him.

He probably would have been OK if it had been a police officer from any of the more professional organizations who stumbled upon him first. But the toy cops who worked for the Regents were first on the scene, and they were panicked by the gunplay on the campus, something hardly any of them had ever experienced. A real youngster, one only three months on the force, was the very first to spot TS and call for him to surrender. When TS attempted to raise his hands, he raised his cane gun, too. When they counted them up, there were five separate bullet holes in various parts of TS's by then very dead body.

Leticia fared better. Shot in the chest and shoulder, she made a full recovery. With two hundred eyewitnesses and Alicia Burden as her counsel, Leticia happily consumed what remained of TS's net worth, leaving Ellen Smiley with zero. Baby Ellen dreamed beautiful dreams and knew nothing of it.

About the Author

Will Nathan is a 2010 NorCal Superlawyer who wishes to remain anonymous.